ACCLAIM FOR COLLEEN COBLE

"Coble's clear-cut prose makes it easy for the reader to follow the numerous scenarios and characters. This is just the ticket for readers of romantic suspense."

—*PUBLISHERS WEEKLY* ON *THREE MISSING DAYS*

"Colleen Coble is my go-to author for the best romantic suspense today. *Three Missing Days* is now my favorite in the series, and I adored the other two. A stay-up-all-night page-turning story!"

—CARRIE STUART PARKS, BESTSELLING AND AWARD-WINNING AUTHOR OF *RELATIVE SILENCE*

"You can't go wrong with a Colleen Coble novel. She always brings readers great characters and edgy, intense story lines."

—BESTINSUSPENSE.COM ON *TWO REASONS TO RUN*

"Colleen Coble's latest has it all: characters to root for, a sinister villain, and a story that just won't stop."

—SIRI MITCHELL, AUTHOR OF *STATE OF LIES*, ON *TWO REASONS TO RUN*

"Colleen Coble's superpower is transporting her readers into beautiful settings in vivid detail. *Two Reasons to Run* is no exception. Add to that the suspense that keeps you wanting to know more, and characters that pull at your heart. These are the ingredients of a fun read!"

—TERRI BLACKSTOCK, BESTSELLING AUTHOR OF *IF I RUN, IF I'M FOUND*, AND *IF I LIVE*

"This is a romantic suspense novel that will be a surprise when the last page reveals all of the secrets."

—*THE PARKERSBURG NEWS AND SENTINEL* ON *ONE LITTLE LIE*

"There are just enough threads left dangling at the end of this well-crafted romantic suspense to leave fans hungrily awaiting the next installment."

"Colleen Coble once again proves she is at the pinnacle of Christian romantic suspense. Filled with characters you'll come to love, faith lost and found, and scenes that will have you holding your breath, Jane Hardy's story deftly follows the complex and tangled web that can be woven by one little lie."

"Colleen Coble always raises the notch on romantic suspense, and One Little Lie is my favorite yet! The story took me on a wild and wonderful ride."

"Coble's latest, One Little Lie, is a powerful read . . . one of her absolute best. I stayed up way too late finishing this book because I literally couldn't go to sleep without knowing what happened. This is a must read! Highly recommend!"

"I always look forward to Colleen Coble's new releases. One Little Lie is One Phenomenal Read. I don't know how she does it, but she just keeps getting better. Be sure to have plenty of time to flip the pages in this one because you won't want to put it down. I devoured it! Thank you, Colleen, for more hours of edge-of-the-seat entertainment. I'm already looking forward to the next one!"

"In One Little Lie the repercussions of one lie skid through the town of Pelican Harbor, creating ripples of chaos and suspense. Who will survive the questions? One Little Lie is the latest page-turner from

Colleen Coble. Set on the Gulf coast of Alabama, Jane Hardy is the new police chief who is fighting to clear her father. Reid Dixon has secrets of his own as he follows Jane around town for a documentary. Together they must face their secrets and decide when a secret becomes a lie. And when does it become too much to forgive?"

"Coble wows with this suspense-filled inspirational . . . With startling twists and endearing characters, Coble's engrossing story explores the tragedy, betrayal, and redemption of faithful people all searching to reclaim their sense of identity."

"Just when I think Colleen Coble's stories can't get any better, she proves me wrong. In *Strands of Truth*, I couldn't turn the pages fast enough. The characterization of Ridge and Harper and their relationship pulled me immediately into the story. Fast-paced, with so many unexpected twists and turns, I read this book in one sitting. Coble has pushed the bar higher than I'd imagined. This book is one not to be missed. Highly recommend!"

"Colleen Coble's latest book, *Strands of Truth*, grips you on page one with a heart-pounding opening and doesn't let go until the last satisfying word. I love her skill in pulling the reader in with believable, likable characters, interesting locations, and a mystery just waiting to be untangled. Highly recommended."

"It's in her blood! Colleen Coble once again shows her suspense prowess with a thriller as intricate and beautiful as a strand of DNA. *Strands of Truth* dives into an unusual profession involving mollusks and shell beds that weaves a unique, silky thread throughout the story. So fascinating I couldn't stop reading!"

"Once again, Colleen Coble delivers an intriguing, suspenseful tale in *Strands of Truth*. The mystery and tension mount toward an explosive and satisfying finish. Well done."

—CRESTON MAPES, BESTSELLING AUTHOR

"*Secrets at Cedar Cabin* is filled with twists and turns that will keep readers turning the pages as they plunge into the horrific world of sex trafficking, where they come face-to-face with evil. Colleen Coble delivers a fast-paced story with a strong, lovable ensemble cast and a sweet, heaping helping of romance."

—KELLY IRVIN, AUTHOR OF *TELL HER NO LIES*

"Coble . . . weaves a suspense-filled romance set during the Revolutionary War. Coble's fine historical novel introduces a strong heroine—both in faith and character—that will appeal deeply to readers."

—PUBLISHERS WEEKLY ON *FREEDOM'S LIGHT*

"This follow-up to *The View from Rainshadow Bay* features delightful characters and an evocative, atmospheric setting. Ideal for fans of romantic suspense and authors Dani Pettrey, Dee Henderson, and Brandilyn Collins."

—LIBRARY JOURNAL ON *THE HOUSE AT SALTWATER POINT*

"*The View from Rainshadow Bay* opens with a heart-pounding, run-for-your-life chase. This book will stay with you for a long time, long after you flip to the last page."

—RT BOOK REVIEWS, 4 STARS

"Set on Washington State's Olympic Peninsula, this first volume of Coble's new suspense series is a tensely plotted and harrowing tale of murder, corporate greed, and family secrets. Devotees of Dani Pettrey, Brenda Novak, and Allison Brennan will find a new favorite here."

—LIBRARY JOURNAL ON *THE VIEW FROM RAINSHADOW BAY*

ALSO BY COLLEEN COBLE

PELICAN HARBOR NOVELS
One Little Lie
Two Reasons to Run
Three Missing Days

LAVENDER TIDES NOVELS
The View from Rainshadow Bay
Leaving Lavender Tides Novella
The House at Saltwater Point
Secrets at Cedar Cabin

ROCK HARBOR NOVELS
Without a Trace
Beyond a Doubt
Into the Deep
Cry in the Night
Haven of Swans (formerly
titled Abomination)
Silent Night: A Rock Harbor
Christmas Novella (e-book only)
Beneath Copper Falls

YA/MIDDLE GRADE ROCK HARBOR BOOKS
Rock Harbor Search and Rescue
Rock Harbor Lost and Found

CHILDREN'S ROCK HARBOR BOOK
The Blessings Jar

SUNSET COVE NOVELS
The Inn at Ocean's Edge
Mermaid Moon
Twilight at Blueberry Barrens

HOPE BEACH NOVELS
Tidewater Inn
Rosemary Cottage
Seagrass Pier
All Is Bright: A Hope Beach
Christmas Novella (e-book only)

UNDER TEXAS STARS NOVELS
Blue Moon Promise
Safe in His Arms
Bluebonnet Bride Novella (e-book only)

THE ALOHA REEF NOVELS
Distant Echoes
Black Sands
Dangerous Depths
Midnight Sea
Holy Night: An Aloha Reef
Christmas Novella (e-book only)

THE MERCY FALLS SERIES
The Lightkeeper's Daughter
The Lightkeeper's Bride
The Lightkeeper's Ball

JOURNEY OF THE HEART SERIES
A Heart's Disguise
A Heart's Obsession
A Heart's Danger
A Heart's Betrayal
A Heart's Promise
A Heart's Home

LONESTAR NOVELS
Lonestar Sanctuary
Lonestar Secrets
Lonestar Homecoming
Lonestar Angel
All Is Calm: A Lonestar Christmas
Novella (e-book only)

STAND-ALONE NOVELS
Strands of Truth
Freedom's Light
Alaska Twilight
Fire Dancer
Where Shadows Meet (formerly
titled Anathema)
Butterfly Palace
Because You're Mine

A STRANGER'S GAME

COLLEEN COBLE

THOMAS NELSON
Since 1798

Published in Nashville, Tennessee, by Thomas Nelson. Thomas Nelson is a registered trademark of HarperCollins Christian Publishing, Inc.

Thomas Nelson titles may be purchased in bulk for educational, business, fundraising, or sales promotional use. For information, please e-mail SpecialMarkets@ThomasNelson.com.

Scripture quotations are taken from the ESV® Bible (The Holy Bible, English Standard Version®). Copyright © 2001 by Crossway, a publishing ministry of Good News Publishers. Used by permission. All rights reserved.

Scripture quotations are taken from the (NASB®) New American Standard Bible®, Copyright © 1960, 1971, 1977, 1995, 2020 by The Lockman Foundation. Used by permission. All rights reserved. www.Lockman.org.

Publisher's Note: This novel is a work of fiction. Names, characters, places, and incidents are either products of the author's imagination or used fictitiously. All characters are fictional, and any similarity to people living or dead is purely coincidental.

ISBN 978-0-7852-2857-8 (trade paper)
ISBN 978-0-7852-2858-5 (e-book)
ISBN 978-0-7852-2859-2 (library edition)
ISBN 978-0-7852-2860-8 (downloadable audio)

Library of Congress Cataloging-in-Publication Data

Library of Congress Cataloging-in-Publication Data
Names: Coble, Colleen, author.
Title: A stranger's game / Colleen Coble.
Description: Nashville, Tennessee : Thomas Nelson, [2022] | Summary: "A gripping new stand-alone novel from USA TODAY bestselling romantic suspense author Colleen Coble"-- Provided by publisher.
Identifiers: LCCN 2021029496 (print) | LCCN 2021029497 (ebook) | ISBN 9780785228578 (paperback) | ISBN 9780785228592 (library binding) | ISBN 9780785228585 (epub) | ISBN 9780785228608 (downloadable audio)
Subjects: BISAC: FICTION / Christian / Romance / Suspense | FICTION / Romance / Clean & Wholesome | GSAFD: Christian fiction. | Romantic suspense fiction.
Classification: LCC PS3553.O2285 S79 2022 (print) | LCC PS3553.O2285 (ebook) | DDC 813/.54--dc23
LC record available at https://lccn.loc.gov/2021029496
LC ebook record available at https://lccn.loc.gov/2021029497

Printed in the United States of America

HB 08.17.2022

For Lori Leonard
Thank you so much for your help researching
the hotel—you're wonderful!

CHAPTER 1

VICTORIA BERGSTROM ALMOST FORGOT TO breathe at the beauty of Georgia's Jekyll Island. Standing at the railing, she watched the sunset gild the undulating tidal grass with gold and orange and continue to paint its spectacular hues on sand and sea as the boat made its way along the Intracoastal Waterway to the wharf. The Golden Isles was an apt name this time of day especially. Her gaze landed on the hotel, and her chest compressed.

Then again, maybe dread stole her oxygen instead.

The garrulous captain gestured toward The Wharf restaurant, perched at the end of the wooden walkway. "There she is. It's a much prettier approach this direction instead of coming over the bridge. I still can't believe those people blocked the bridge."

Torie had planned to drive, but protesters advocating for the abolishment of the Federal Reserve had filled every inch of the bridge over the causeway to the island, and she hadn't wanted to be stuck in traffic for hours. She shook her head. Did the protesters really believe marching would accomplish their goal? And besides, the Fed helped to protect against bank runs and depressions. It seemed insane to protest about it.

The boat docked, and she grabbed her carry-on bag to disembark. The rest of her luggage would be delivered tomorrow once she knew where she was staying. "Thanks for the ride, Captain."

He tipped his hat. "You're welcome, Miss Torie."

Her heels clattered on the wooden planks past the restaurant and a storefront for boating excursions, and onto the sidewalk onshore. Time slipped past in a shimmering haze as she crossed Riverview Drive, avoiding the ever-constant bikers, and approached the Jekyll Island Club Resort hotel.

It had been eighteen years since she'd run and played along this water. Eighteen years since she'd smelled the river and listened to a bull alligator roar at Horton Pond. Eighteen years since she'd seen stiletto-tipped palmetto groves and moss-draped oak trees. The narrator on a passing tram droned on about the history of this place she'd once loved so much.

There it was.

The hotel that lived both in her dreams and her nightmares.

The tower in the left corner rose above the four-story structure, and the large wraparound porch beckoned visitors with thoughts of sweet tea and laughter with friends. She paused to tuck her white blouse into her navy skirt before she mounted the steps to the outdoor receptionist box guarding the doorway inside. It was unmanned at the moment, so she stepped into the hotel lobby. The scents of sandalwood and pine took her back to her childhood in an instant, and she swallowed past the constriction in her throat.

Audentes fortuna juvat. "Fortune favors the bold," the Roman poet Virgil had said, and though being here brought out all her insecurities, Torie had to find her courage.

Little had changed through the years other than fresh paint and attentive maintenance. The ornate Victorian moldings gleamed with a gentle glow of wax, and the wood floors were as beautiful as ever. She had never wanted to step foot in this lobby again, yet here she was.

Torie raised her head with a confidence she didn't feel and approached the resort's front desk. "Torie Berg. I'm your new IT specialist."

The alias flowed smoothly off her lips. She'd used it on her last assignment, and it was close enough to her real name to feel natural.

"Welcome to Jekyll Island Club Resort," the young woman said.

The blonde looked to be about Torie's age of twenty-eight and wore an engagement ring. Her open, friendly expression was perfect for the check-in desk.

"Marianne," a familiar voice said behind Torie.

Torie froze and didn't turn. While she didn't think the older woman would recognize her, she couldn't take the chance. The click of high heels went past her to the left, and she caught a glimpse of Genevieve Hallston's lavender blouse, her signature color.

"Come to my office, please," Genevieve said to the housekeeper she'd hailed.

The stricken look on the middle-aged woman's face said it all. Genevieve was on a tear about something, and it took all of Torie's resolve not to intervene. She'd been sliced by the older woman's razor-sharp tongue enough to know it wouldn't be a pleasant conversation.

But she had to remember her mission. If anyone recognized her, her cover would be blown and all of her plans would be in ruins.

Torie forced a smile and focused on the desk clerk again. "I was told there were rooms or cottages for employees?" The cottages had been added since she was a child, but she'd seen pictures.

The young woman nodded and handed over a key card. "You're in Stingray Cottage, Ms. Berg." She traced a path on the map in her hand and showed Torie the way to a cottage along Riverview Drive she could find with her eyes closed.

"Thank you. I believe I can find it. What's your name? I'm sure I'll be seeing you."

"It's Bella Hansen. I look forward to getting to know you." Her gaze went over Torie's shoulder, and she gave a reflexive smile to someone behind Torie.

Torie thanked her again and grabbed the handle of her suitcase. The wheels rolled smoothly over the floors, and she exited to follow the path around the pool and the entertainment area with its game tables and exercise room. Palm trees swayed in the breeze overhead, and the groundskeeper had done a great job with the banks of brightly blooming flowers and greenery lining the walk. She recognized Rozanne geraniums, hydrangeas, cosmos, baby's breath, and zinnias. There wasn't much she would change in the landscaping arrangements. It was perfect in every way.

She'd asked her dad to arrange for her to have the Stingray Cottage where Lisbeth had stayed. When she rounded the corner, she caught a whiff of artisan pizza baking in the wood-fired oven, and the aroma transported her back to her ten-year-old self. They'd had pizza every Friday night.

With a Herculean effort she moved past the temptation toward her cottage. Funny how things seemed smaller than she remembered. Perspective, she supposed.

She couldn't wait another minute to get her toes in the sea of her childhood, so she unlocked the door and put her bag inside. A bike had been left for her convenience, and she changed into shorts and a tee before she mounted it and set off for St. Andrews Beach, a four-mile trip. The ride would blow away the memories trying to surface.

==

The cedar trees around St. Andrews Beach had been perfect for hide-and-seek when Torie was a little girl, and they'd grown in eighteen years. Dead trees that had once been part of the maritime forest lay toppled on the perfect beach just past the two-story viewing platform, and she caught a glimpse of sand and blue water melding into the twilight sky.

She kicked off her shoes and carried them as she walked along the wet sand. A thousand memories vied for space in her thoughts. The wind teased strands of hair from her coronet of braids, and she inhaled the aroma of salt and sea, a heady combination that made her feel as if she could actually accomplish the task before her.

"Hailey!"

She turned toward the frantic sound of the male voice. A man in his midthirties stood in front of a forest of oak and cedar trees. His light-brown hair fell across his forehead above clear green eyes. He was taller than most, even topping her six-foot height, and she estimated him to be six four.

There was no missing the sheer terror on his face. She dropped her shoes and ran toward him. "Can I help?"

"My daughter." He raked his hand through his hair. "She's missing. She's eight."

"How long?"

His gaze continued to scan the beach and water. "Couple minutes. I had a woman check the bathroom, and Hailey's not in there."

"Does she have a favorite place to go?"

His expression cleared and he nodded. "Of course. The turtle nest! She probably didn't wait for me."

He still seemed panicked even after such a reasonable explanation, but she chalked it up to an overly protective father. "I'll be glad to help you find her."

He set off at a fast clip, and she followed across the soft sand. It was none of her business, really, but she had to make sure the little girl was all right. His long legs ate up the distance, but she had no trouble keeping up.

The Sea Islands of Georgia were known for loggerhead turtle nesting sites, and residents made huge efforts to protect them. The thought of seeing a nest after all these years made her pick up the pace. They went up a dune and down the other side near a clump of sea grass, and she spotted a young girl on her knees.

"There she is. Thank you, Lord." He stopped a few feet away. "Hailey, you scared me to death. You know better than to run off."

The girl didn't take her gaze from the turtle nest containing dozens of squirming black hatchlings. "They aren't getting out, Dad. I think we need to scoop some sand away."

"Yeah." The man squatted beside her and brushed the sand away.

The sea turtle "boil" was always mesmerizing to Torie. All those squirming black flippers held her in place. The hatchlings began to squirm out of the hole and their flippers scissored back and forth to propel them across the sand toward the sea.

The girl stood and walked beside the babies. "There are seagulls around. Pelicans too. I got here just in time to save the babies."

A lot of nests were logged and checked daily, but Torie found no glimpse of yellow rope or signs here, which wasn't too surprising. In good years Jekyll Island would have six hundred nests, and if the mother had come ashore just before a rain, her tracks would have been washed away.

Torie moved closer and shooed away a pelican. The last time she'd seen this sight she'd been with her best friend Lisbeth. Lisbeth had worn the same mesmerized expression as was on Hailey's face. It had been a perfect day of sun and sand, togetherness and giggling.

And it would never come again.

She bit her lip and exhaled. These trips back through

memory lane weren't helping. She had to focus on the task at hand.

The man turned back to face her. "Thanks for your help. I'm sorry to bother you."

"I'm glad she's okay." She extended her hand. "Torie Berg."

His big hand closed around hers. "Joe Abbott. Vacationing?"

She shook her head. "Just moved here. I'll be working in IT at the Club Hotel."

"You'll like it here."

"Daddy trains sea lions to keep bad guys away," Hailey said.

Torie already liked the little girl. "How interesting. I've heard of the military using dolphins for defense, but I didn't know about sea lions." Hailey stepped close to Torie, close enough for Torie to smell the fresh scent of her shampoo.

"Simon is really cool," Hailey said. "He's Daddy's favorite, but he's not fully trained yet."

Joe fixed his daughter with a stern look. "It's a good thing I'm not a spy or something. Hailey would give away all the secrets."

What was bugging him? Torie moved away a few feet. A couple more minutes and she could mount her bike and get out of here.

CHAPTER 2

JOE WASN'T USED TO BEING AT NEARLY EYE level with a woman. She was what—six or six one? And she didn't slouch as if ashamed of her height. The way she wore her long hair in a kind of braided crown was unusual too. The sea breeze had teased a few dark-brown strands loose, and they blew across her face with its planes and angles. She wasn't beautiful in the conventional sense but striking like an intriguing painting, especially with the fading sun casting shadows across her face. Her arresting features would draw the attention of men and women alike.

Her gaze remained on the hatchlings still making for the water with every ounce of their strength. They moved fast for such small creatures.

He wanted a little more information about Ms. Berg. "So, Ms. Berg, you just got here today?"

She smiled and nodded. "Call me Torie. I dropped my shoes and ran when I heard the panic in your voice." Her gaze tracked the baby turtles still struggling toward the waves.

9

He and Hailey followed her. Not many people would get involved so quickly. It wasn't like he'd shouted for help. "You must be intuitive."

Those deep-brown eyes went guarded. "People have mentioned that before, but I don't know about that. How long have you lived here, Joe?"

"Three years. Since Hailey was five."

"Does your wife work for the Navy too?"

"She's dead." He let her know with a clipped tone that he didn't welcome any questions about his wife.

He squatted in the sand and watched the hatchlings leave their distinctive tracks through the sand as they headed for the haven of the Atlantic Ocean. "Jekyll Island's history is interesting. During World War II after the millionaires vacated the place to stay safe, the Coast Guard patrolled here in case of an attack by a submarine or U-boat. A guardsman saw turtle tracks and roused the caretaker to tell him an enemy tank was ashore. It was only a loggerhead laying eggs. I'll bet the residents had a good laugh about that."

She smiled, and her gaze went back to his daughter. "Hailey seems smitten with them. Has she always loved them?"

"From the first moment she saw a clutch of eggs."

"I've been watching the news ever since I knew I was coming here, and I saw a hotel employee died a few days ago."

Strange comment out of the blue. "Yeah, a drowning."

"Lisbeth Nelson?"

He nodded. "She was a nice lady and kind to Hailey."

Why had he admitted that? It wasn't relevant, and he wasn't in the habit of engaging in idle gossip.

She brushed a strand of hair out of her eyes. "I heard there was some question over whether it was an accidental drowning or murder."

He raised his brows. "Who would have told you something like that? I found her on the beach with seaweed in her hair. The police are waiting on the autopsy to come back, but the cause of death doesn't seem to be in question. I have to say, your interest seems a little macabre."

She looked down, and the sunset gilded her hair. "Just trying to figure things out in my new home."

Why did she seem so interested in the drowning of a stranger? Did she know the Nelson woman? He opened his mouth to ask, but Hailey stood and waved her hands.

"Get away, gulls!" she shouted.

Four gulls were dive-bombing the hatchlings, and Joe leaped forward as one had a turtle in its beak. He grabbed the bird by the wing, and it dropped the hatchling, then gave an indignant squawk before it flew away. The other gulls kept circling, and Torie went into the fray with waving hands too.

The little turtle flailed around on its back, and Joe gestured to his daughter. "Want to get that one on its way again?"

Hailey nodded and gently turned the little creature right side up. It began its determined movement to the water again. And more turtles kept on coming out of the nest. He estimated the clutch had been around fifty eggs, and another twenty still needed to reach the water. He and Torie lined the path and shouted at the gulls and terns as the little procession marched on.

When the last turtle reached the waves, he exhaled and smiled. "I don't think we lost a single one."

"We didn't, Dad. I was watching. I'm glad I found them in time. There were a lot of birds out here. The turtles should have waited until they went to sleep."

He put his arm around her shoulders and hugged her. "What do you say we get some fudge to celebrate? Care to join us, Torie?"

Her brown eyes flickered, and she bit her lip. "I wish I could, but it will take a while to bike back. I smelled the fudge as I went past. What's your favorite, Hailey?"

"Peanut butter and chocolate. Or maybe rocky road. And the butter pecan is good, but I like anything with chocolate."

"A girl after my own heart," Torie said. "Maybe I'll come find you when I get back." She looked around. "Now where did I drop my shoes?"

"I'll help you find 'em, and you can ride with us back to the hotel. I can put your bike in the back of my truck," Joe said.

Why was she questioning what had happened to Lisbeth when she'd just arrived?

≡≡

If Torie had hoped to grill Joe in a subtle way, it wasn't going to happen easily. Hailey was at that age where she talked constantly.

Hailey slurped her chocolate shake while sitting on a

bench under a wash of dim light from the streetlamp. "Did you know loggerheads lay their eggs on the same beach where they hatched? They are migratory, so they swim over three thousand miles to get back to their site. I wonder if the hatchlings we saw just now were boys or girls? The temperature of the nest determines the gender. And we're not supposed to use bright lights because it can disorient them."

Which explained why the lights all over the island were so dim. Torie nibbled on her chocolate peanut butter fudge and listened to the child ramble on. She was a cute kid with red hair in a ponytail that swung with the girl's constant motion. Her green eyes held a world of interest and enthusiasm.

Torie must have looked as dazed as she felt because Joe grinned. "In case you're wondering, she never shuts up. Except when she's sleeping. The rest of the time, the mouth is engaged."

Hailey wrinkled her nose. "Dad, that's mean. You didn't listen very well to the sermon last week. 'Let no corrupting talk come out of your mouths, but only such as is good for building up, as fits the occasion, that it may give grace to those who hear.'"

He tugged on her ponytail. "Oh yeah? Well, what about, 'Therefore, having put away falsehood, let each one of you speak the truth with his neighbor, for we are members one of another'?"

They were quoting Bible verses to each other? Who did that? Certainly not her father or any of her friends' families, even though she attended church every Sunday. The affection between them was interesting though. Maybe it was because they had only each other.

Silence settled between them as they ate their treats. Guests strolled the path to the shops and the hotel, and Torie closed her eyes a moment to breathe in the aroma of the resort: suntan lotion, ocean, freshly mown grass, lavender, and Russian sage—all blended with the sweet scent of myriad fudge flavors. She could almost hear Lisbeth's voice calling for her to hurry to the beach with her. Or asking if they could please have two flavors of fudge this time.

Torie's eyes stung, and she opened them to stare down at the treat in her hand. It had suddenly lost its allure.

"You okay?" Joe asked.

"Fine." She opened her mouth to blurt out her questions about Lisbeth's death when she heard Genevieve's voice calling to Joe.

"It's Miss Genevieve!" Hailey bolted from her chair and raced to intercept Torie's aunt.

"There's my favorite girl." The older woman embraced the child, hugging her around the waist.

Torie turned her face away from Genevieve. Was that actually affection in her aunt's voice? Growing up, all Torie had heard from her starchy voice were criticism and orders. Aunt Genevieve had no children of her own. She'd always said the hotel was the only child she needed, and Torie had always understood she was to stay out of the way and not draw attention to herself.

Her mother had tried to protect her, but Lily Bergstrom's gentle voice and manner was no match for the juggernaut named Genevieve. When Dad was around, his sister-in-law backed off, but he was often gone visiting other hotel properties.

While her aunt's attention was on the little girl, Torie rose to her feet. "I have to go. Catch you later, Joe." Her pulse pounded in her neck as she hurried off.

Her aunt's voice carried on the sea breeze. "Who was that young lady rushing off?"

"Torie Berg," Joe said. "She's working at the hotel in the IT department."

"I hadn't realized we'd hired someone. I will have to meet her. She should have introduced herself when she arrived."

Torie rounded a cottage far enough away to catch her breath and let her heart rate resume its normal rhythm. Surely her aunt wouldn't recognize her after all this time. Torie's hair had darkened from its corn silk color to dark brown, and she was pale-skinned now, too, not the tanned urchin running around the property the way she'd done when she was a child.

It would be impossible to work at the hotel and evade the attention of Genevieve Hallston, who micromanaged the resort down to how many tea lights to order. Her aunt's reputation meant everything to her, and Torie was under no illusions that an IT employee would go unnoticed. Her aunt attended to every detail of the guests' wants, and Torie didn't expect the job to be easy.

But she wasn't ready to face her aunt just yet. She had to be able to mask her heartache. Right now things felt too raw.

With her heartbeat finally at a normal rhythm, she hurried to her cottage. Her luggage was just as she'd left it inside. She shut and locked the door, then rolled it out of the way. Leaning against the closed door, she exhaled. She was finally alone and didn't have to manage every word, every expression. This was already harder than she'd ever dreamed it would be.

She panned her gaze around the cottage, and she began to walk through it. Medium-tone wood floors gleamed in the light from the lamps. The coastal vibe of the comfortable sand-colored furniture and pale-aqua walls made her feel at home. The perfect touches of beach décor on glass-topped tables and shelves made her wonder if her aunt had decorated this place. Either that or the designer had followed Aunt Genevieve's explicit instructions.

The living room opened into a dollhouse kitchen. The white cabinets looked new, and she ran her hand along the smooth surface of the pale-gray quartz countertop. She'd be very comfortable here. At least she'd have this sanctuary for escape. She'd have to order in groceries. There was nothing in the house to eat, and though she wasn't hungry, she would be by morning.

She went back to her luggage and unzipped the outer pocket of her suitcase to pull out her laptop. When she'd gotten on the plane in Phoenix, there'd been no details online of her friend's funeral service yet.

No matter what the danger, she couldn't miss the opportunity to say good-bye to Lisbeth.

Torie sank onto the comfortable sofa and checked the local news.

There it was. The service was later than she expected— not until next weekend on Sunday morning. Ten days away, probably to allow for the autopsy, but it was still not nearly enough time to prepare her heart for what she had to do. She'd be there though. Didn't cop shows mention the killer often showed up at the funeral of his victim? Torie planned to sit in the back and examine every person who came through the door. The hard part would be ignoring her father, who was flying in later tonight. She could only hope he didn't let her identity slip.

She was going to bring Lisbeth's killer to justice no matter what it took.

CHAPTER 3

ZACHRY'S RIVERHOUSE WAS HOPPING TONIGHT. Joe and Hailey were lucky enough to get seated at a table with a view of the marina. The mouth-watering aromas of crab cakes and shrimp vied with those of fries and burgers.

While Joe waited to order, he spotted Craig Hall waiting to be seated. They had room at their table, so he rose and asked the hostess to bring him over.

Craig, a Georgia state trooper, high-fived Joe when he arrived at the table. "Thanks for saving me from a long wait. It's been quite the day." He tugged on Hailey's ponytail. "Hey, squirt."

They'd met when Joe's moving truck broke down on the causeway over to the island, and the trooper stopped to help. They were about the same age, and Craig had been recently divorced so the two had bonded over their losses in life. He'd been the one Joe had called when he found Lisbeth's body. The trooper's sharp eyes and nose for truth had seen him promoted six months ago.

They ordered sweet teas, and the server brought their drinks with cheese sticks while they waited for their meals. "So what was up with your day?"

Craig took a sip of his drink. "Protesters had the bridge closed most of the day. Some drivers got out and started slinging their fists around. Two people were taken to the hospital. Wild scene."

"Hey, Craig," Joe dipped a cheese stick in marinara sauce, "what's the latest on the Nelson drowning? Someone told me today she'd heard it wasn't accidental."

Craig frowned and shook his head. "I don't know where that came from. It's pretty straightforward according to the initial investigation. Water in her lungs, no sign of foul play that the coroner found. We've sent fluids off, including the water in her lungs, for a toxicology report. We don't have everything back yet, but it doesn't seem to be anything hinky. Sounds to me like someone was just trying to cause drama."

Torie didn't seem the drama type. She'd jumped into action at the first sign his daughter might be in danger, and she had the kind of personality that felt calming. Or maybe it was just he'd been so relieved to find Hailey in one piece.

"So definitely didn't look like a homicide."

"Nope." Craig took a swig of his sweet tea. "We will be releasing the body in a few days, and I hear the service is going to be at Faith Chapel next weekend, Sunday morning. I thought I might go."

"I will too, just to pay my respects." And maybe if he was honest, he wanted to see if Torie showed up. Her curiosity seemed unusual.

Craig reached for a chip. "So who is questioning the death?"

"A new employee at the hotel. Torie Berg. She said she was watching the news because she was moving here and heard something about it being suspicious."

"That's a crock. I've seen every bit of news coverage. Nothing's been mentioned but accidental drowning. Seems strange to me that she's saying anything when she just got here. What do you make of her questions?"

"I wasn't sure where she was coming from, and I thought she seemed too interested in the case."

She was an enigma. She was attractive but reserved. And she wore expensive clothes and shoes. Even he could recognize quality when he saw it. So she was likely a spendthrift unless she came from money, and if that was the case, why would she be working an IT job on a remote island?

His initial reservations about her surged, but maybe he was the one causing drama this time. For all he knew she bought good clothes secondhand. His wife used to do that. It wasn't a crime to like quality.

So why was he mentally defending her? He barely knew the woman, but something about her intense interest in the case had him wondering if everything she had told him was true. She was a neighbor so it shouldn't be hard to learn a little more about her.

Joe glanced at his daughter, but she was busy tossing pieces of her bun to the birds. He touched her arm and shook his head. She scowled but obeyed his silent order. The last thing the restaurant needed was to have birds demanding to be fed and making a mess everywhere.

"How's work?" Craig asked.

"Busy month coming. We've got a new nuclear sub arriving soon, and there will be war games."

"You meet anyone new yet?"

A vision of Torie's slim neck holding her crown of braids high flashed through his head. "I don't have time to date."

"I say that to acquaintances all the time, and we both know it's a lie. I'm getting over my divorce and you need to get over Julie's death." Craig's gaze slid to Hailey, who seemed to be paying no attention. "We're both too young to be alone the rest of our lives. At least I'm trying to move on. You don't seem to even notice an attractive woman when you see her."

Craig gave a nod toward the hostess seating a family two tables away. "She's not married and not dating anyone. We went out once, but there was no spark, you know. You should try."

Joe glanced at the attractive brunette. "I've talked to her a few times, but I don't like being gone from Hailey. Any woman will want more attention than I can give her. It wouldn't be fair."

"Maybe you'll find a woman who loves your daughter."

Joe didn't see that happening. Every teacher Hailey had so far was married. And talking to a stranger's child didn't happen all that often.

The server brought their plates of food, and his stomach rumbled at the aroma of crab cakes. He shoved away the questions he had about Torie. She wasn't his business.

≡≡

Torie found nothing belonging to Lisbeth anywhere in the cottage.

She exhaled and shut the drawer of the bedside table. It had been a vain hope to think that something of Lisbeth's might be hidden here, but Torie wasn't ready to give up yet. She glanced around. Where else might she look?

She wandered the bedroom. There had been nothing under the bed or in the closet. The bathroom drawers were spotless and empty, as was the space under the sink. She'd searched everywhere in the living room and kitchen, but maybe she'd missed something.

She gave a last glance around the room, then went back to the main living area. Her gaze landed on the glass bookshelf. About ten books, arranged by color, were interspersed with large seashells. She hadn't checked inside the books.

The first book was on the history of Jekyll Island with the cover depicting the ruins of the Horton House. The pictures of the old days made her pause to read a few tidbits about the club era and the members who used the place as a hunting club during the turn of the century: Rockefeller, DuBignon, Morgan, Vanderbilt, Pulitzer. The prominent names went on and on. There were pictures of lavish dinner parties with ladies in exquisite dresses followed by ones of men with cigars and whiskey glasses in the library.

She flipped through the pages and found nothing suspicious, then laid it on the desk and pulled out the next book, a book about loggerhead turtles. Hailey might be interested in it. The third book was titled *The Creature from Jekyll Island* and was about the Federal Reserve. She laid it aside to read herself. The next book felt off when she pulled it out. The dust jacket felt loose and too big for the book it covered.

She opened it and gasped when she saw a Moleskine notebook decorated with Lisbeth's customary swirling design on the outside. She opened it to the first page and recognized her friend's distinctive writing: half-script and half-printed letters. She lifted it to her nose and inhaled the scent of Versace Bright Crystal, a fragrance Torie had first bought for Lisbeth's birthday when she was fifteen. She'd kept Lisbeth supplied ever since.

Torie closed her eyes and could see Lisbeth's smile. She began to tremble and opened her eyes. The notebook shook in her hands. While she'd hoped for a message from her friend, she hadn't expected to find anything, not really. Whatever Lisbeth had written here had been important enough for her to hide. What did that mean?

Torie carried her find to the sofa, where she settled to read it. The entries appeared to be dated daily, almost like a diary or a recounting of her events. As Torie scanned it, she realized it was a journal of Lisbeth's first days here. But it felt off somehow. She flipped through the pages, and looking closer, she discovered several pages had been cut cleanly from the book with a razor. Why?

The task of figuring it out felt overwhelming tonight. She was tired, discouraged, and scared of facing her aunt. Even though she told herself she'd feel better after a good night's sleep, she couldn't bring herself to believe it. Not right now.

The first entry was dated the day after Lisbeth had arrived, one month ago today.

June 2

Genevieve didn't recognize me, and I decided not to make myself known to her. There will be time enough for that later. Granted, I was in the back row of the orientation for new employees, but I must admit I felt slighted when her gaze zipped right past my face without so much as a flicker of recognition. To be fair, she wouldn't have expected to see her niece's best friend from childhood in that setting, and she also hadn't seen me in eighteen years, not since Torie had left the island. The last time we'd been eyeball to eyeball was when I was ten. At the orientation I was next to Bella Hansen, who was going to work the front desk. She seemed nice, and I think we're going to be friends. In fact, I know we are because I found out she'll be sharing my cottage since there are two bedrooms here. She's moving in tomorrow.

June 4

I started work today, and I was able to meet the head of IT. It's too soon to ask about Lily, so I made small talk and flirted a little even though Kyle Ballard gave me the creeps just a little. He reminded me of an orangutan with his spiky red hair and big hands and feet. I didn't like the amorous way his gaze wandered either. I wanted to grab him by the shoulders and yell, "My face is up here, Bucko." I was glad I wasn't wearing a V-neck top or anything revealing. Ick. But he showed me my office, a tiny cubicle in the back. Today Kyle was in and out too much. I have a feeling he's going to be a problem. Bella moved in yesterday, and we are getting along okay, though I couldn't help meddling a bit. She's engaged, but she's been hooking up with another guy. I caught a glimpse of him outside the door, and I wasn't impressed. For one thing he's too old for her. She got mad when I told her it wasn't right, but I've always found it hard to shut up when I should.

June 6

Someone broke into my cottage last night. I didn't know it until I got up this morning and found the back door standing open. There was a note on the dining table that read, "I KNOW WHO YOU ARE. GO AWAY OR FACE THE CONSEQUENCES." I cried when I read it because I knew then for sure that something bad had happened to Torie's mother. If her death was truly an accident, no one would be trying to scare me off. And it made me more determined to find out who was behind this. If I can, maybe Torie can finally move on and have peace.

Torie closed her eyes and inhaled. Lisbeth hadn't said a word about wanting to find out what had happened to Mom. Was that the real reason she'd come back to the island? She'd told Torie she missed the water and wanted to come back to her hometown. Torie had been happy to arrange a job for her, but she wouldn't have done it if she'd realized Lisbeth's true purpose.

Had it gotten her killed?

She should have known though—Lisbeth had told her the reason Torie was so walled off from other people was she'd never dealt with her mom's death. And maybe it was true, but if probing Mom's death had led to Lisbeth's death, it would be an even harder truth to deal with.

Torie jumped when someone knocked at her door. Her heart rate doubled, and her mouth went dry. Could someone have figured out who she was already? She shut the notebook and tucked it down into the sofa before she went to peer through the window.

It was Joe with Hailey. She let out a breath and opened the door to the moon above the palm trees. "Well, hello."

Joe held up a take-out box. "We ate at Zachry's Riverhouse, and I decided you needed to know about the best crab cakes around. Hope you like them."

She took the proffered Styrofoam box. "I love crab cakes." She opened the door wider. "Want to come in?"

He caught Hailey's shoulder as she started forward. "Another time. It's nearly nine, and you want to eat those while they're hot."

Hailey scowled but held out a white bag. "I got you chips and salsa too. Want to go look for nests with me tomorrow?"

"I think I can do that," Torie said. "I don't start work until Monday so I have a few days to acclimate."

Joe turned his daughter away from the door. "Enjoy your dinner."

Torie shut the door behind them, and her stomach rumbled at the aroma wafting from the box. While she wanted to believe he'd brought her a meal out of friendliness, she didn't quite buy it. Was he suspicious of her already?

The flavor from the crab cakes lingered on her tongue after scarfing them down. She hadn't realized how hungry she was. Her lids were heavy, and it was hard to think. She'd study more of Lisbeth's notebook tomorrow.

CHAPTER 4

THE COAST WAS CLEAR. NO SIGN OF AUNT
Genevieve.

Torie followed the rich scent of espresso and slipped into the coffee shop inside the hotel lobby. She got into the line of five people. Just ahead of her, she spotted the desk clerk from yesterday when she'd checked in. "Bella, isn't it?"

The blonde turned with a practiced smile. "That's right. And you're Torie. Did you get settled into your cottage okay?" Her smile faltered. "It's a nice place."

"I did. It's lovely." She started to mention that she knew Bella had lived there before Lisbeth's death, but she caught back the remark. Bella would want to know how she'd heard that news, and Torie didn't want to mention Lisbeth. Not yet.

"It's a favorite with staff."

"Has it been empty long?"

Bella's smile totally vanished at the question, and

she looked away to move forward as another customer stepped to the counter. "Just a few days."

Why hadn't she admitted she'd lived there? It could be an innocent decision made so she wasn't asked questions, or it could be something more.

Torie wet her lips and told her racing heart to slow. She needed to get to know Bella. "You have time to sit out on the patio with me for a bit?"

"Sure. I know what it's like to come to a new place."

Torie ordered lattes for them both, and they found an empty table under the patio awning. An aerobics instructor barked orders at a group of five people on the lawn. Gulls seeking a handout waddled close to her feet, and she shooed the boldest one away, but it quickly returned to sidle close again.

Bella sipped her latte, and her blue eyes peered over the rim of her cup. "They are pesky. Where are you from, Torie?"

All over would be the best reply, but Torie didn't want to dig into her nomadic childhood. Not yet anyway. "Scottsdale. The landscaping is a little different here, though we like our flowers in the desert. They take a lot more watering. The grounds are lovely here."

"Miss Genevieve is crazy picky about the gardens. And the happiness of the guests with our internet."

Bella wasn't telling Torie anything she didn't know. She nodded. "I hope I'm up to the challenge of working for Miss Genevieve. There's a lot to keep up with."

She wasn't trying to be modest either. If there was one thing she knew about herself, it was that she *had* to perform her job well. It was part and parcel of her personality and her work ethic. While her goal here was to bring justice for Lisbeth, she couldn't dismiss her drive for excellence any easier than she could change her brown eyes to blue. Even when she was a little girl, her pictures of flowers had to be just so with neat rows and complementary colors. Her own garden in Scottsdale had won awards, and she'd put the same effort into the IT job. She loved computer work because it was so regimented and exact.

She took a sip of her latte. "Where are you from, Bella, and how long have you been here?"

"I'm from a small town in Indiana, so this place felt perfect. I love everyone riding bikes and strolling the beaches. No big box stores either. I came here a year ago, and I stayed in your cottage until a few days ago. I, um, my roommate drowned, and I couldn't bring myself to stay there and think I heard her in the other room."

Tori relaxed once Bella mentioned she'd been in the cottage. "Your roommate drowned?" She had to pretend she knew nothing so she could uncover every bit of evidence.

Unexpectedly, Bella's eyes filled with tears. "She was a good friend. I still can't believe it. I've never even known her to go swimming, so I don't know how it even happened. But the currents can be treacherous." She wiped at her eyes. "Look at me, bawling like a baby. I'm normally not so emotional, but Lisbeth's death has left me rattled."

It was all Torie could do to keep her own tears at bay. "I'm so sorry." *More than you know.* "When did this happen?"

"Almost a week ago. I didn't even get to say good-bye.

Her body is still with the police, but there will be a service in about nine days. I'd also thought about having a little wake with friends, just to celebrate who she was, you know? A lot of us really cared about her. She was the kind of person who made you feel good about yourself."

"You could hold the wake before the funeral. I'd like to come if you do."

Bella wiped her eyes with her napkin. "Why would you want to do that?"

"I want to feel part of the community here, and it's clear she was a good person if you loved her."

"That's very sweet. I'll think about it and let you know. I'm glad you're here. I think we will be friends."

Torie stared down at the gulls to hide the moisture in her eyes. She couldn't let anyone know why she was here. Not yet. But maybe someday Bella would be an ally.

"I hear the hotel has game nights. That sounds like fun. Do you usually attend?"

Bella sipped her latte and nodded. "I try to be there once a week. Usually Fridays. It's loads of fun. I like charades, though it's very old-school. Lisbeth was good at it."

She was indeed. Torie had played it with her often. "I'll have to come. Is it every night?"

"Every day but Sunday. Our guests love it. You'll find a cupboard full of board games, too, just about every kind. Guests sit at tables and play all sorts of games." She picked up her phone and glanced at it. "Gosh, I need to get to work. It's been nice getting to know you, Torie. We should do lunch or dinner one night."

"I'd like that."

What kinds of secrets did Bella know about the resort

and what went on here? At least Torie had an ally, even if Bella didn't know it yet.

==

Dusk lit the sky with red and orange as Joe tied up the boat and shooed away a gull trying to land on his passenger's head. Hailey was helping "babysit" his coworker Danielle's twins while he did a little work for the hotel. The three-year-olds adored Hailey, and she was a little mother to them.

He extended his hand. "Good evening, sir."

Anton Bergstrom, hotel magnate of the worldwide chain of Bergstrom Hotels and Resorts, ignored Joe's offer of assistance and stepped easily onto the dock.

Joe had never met the famous man, but he'd read up on him last night when he'd realized he was transporting him to the island. Bergstrom started his massive hospitality business on a modest inheritance from his grandmother and now owned one of the most well-known hotel brands in the world. He was a widower with one daughter, Victoria, and they both avoided media interviews.

Though sixty, Anton looked forty with wings of gray at the temples only beginning to shimmer in his brown hair. He wore a gray Armani suit with a white dress shirt and red silk tie. His black shoes oozed money, as did the cologne he wore. Joe didn't recognize it, but the robust scent suggested it cost plenty.

Steely blue eyes took in Joe's measure, and he extended his hand in a firm shake. He was as tall as Joe's six four.

"I don't believe you worked here the last time I was in Georgia, Mr. Abbott."

"No, sir. I've been working at the hotel part-time for three years. I've been looking forward to meeting you. I have a table reserved for you here at the Grand Dining Room."

"Excellent. It's always my first stop. Have to make sure the food and service stays five star."

Joe fell into step beside Bergstrom as they walked the oyster shell–embedded concrete sidewalk around to the hotel. The briny scent of the water vied with the aroma of steaks and seafood wafting their way.

Bergstrom stopped inside the hotel door on the polished floors and sniffed. "Ah, the scent of this hotel always takes me back years. My wife came up with it, you know. Lily was quite entranced with essential oils and fragrances. That pine and sandalwood fragrance always reminds me of her."

There was no self-pity or pain in his voice so Joe held back an automatic "I'm sorry for your loss" comment. Lily's death had been eighteen years ago, and Bergstrom spoke of his wife in easy tones that indicated he'd healed from the trauma. Joe wasn't sure how Lily had died, but he'd heard it had been on this property.

Joe led him past the lobby toward the dining room. A few wide-eyed employees greeted Bergstrom by name. He stopped and inquired after their families as if they were old friends. His easy manner made it clear to see why Joe had heard only glowing stories about him. Bergstrom seemed to truly care about other people, and Joe's estimation of the man went up even higher.

The hostess, a young woman Joe hadn't met yet, greeted them at the entrance to the restaurant. Her bright smile brushed past him and landed on Bergstrom.

"Mr. Bergstrom, the staff has been eagerly awaiting your visit. If you'll follow me, your table is ready."

"Come with me, Joe. I hate eating alone," Bergstrom said.

Joe nodded and swept his gaze over the busy tables draped in white linens as he listened with half an ear to Bergstrom getting acquainted with the hostess.

Joe took the chair facing the rest of the room, and Bergstrom seated himself facing the window. The hostess unfurled Bergstrom's napkin and placed it across his lap, then handed them their menus before she lit the candle in the center of the table.

"Your server will be right with you. Enjoy your dinner."

Anton glanced around. "Looks like they have a full house."

Joe settled into his chair with his back to the window, allowing him to see anyone approaching. "Holiday weekends are usually packed, and the fireworks will be starting in another couple of hours."

The older man smiled. "Ah, the fireworks. I haven't been here on Independence Day to see them in four years. I'm looking forward to mingling with guests at the hotel too."

"Is that safe, sir?" In this day and age Joe didn't trust large crowds, especially with a person commanding Bergstrom's wealth and power. Someone might try to grab him when everyone was distracted by the fireworks.

Bergstrom picked up his menu. "No one has ever tried to harm me in a crowd."

"There's always a first time, Mr. Bergstrom."

"I have faith the security team will see any threat approaching." Bergstrom steepled his fingers. "So, Joe, how did you end up here? I reviewed your résumé. Your main job is training sea lions, but the Navy is down in King's Bay. Jekyll Island seems off the beaten path for the job's location, and working part-time as a security officer is different from training sea mammals."

Joe's gut tightened. He hadn't wanted to go there. Not yet. "My family and I lived in San Diego, where I trained sea lions. My wife died, and I needed a change from Southern California. I wanted to raise my daughter in a small area that wasn't part of a naval base. Genevieve Hallston is my godmother. She was best friends with my mother, so I've known her all my life. She offered me the use of a cottage here if I worked twenty hours a month for her. Hotel security isn't hard, and I'm close by if she needs to call me. I leased some space here and put together a team to train my animals. When the sea lions are ready, the Navy takes them."

"I'm sorry about your loss. We have a similar heartache in our background. She must have been young. You're what—thirty?"

"Thirty-four. I was thirty and she was twenty-nine." The man's kind expression eased Joe's discomfort of talking about a painful subject. "Freak accident. I tried to help her, but I failed."

His throat closed at the image in his head of her wide, panicked brown eyes. And that horrific scream. He closed his eyes at the memory.

"How terrible." Bergstrom shook his head. "My wife fell from our apartment rooftop deck. No one really knows how it happened. Victoria was ten at the time, but it's still not something she talks about."

Joe caught his breath. Bergstrom's daughter hadn't been much older than Hailey.

"Poor child," Bergstrom said. "Well, I'm glad you've found a haven here."

The server arrived to take their drink orders and Joe was glad to leave those awful memories behind.

CHAPTER 5

THE MOON PEEKED THROUGH A BIT OF THE LEAFY bower overhead.

The live oak along the tree line by Driftwood Beach was larger than Torie remembered, but she spied a few weathered boards through the canopy of leaves. Had her tree house survived all these years? She kicked off her heels and reached for the first handhold. Stupid of her not to change into shorts. She wasn't sure if she could climb the tree as easily as she did when she was ten, especially in the dark, but her feet remembered the footholds and hand spaces for the ascent.

She wasn't even breathing hard when she clambered past the Spanish moss and onto the platform. The floor barely wobbled when she crawled across it to the side overlooking the ocean.

She sat with her legs dangling over the edge and stared out at the moonlit waves, inhaling the familiar scent of salt, sand, and pine. The fireworks would be starting soon, and she wanted a chance to talk to her dad before the noise started. Where was he?

While she waited, she looked around her favorite spot from her childhood. She'd spent many afternoons perched up here with her Mary Janes dangling at the ends of her spindly tanned legs. Her mom would scold her when she came home with torn clothes and mud on her shoes and socks.

The image of the perfect daughter of the hotel magnates was a heavy mantle on Torie's shoulders, and she'd never measured up, not really. The thought that her inadequacies might have contributed to her mother's death had nearly driven her crazy when she was growing up. Now that Torie was older, she realized in her head that Mom's death had to have been so much more than that. But that truth had yet to penetrate her heart.

Shiny new nails glimmered in the moonlight on several new boards on the platform. Who had repaired it? Had another child found this spot? She didn't want to be interrupted or overheard tonight when her father got here.

Someone cleared his throat below her, and she looked through the leaves into her father's face. "Dad, you made it. I can come down."

"No, I'll come up. We can watch the fireworks like old times."

He'd changed into shorts and a tee, and she couldn't remember the last time she'd seen him out of a suit. Most of the time they were at resorts in Europe or bigger cities where he had to maintain his image. This place brought out the real Anton Bergstrom. Here, he was the old Dad, the one who'd taken her out to hunt seashells and rescue turtle clutches. They'd examined tide pools, and he taught her the names of the various sea creatures inhabiting them.

She watched him climb the tree with alacrity, and he settled beside her and dangled his deck shoes over the edge beside her bare feet.

He gave her a fierce hug before he released her. "Any clues yet?"

"A few. I spent most of the day getting settled in the cottage." She told him about finding Lisbeth's notebook. "I haven't read all of it. Honestly, it's a little painful hearing her voice in my head and knowing she's gone."

And knowing it was because of me.

"I found out why she really wanted to come here though, Dad. When she had visited us in Copenhagen, she told me she thought the reason I keep people at arm's length was because of Mom's death. I told her she was wrong, but she came here to see if she could find more answers. That's a little nutty."

He frowned. "I wouldn't have hired her if I'd known that. We didn't need anyone poking into our business—not even Lisbeth."

"She wanted to help me."

"I have been concerned about how you go to work and then home. You don't let people get close to you. That's no way to live, honey."

"Why haven't you ever talked to me about it then?" She couldn't look at him right now, so she stared out over the waves. "I'm happy just like I am, Dad. I don't need a boyfriend or a husband to live a full life."

"It's not just that you don't date. You don't even go out with friends. No one is meant to be alone. That's why

Lisbeth's death has hit you so hard. She was your one true friend. Your confidant. I'm sorry you lost her."

The truth slammed into her heart, and her eyes flooded. "I miss her. And it's even harder now that I know it was my fault. When she got here, she started asking questions about Mom. And someone sent her a message telling her they knew who she was. I think she was killed because she was poking around."

Her dad squeezed her hand. "It's not your fault, baby girl. You didn't know what she was planning."

She took comfort from the warmth of her dad's grip. "I would have stopped her if I'd known."

He rose and leaned against the tree trunk where the branches split off. "You say someone knew why Lisbeth was here? It seems preposterous that someone might have killed her for that. There was no mystery to your mom's death. It was an accident."

"You believe it's all cut-and-dried? There's no chance of foul play or suicide?"

"No, honey. It was an accident."

Then why did he look away when he tried to reassure her? Torie pressed her fingers to her forehead. But her mother's death had been a long time ago. How many people who were there that day still lived on Jekyll Island? It seemed a wild-goose chase to Torie. And what good would it do after all these years?

"I'm sure Lisbeth was murdered, Dad. The ocean terrified her. She wouldn't have gone in willingly. She nearly drowned when she was five. I remember it. She refused to go on a boat after that. I've never seen her put so much as a toe into the water. In all these years, she's never overcome that terror of the water. Something much worse is going on here."

He didn't answer for a long moment. She jumped when the fireworks exploded overhead and flooded the night sky with blooming color, then the embers bled down to the water. The sight stirred something inside, like a memory shrouded in mist. But it still wouldn't come.

Her mother had died on Independence Day. Was it something about the fireworks? She hadn't watched them in all these years. Maybe there was a reason.

==

The sky exploded with color in the fireworks finale.

Beside a twisted tree thrown onto the sand by the waves, Joe sat on a blanket with Hailey on one side and Genevieve on the other. The older woman had changed into gray slacks with a lavender top, and her flats matched her shirt. He'd never seen her in jeans or capris, only skirts and slacks. He supposed she thought if she didn't look in control, the hotel might suffer. She lived and breathed corporate protocol.

Hailey jumped and covered her ears as the last, final boom shook the ground. "That was loud!" She leaned against Genevieve, who put her arm around her.

"So what did you think of Anton when you met him?"

Joe lifted a brow. "Impressive guy. Seemed to genuinely care about the people who work here. What's up? You don't know the meaning of idle chatter, so you're asking for a reason."

The lights in the sky were fading, and people started

picking up their blankets to leave. The moonlight showed the older woman's furrowed brow. "He uses his likability factor well, but don't let it fool you. There's a shark hiding behind those smiling teeth."

"You sound like you don't like him. He's your brother-in-law."

"He might be family, but that doesn't mean anything. I had to fight him tooth and nail for my job here. He thought I should have just gone home to Florida and left hotel life behind. He's built his empire, but he didn't want to share it with Lily's family. I put my heart and soul into this place, and it meant nothing to him."

"It must have meant something, or he wouldn't have agreed to let you stay on."

She gave him a withering look. "It was only after I told him Lily would have been ashamed of him that he relented. Luckily, I haven't had to be around him much since he travels to his other hotels so often. I haven't seen my niece in eighteen years. Who treats family like that?"

He loved Genevieve, but he didn't know the other side of the story. Anton hadn't seemed the kind of man to toss family aside, not when Joe had seen him talking to the staff in such concerned tones. But his godmother wouldn't care to hear his views on that, so he said nothing.

She stood and picked up the picnic basket she'd brought. "I'm going to head back to the hotel."

He stood and started to embrace her but backed off when she stiffened. "Talk to you soon."

She'd expected him to trash Anton, which wasn't in his nature. Let her fight her own battles without drawing him into something that had gone on for decades. The intricacies of a longtime feud were more than he wanted to delve into.

"Aunt Genevieve was mad at you."

He chucked his daughter under the chin. "You've got a lot of perception, Peanut. She'll get over it. Ready to go home?"

She looked past him and her face lit up. "There's Alexa. Can I go talk to her?"

"Sure." He watched his daughter run to talk to a school friend. Her parents waved to him, and he waved back, then turned to look up and down Driftwood Beach. A familiar erect figure walked along the tree line and onto the sand. Torie.

He wasn't aware he'd moved until he stood two feet in front of her, blocking her path. "You just get here?"

She wore a white shirt tucked into gray slacks and carried her heels in her hand. He gestured to them. "You're always carrying your shoes. Maybe you should consider getting different clothes for living at the beach. We're pretty casual around here."

She glanced at the shoes in her hand. "I do own other clothes, you know. They just aren't here yet. Tomorrow I should have my other things, and you might see me in jeans." She patted her white top. "Though I don't think I have a red, white, and blue shirt."

He wouldn't mind seeing her in jeans that hugged those long legs. The more he was around her, the more he felt the pull of her attraction. Not that she was flirting with him or anything like that. She held herself too aloof for him to imagine she found him attractive in any way.

She glanced around. "Where's Hailey?"

He pointed to his daughter standing with a gaggle of little girls. "Right there."

"Ah, I see her now." Torie waved when Hailey looked their way, and the little girl left her friends and ran to join them.

Hailey nestled in for a hug with Torie. "I wondered if you were here somewhere. Some people don't like fireworks."

"This is the first time I've watched them in a long time," Torie said. "I'm glad I ran into you, but I'd better get back to the cottage."

There was a touch of pathos in her voice that caught Joe's attention. He knew so little about her. He couldn't begin to guess how she usually spent the Fourth, but he'd like to learn. It was the first time a woman had intrigued him since Julie had died.

CHAPTER 6

HOME TO AN EMPTY HOUSE. AGAIN.

The sweet aromas of jasmine and roses wafted to Torie's nose when she inserted her key into the door of her cottage, but the door opened before she could turn the lock. The door stood slightly ajar, but she distinctly remembered locking it.

Her pulse surged. "Hello? Anyone here?"

Her chest compressed at the thought someone might be inside, but maybe she was overreacting. It was possible maintenance had come by to tend to something and hadn't locked up properly.

Maintenance. Who was she kidding? They wouldn't come in without informing her. Her dad's rules were very specific. She stood on the stoop and peered into the cottage, but it was too dark to see more than a few inches inside the door with the way lighting in the area was low and dim.

She reached inside and felt along the wall, then flipped on the light. The sudden illumination made her blink, and she stood in the open doorway for a minute until her eyes adjusted. She slid her gaze to a giant bouquet on the coffee table.

Someone had been here. A song played on the Apple TV, and she recognized the tune as "Games People Play."

Backing out of the open doorway, she pulled out her phone, but her hands trembled so much she found it hard to call up the number for security.

"Everything okay?"

She nearly dropped the phone when a male voice spoke behind her. She whirled to see Joe standing with Hailey in the faint glow of an overhead security light.

"I was about to call security. Someone broke into my cottage."

His smile vanished, and he flagged down an employee Torie had seen before. "Can you take Hailey to Genevieve for a bit while I handle this?"

"Sure." The woman set her hand on his daughter's shoulder. "We can get ice cream on the way, Hailey."

The little girl nodded and tramped down the sidewalk with her toward the lights of the hotel lobby with the American flag in her hand waving in the wind.

Torie's heart thudded against her ribs as she stared at the entry. "Someone left flowers. And there's music playing. The door was ajar when I got here."

It wasn't until his hand grazed the pistol grip in a holster at his waist that she realized he was armed. He worked security at the hotel so that made sense. A bit of her anxiety lifted, and she hung behind him as he pushed the door open wider.

Joe entered the cottage, but she stayed on the stoop.

The enormous bouquet inside drew her attention. It had to have cost quite a lot of money with the masses of exotic flowers mingling with the roses and jasmine. The thing nearly took up the entire coffee table, and the sickeningly sweet aroma made her want to throw up.

The music jangled her nerves, but she couldn't make herself move into the house to end the song. The title might mean something so she listened to the familiar words. The lyrics to "Games People Play" made her shudder, and she had to fight a wave of nausea. She clenched her hands so tightly her nails bit into her palms.

The sharp taste of bile hit her throat, and she stepped back to draw several deep breaths of the night air. Once she felt strong enough, she sidled a few feet closer to the doorjamb.

Joe leaned over and peered at the card on the flowers. "Don't come in. I want to check out the house. In fact, why don't you go get some ice cream with Hailey? I can come find you once it's clean."

She shook her head. "This is not some casual break-in. I need to try to figure out what the intruder is trying to tell me."

"What makes you think he's trying to tell you anything? Maybe you just have a secret admirer."

"One who breaks in to leave flowers and turn on ominous music? You know better than that, and I'm not a child. I can handle the truth."

The bold words had an immediate effect on her courage, and she stepped into the living room. She verbally ordered the music to stop, but the immediate silence felt worse somehow. As if something or someone in the house *waited*. And *laughed*.

Joe moved through the small space flipping on lights and opening doors. It didn't take long for him to peer under the beds and into the closets before he rejoined her in the living room. "No one's here now. How long were you gone?"

"A couple of hours. Long enough to see the fireworks."

Joe had appeared right when she found the break-in. Coincidence? She didn't want to be the suspicious sort who saw danger behind every bush, but it was odd he'd appeared the moment she needed help.

If Lisbeth had shown more caution, she might not be dead right now, and Torie had to stay alert. Joe seemed the dependable sort, but a handsome face and a cute daughter could hide all kinds of darkness. She didn't intend to be a victim. Lisbeth's killer had to be brought to justice.

Joe moved toward the door. "I'll report this to the state police. You could stay at the hotel if you're afraid to sleep here tonight."

She forced a reassuring smile. "I'll be fine. You checked out everything, and I'll lock up behind you. Maybe it was a prank. Someone trying to rattle me."

His green eyes narrowed. "You just got here, Torie. Why would someone want to rattle you?"

She gave a casual shrug. "I have no idea, but what else could it be? Like you said, I'm a stranger here."

The skeptical twist to his lips didn't change, but he didn't argue. "Well, I'll go get my daughter then."

"Ah, you must know the hotel manager well if you sent Hailey to her."

"She's my godmother. I've known her all my life." He pulled a card from his pocket. "Here's my number. If you hear anything, my place is just down the walkway."

"I'm sure I'll be fine," she said again and turned toward the door. Everything in her wanted to beg him to stay, but he was as much of a stranger as everyone else here.

This was her task to accomplish, and she could only pray she was up to the challenge.

==

The dark pressed in on her, and Torie went from room to room closing the blinds and curtains, but she still felt eyes on her.

Silly, she knew. No one was here. She stared at the vase of flowers and wrinkled her nose. The cloying scent overpowered her, and she couldn't stand it. Carrying the heavy vase, she opened the trash drawer and dumped the flowers inside, then washed the water down the kitchen sink. But even with the flowers in the garbage bin, she could still smell them.

She eyed the back door, but the thought of stepping out into the dark made her quail. This was why she was here. *Suck it up.*

She tightened her jaw and pulled out the trash drawer, then quickly tied the bag up with a wire twisty. Holding it away from her, she marched to the door and flipped on the outside light. The dim glow did little to reassure her, but she unlocked the latch and stepped through the door. The trash bin was to her right, and she hurried to deposit the bag in it, then practically ran back to the kitchen.

As she started to enter, she heard Tennessee Ernie Ford's deep voice singing "Sixteen Tons." The sound rooted her in the doorway, halfway between inside and outside. Her throat constricted, and she struggled to breathe. Mom had been a huge Tennessee Ernie Ford fan and had played this song a lot. Her phone was inside, so she couldn't even call Joe. His place was two cottages down though, so she turned to her left and ran around the side of the house. Once she reached the street, she felt her chest ease, and she was able to draw in sweet air.

His lights were on even though it was ten. Should she ring the bell and risk awakening Hailey, or should she just knock? The blinds were open, and she spotted him sitting on the sofa with a book in his hand. A tap on the window should get his attention, so she tapped her knuckles against the glass.

He looked up and his face tightened with concern. He bolted to his feet and rushed to throw open the door. "Are you okay? What's happened?"

"The music started playing by itself. A different song." She told him the sequence of events. "I didn't see anyone though."

"Come in." He stepped aside and looked both ways down the street as she moved past before he locked the door behind her.

"I left my phone inside, then remembered you'd pointed out your cottage. I'm sorry to bother you so late."

"It's no bother. I was awake." He gestured for her to have a seat.

She settled on the sofa, an overstuffed one clad in a navy plaid. The room held very little in the way of decoration, just some pictures of Hailey. It had a similar floor plan to hers.

"If you stay here with Hailey, I'll go take a look."

"Of course."

He opened the door. "Lock it behind me."

She nodded and did as he said. Once the lock clicked, she wandered around the room to have something to do. If this house was like hers, Hailey's room would be to the right, so she went down the hall and peeked in on the little girl, who slept peacefully with her hand thrown up over her head. She was half uncovered, so Torie tugged the pink-and-white quilt up to her shoulders, then kissed her forehead.

She'd never been around kids much, but something inside her had responded to Hailey immediately. Maybe it was that their circumstances were so similar with her losing her mother too. They were kindred souls, though Hailey's mother had likely died of an illness. Joe had never said.

She turned at a sound and saw Joe standing in the doorway. Tiptoeing out of the room, she shut the bedroom door behind her. "I was just checking on her. She didn't wake up."

"Thanks." He ran his hand through his thick brown hair. "I didn't find anything in your place. The music wasn't even playing, and the doors were all shut."

"Even the back door? I left it open when I ran down here."

"It was shut and locked."

"I'm not crazy. It really happened."

"I never said it didn't." He took her arm and steered

her back down the hall to the sofa. "You've got all that electronic stuff in there. Apple TV responds to voice commands. Could it be controlled with a remote?"

She sank onto the sofa's cushion. "Sure."

"Do you know where it is? Maybe the guy took it or programmed another one to the same frequency."

"Possible." She gave a shaky laugh. "I'm in IT. I should have thought of that first."

"It's hard to think when you're scared. Is there any significance to you in the music itself? 'Sixteen Tons' lyrics mean anything to you?"

She shook her head. "I've heard it but that's about it. My mom was a Tennessee Ernie Ford fan."

"It's very strange." He gestured to the other side of the room. "You can sleep in my bed, and I can bunk on the sofa."

She got to her feet. "Absolutely not. Now that I know it's someone playing a harmless prank, I'm not frightened. Thank you for figuring it out."

He called after her, but she rushed out the door before her resolve weakened. She held the fates of thousands of workers in her hand. She knew the hotel business inside and out and could hold her own in a boardroom full of executives. So why did this situation make her feel weak when she knew she was strong?

Torie had to remember who she was and why she was here.

CHAPTER 7

THE START TO JOE'S WORKWEEK WAS A WELCOME respite from the weekend, but he'd found himself wondering how Torie was all morning. It made him a little short-tempered with his sea lion, Simon.

Joe gave a lazy kick with his fins and swam close to a sunken ship teeming with fish. Best-case scenario would be if he didn't see the big sea lion coming. Usually Simon was like a bull in a china shop. He wasn't good at a sneak attack, and the last thing Joe wanted was for his favorite mammal to be injured or killed by a hostile diver in a real-world situation.

The sea was busy taking over what was left of the old ship. It had become a favorite artificial reef for divers, and he spotted barracuda, rays, and spadefish. He couldn't wait until Hailey was old enough to dive and experience all the underwater wonders.

The thought was barely gone when Joe felt something clasp around his leg. The cuff was made to clamp as soon as the sea lion bumped it against something. He caught the gleam in Simon's eye as the big sea lion zipped through the water back to the inflatable craft rolling with the waves above Joe's head.

Joe grinned and gave a hand signal of approval to the sea mammal before a tug on the line attached to the cuff reeled him in like a caught fish. He didn't fight and let his teammates bring him to the side of the boat.

When his head broke the surface of the waves, he spit out his mouthpiece to breathe in fresh salt air, then clambered over the side of the rubber raft. "I didn't even see Simon coming this time."

Danielle Maine handed him a bottle of water. "He's getting it."

His coworker was in her early thirties with short, curly brown hair and merry blue eyes that went even more cheerful when talking about her three-year-old twin girls. She had a special connection with the sea lions. Joe's training team was a tight-knit group. They all lived on Jekyll Island and worked at the small compound Joe had leased from the state.

"I'll bet you gave him crab, didn't you?"

She sent an impish smile his way. "And what if I did?"

"Nothing. Just figuring out where I went wrong." Joe took a swig of water and turned to Tyrone Walsh, the third member of the team. "How long did he take to find me?"

"Three minutes."

Tyrone had a deep voice that reminded Joe of James Earl Jones, and he even looked a little like a young version of the actor. In his late twenties, Tyrone had tremendous focus and determination.

A flipper slapped against the side of the boat, and Joe turned around with a grin when Simon barked. "Come for more crab, Simon?" He reached into the bucket and tossed a soft-shelled crab to the sea lion, who gobbled it up before it had time to sink an inch.

Something in the sea lion's mouth glinted in the morning sunshine, and Joe squinted at Simon. "What do you have, big guy?"

He held up another crab, and the sea lion swam near enough for Joe to reach into his mouth to retrieve what Simon had found. The item on Joe's open palm was a small propeller that he recognized immediately as part of a thruster system on an underwater drone. It might belong to a fisherman or a hobbyist, but it might be something more ominous.

He showed it to his team. "I'm going down to take a look around. I'll have Simon show me where he found it."

He bit into his mouthpiece and inhaled stale canned air, then adjusted his mask before he fell backward into the blue water. The waves embraced him in a warm caress, and he swam past a school of rock beauty angelfish. Their striking yellow-and-black markings stood out in stark contrast to the gray rocks. Simon swam beside him, and the fish scattered at the sea lion's approach. Simon seemed to realize why Joe was in the water, and he propelled ahead toward the seafloor just under a rocky outcropping.

Joe followed Simon down toward the HLHA artificial reef. The reef included Liberty ships, concrete rubble, subway cars, barges, and even M60 battle tanks. Coral grew everywhere, and the interesting shapes and sunken ships made for an exciting dive. A sea turtle swam lazily by, and colorful fish darted out of its way. Simon looked back as if to make sure Joe followed before he slipped through the coral-encrusted window of a subway car.

Joe paused and peered inside. Simon had disappeared. He kicked his fins and focused on the steady in and out of oxygen until he was inside, where he clicked on his flashlight. The beam of light found Simon waiting for him in the corner. Joe swam over to join the sea lion and saw what the mammal had found—a broken underwater drone.

The thing was no toy and clearly cost a lot of money. It wasn't a hobbyist drone but something a hostile swimmer or spy would use.

Joe glanced around the dark compartment but only fish and stingrays moved past the window openings. He'd have to report this to the Navy commander over the sea mammal project, who would know if a threat had been reported.

Joe gave the hand signal of approval to Simon, who swam around him a few times in delight before they both exited the subway car and headed for the surface.

Hopefully this was nothing.

==

Lisbeth was the last person to have sat in this office chair.

Torie ran her fingers over the top of the chair bathed in blue light from the computers. She could almost hear her best friend's tinkle of laughter. No one laughed like Lisbeth, that special combination of pure joy and sweet spirit. Torie's vision blurred, and grief tightened her throat.

The room was tiny, and her claustrophobia made her feel antsy so she opened the blinds on the small window. Being able to look out onto the lawn made her breathe a little easier.

Her suitcases had arrived yesterday, so she'd spent all day unpacking and organizing things to her liking after receiving a grocery order through Instacart. She'd thought to find a church, but it could wait a week. She had no car, but it was a short bike ride to the hotel and anywhere else on the small island.

She swept her gaze over the room filled with computers and monitors. Three desks were crammed together by the walls, and the beige wall color did nothing to brighten the room's feel. Her new boss stood in the doorway behind her.

Kyle Ballard's red hair didn't appear to have been combed this morning, and it stuck out in clumps all over the top of his head. His shirt looked like it had been slept in. "This bank of computers is connected to all our security cameras around the complex."

Torie turned toward him. "How long do we keep the footage?"

"About six months."

"Whoa, that's a long time."

"Mr. Bergstrom is adamant about providing security." The man dropped his tall frame in front of a large desk that was as messy as he was. "Our internet system is state of the art, and it seldom goes down, but when it does, you might be summoned in the middle of the night to help fix it. High rollers like our guests expect the very best in service. They aren't content to wait until breakfast if they need to be online at two in the morning."

No surprise there. Torie cut her teeth on learning the importance her parents put on customer service and happy repeat guests. "I'll make sure my phone is on the nightstand. Are we able to log in remotely to handle problems?"

He lifted a brow. "You're like less than a five minute walk from the office, so no. I'll expect you to get your butt in here and take care of the problem. You'll follow up with a personal call to the guest, and you'll wait around to ensure everything is working as it should."

That was something she would change when this was all over. The employees didn't need to go to the office to fix things. Not in this day and age. "Got it."

"The majority of our time is spent keeping an eye on the cameras around the property and notifying security if we see anything out of the ordinary or suspicious."

She suspected that was a duty he enjoyed. Kyle's brown eyes seemed too likely to roam away from a woman's face and head south. Hopefully he didn't hang out in the office all the time.

She stashed her bag in an empty desk drawer and logged on to the computer with her new credentials. Once he left the office, she planned to go over every byte of security footage of Lisbeth's time here. Especially on the day she died. The fact the footage still existed was an unexpected boon.

Kyle plopped into his chair. "I heard you had a

break-in on Saturday night. When Joe told me about it, I pulled the recording from the camera nearest your cottage. We don't have as many in the cottage quarter as we do in the guest section, but there's one that picks up your back door. I didn't see anything."

"The front door was open, so I assume the intruder got in that way."

"Any trouble after Joe cleared the place?"

"No."

Unless he considered someone accessing her music "trouble." She had been on edge ever since Saturday night and had heard every croaking frog and loud cricket. She'd bought alarms for the doors that went off if anyone touched the doorknob, but the place had stayed blessedly quiet after Joe had mentioned the possibility of a hijacked remote. Her remote was still on the component shelf, but anyone could have programmed another one.

His speculative stare gave her the creeps. Could he have done it? Possibly. But why? She should take a look at the footage herself.

Kyle jiggled his mouse, and a screen lit up. "Just a warning: things will be very busy tonight, and you'll need to work. Game night tonight."

"Game night?" Hailey had mentioned it to Torie, but she wanted to know more about it and her duties here.

"Guests love it. We don't run it on Sunday since it tends to be an off day, but every other night, we have rotating games. Tonight is charades."

With a lot of chaos and interaction, the chance of theft would be higher, though that didn't seem to be a problem here. Torie had gone over all the issues the resort had seen in the past five years before she came. It had been remarkably quiet.

"How late should I plan to stay?"

"About ten. Things die down after that."

She glanced at the clock on her desk. Starting time had been seven, and it was now half past. A long day, but if things stayed truly quiet, she'd have time to review that footage. "No problem."

His mouth twisted as if he'd hoped she'd object. Was he looking for an argument or a way to throw his weight around? She'd dealt with people like that over the years, and it was best to defuse the situation when possible.

"Okay then." He moved toward the door. "I'm going to get coffee. Want anything?"

"Not yet, thanks. I had coffee with breakfast this morning. I'll grab some later. Thanks for showing me the ropes." She kept her tone light and polite and prayed he'd just leave her alone.

In another moment the door latch clicked, and she glanced back to make sure he was gone. If only her screen didn't face the room's entry. She'd need to listen for any approaching footsteps.

She found the footage from Saturday night and set it to running. At first she thought Kyle was right and it showed nothing, but five minutes from the time she'd come home, she saw something move in the shrubbery. She paused the feed and leaned in to study it, then she let it run frame by frame. A figure moved by the tree near the back door. Unfortunately there wasn't enough light to identify the person, but she watched the dark shadow move toward the front of the house until it vanished from sight.

She advanced the footage to just before ten. Her back door opened, and she watched herself take out the trash. Wait, was that a flash of light? She froze the frame and advanced slowly. A red light off in the bushes had briefly flashed. Maybe that was when her tormentor started the music. She played through several more frames and saw a hooded figure run to her back door and flip off the light, lock the doorknob inside, then shut the door.

What on earth? The figure was dressed all in black, and the hoodie obscured the face.

She copied the short footage over to a flash drive she'd brought. When she got home, she could enhance it and see if she could identify more clues.

While Kyle was gone, she called up the saved security files from around the resort and found the ones starting when Lisbeth arrived. She caught a glimpse of her friend three times in the first hour, and each time she had to blink back tears.

When she heard the doorknob rattle, she switched to another screen before Kyle saw what she was doing. There would be time later for more.

CHAPTER 8

AUNT GENEVIEVE STOOD BETWEEN TORIE AND
the coffee shop.

Torie saw her aunt's erect figure turn and stride
toward her along the gleaming wood floors in the lobby.
Coffee could wait. She reversed course and hurried for
the ladies' room, where she leaned against the door for a
moment after it closed behind her.

She didn't think Aunt Genevieve had seen her. She
glanced around the restroom, which had been completely
redone since she'd lived here. Gleaming copper bowls
topped marble counters, and the stalls were sleek stain-
less walls. The mixture of old and new hit exactly the
right note, and Torie knew her aunt had been behind the
renovation. She had impeccable taste.

Torie stepped to the mirror and touched her head. Her
coronet of braids didn't have a hair out of place in spite
of dashing in here. How long could she hide out in here
before someone came in and gave her a suspicious stare?

She had worn jeans today and a pink tee, which looked

way too casual to her, but she'd wanted to fit in with IT. Clothes made the woman, and she felt a little powerless in this outfit.

The decisive click of heels on wood came along the corridor, and she inhaled at the familiar staccato. Aunt Genevieve was coming this way. Torie closed her eyes and gulped.

Don't come in here . . . don't come in here.

Her plea was in vain when the door opened. Torie blinked, pasted on a smile, then turned toward the door.

Her aunt swept into the restroom, and the door shut soundlessly behind her. Her power suit was dark purple, and every hair was in place. Her gaze raked over Torie's jeans and pink top, and she sniffed at the shell-pink polish on Torie's toes. "I thought Kyle had instituted a dress code."

Torie touched the soft denim on her hips. "Not that I've heard. We're in a dungeon and don't interact with the guests except by phone." And Kyle was the last one she could see in a suit.

Her aunt smoothed her perfect blonde bob. "How is your first day going? Any problems?"

What would her aunt say if Torie told her she was working with a guy she could imagine peeping in her bedroom window? "No problems. He told me about the game night."

"There's even more news than that, which is why I chased you down. We have six banking executives arriving next week along with a couple of US senators. The structure of the Federal Reserve was hammered out here back in 1910, so it's appropriate for them to return to discuss changes to the system here. I want it to be enjoyable for them, so I thought we'd do a variation on the usual float hunting the island does in January."

"Float hunting?" It sounded vaguely familiar, but Torie couldn't remember exactly what her aunt was referencing.

Genevieve turned toward the mirror and pulled a lipstick out of a drawer, then applied a coat of pink. She took a tissue and blotted before she turned back to face Torie. "It's a throwback to the glass floats on the nets of fishermen in the nineteenth century. Collecting them was very popular in the 1950s, then fell off when commercial fishermen began to use Styrofoam and plastic ones. The Jekyll Island Authority commissioned glass artisans from all over the country to make floats, and we hide plastic ones in January and February that can be exchanged for the glass ones. Our own Amelia Rogers has agreed to make special floats for our guests to find during a scavenger hunt. Security will need to be very high all through the weekend. If we need to put up extra cameras, I want it done."

"You've spoken to Kyle already?"

"Of course, but I wanted to make sure you realize you'll be working that weekend with very little rest. I've authorized temp help after the officials leave so you and the rest of the staff can take a few days off to rest and recover."

"I came here to work so I'm fine with the overtime."

"Excellent news." Her hazel eyes lingered on Torie's face. "You remind me of someone, but I can't put my finger on it. My sister always wore her hair like that so maybe that's what I'm thinking of."

A denial sprang to Torie's lips, but she hated lies.

When she hesitated, her aunt shook her head. "No matter. It will come to me. I have to attend to a problem in the dining room. Please come to me with any problems you foresee that weekend."

"Of course."

Torie blew out a heavy exhale when her aunt left her alone. That was close. It was only a matter of time before Genevieve figured out who Torie was. Maybe she should confess, but she wanted to poke into things without the doors being slammed in her face. Once her aunt knew the reigning Bergstrom "princess" was on-site, she'd expect her to attend every fund-raising event and every boring tea thrown on the island. She wasn't ready to be thrust into the spotlight like that. Not yet.

She stared at her reflection in the mirror again and touched her hair. Though her mother had been blonde, Torie wore her hair in the same coronet of loose braids as a way of honoring her mother's memory. It was elegant, even if a little old-fashioned, but something about being here made her want to take it down and do things differently.

She waited a few discreet minutes, then slipped back out into the hall. The fragrance of sandalwood and pine was particularly potent when she stepped into the main lobby again, and she found herself moments later on the elevator with the top-floor button lit.

She emptied her mind as the elevator rose. When it stopped on the penthouse floor, she stepped out onto the thick carpet before she could change her mind. She hadn't been sure she'd remember how to get up to the balcony in the tower, but her feet remembered the way to the elevator. *Go back.*

The warning in her head couldn't overcome her compulsion to go up there, to see the place she'd so successfully avoided for nearly two decades. Her steps echoed a bit in the enclosed stairwell, and she pushed open the door out onto the balcony. The sunshine hit her eyes, and she slammed them closed.

Torie's heart wanted to pound out of her chest as the memories flooded back. She could feel them rising, fighting to become clear. But she didn't want to think about the last day of her mother's life.

She turned and ran for the exit.

==

The battered drone and its parts lay on the desk. Joe saw the moment his contact with the Navy tensed and realized his suspicions were on target. "Looks like a Russian military drone, doesn't it?"

Ajax Smith was a bulldog of a man with a thick neck and massive shoulders. In spite of his appearance, he was mild-mannered and thoughtful, never rushing to judgment and carefully considering every response. He'd come as soon as Joe had called, and the heavy scent of his Brut cologne filled Joe's office.

Ajax prodded the propeller with a sausage-like finger. "Any sign of a swimmer or just this broken drone?"

"No. Simon brought me the propeller, and I went down to take a look, but there was no one around it. It was untethered so no way to trace it back to a boat. Maybe we need extra patrols? The new sub will be coming this way next week."

Ajax's massive forehead wrinkled, and he leaned his bulk back in the office chair across from the desk. "Patrols are already beefed up. There's a group of senators and the Federal Reserve Board meeting on Jekyll Island next week to discuss changes to the Fed. And we have war games running for the next two weeks as well. Lots of activity going for fifteen miles."

That news ramped up Joe's concern. "You think the Russians have gotten wind of the war games?"

"They get wind of everything. You've got three lions. They're all trained and ready to go?"

"Simon is making strides but isn't fully trained yet. The other two are experienced. When do the war games start?"

"Next weekend. The subs arrive on Wednesday the fifteenth, and the members of the meeting on Jekyll Island arrive on Thursday."

Today was Monday so Joe had ten days. "So the Federal Reserve VIPs are staying at Jekyll Island Club Resort, just like they did back then. We'll close the club to any other visitors during the meeting."

Ajax nodded. "And we'll treat it with the highest security. We've got several extra patrol boats heading our way."

The whole thing had Joe's spidey senses tingling. He turned toward the door. "We'll be vigilant with the sea lions. Thanks for coming so quickly, Ajax. I'll see you out."

They exited into the bright Georgia sunshine and Smith lumbered to his black Cadillac while Joe strode toward his pickup. It was past time to get Hailey from

Camp Jekyll. He drove out Beachview Drive and pulled in at the camp.

Hailey waved from the front lawn and ran toward him as soon as he parked and got out of his truck. "Hey, Peanut." He hugged her, inhaling the aroma of little girl mingled with sea salt and sunscreen.

These moments with his daughter were ones he treasured. Since his wife died, he didn't take even a moment for granted. Happiness had a funny way of twisting into something unrecognizable, and he had a hard time even letting Hailey out of his sight. His work helped him focus, but worry about her was never far from his mind.

She went around to the passenger side of the truck. "We got to swim with some dolphins today, Daddy."

His gut clenched. "Was that planned?"

"Oh no. We were swimming and they joined us. I touched one. It felt like a warm inner tube."

She'd heard his warnings a thousand times, so he didn't voice them again. "Everything was okay?"

"The teacher made us get out of the water, but I know they'd never hurt me. The little one looked me right in the face and did a flip. It liked me."

He buckled his seat belt. "Of course it did. It could tell you were kind and loving." He gave up the bridle on his tongue. "But remember, you can't get too close. A dolphin could hurt you without meaning to."

She rolled her eyes and fastened her seat belt. "I know, Daddy."

He forced back a grin. "When did you get so old?" He started his truck. "What sounds good for dinner?"

"Can we go to Tortuga Jack's?"

"Will you ever have another favorite? Pizza? Or what about Driftwood Bistro? You like their Og's fried okra. Or what about their cheese grits? We ate at Tortuga Jack's twice last week, and it's the height of the tourist season. We'll have to wait an hour for a table."

"Maybe we'll find someone we know to sit with. All I thought about all day was fish tacos."

"You got those last time. And the time before."

A dimple flashed in her cheek. "And tonight."

"All right, tonight too." He shook his head and drove back toward the village.

Just as he'd predicted, the lot was full. He parked, and they went to the outdoor check-in by the thatched patio seating to put their name in. An hour wait. At least they'd have the sea and surf to watch as they waited for the pager to go off. The restaurant was right on the Atlantic with a killer view that drew tourists and locals alike.

Hailey tugged on his hand. "Look, there's Miss Torie sitting all by herself. We can eat with her." She waved. "Miss Torie!"

Torie sat under the outside thatched hut. She had a chip loaded with guacamole halfway to her mouth that she lowered to wave back, then she pointed to the seats beside her.

The warmth spreading through Joe's midsection surprised him. He hadn't wanted to face how much he liked Torie. He liked the way she carried her height like a badge of honor. The crown of loose braids reminded him of a Victorian lady, but the spark in her brown eyes warned everyone she was no shrinking violet. The quiet

competence in her manner drew him too. She was confident in who she was.

Heaven help him, he wasn't sure he was ready to feel
any kind of attraction again. But he stuffed his misgivings
and followed his daughter under the thatched hut.

CHAPTER 9

TORIE COULDN'T SORT OUT HER FEELINGS AT
the sight of Joe and Hailey. She'd wrestled with her suspicion of the way he'd shown up right after the break-in,
and she hadn't come to any firm conclusion on how much
she could trust him. Torie's suspicion wasn't his daughter's
fault, so she directed a welcoming smile at the little girl.
"You look like you've been swimming."

Hailey touched her tousled red hair. "Yeah, I should
have rinsed out the salt. It's a little sticky."

Torie waited until the server took their orders before
she started to probe. "And you look like you just got off
work, Joe. You're a little windburned. Or sunburned. I
can't tell which."

"Yep. Out on the boat all day so it's a little of both."

"So what exactly do you do for the Navy?" Everything
was too new, and she didn't know who to trust. For all
she knew, this handsome guy could have been involved
in Lisbeth's death. He'd been quick to dismiss her doubt
about how she'd died.

But he didn't answer her question and reached for a chip to scoop up guacamole. The sea wind lifted his light-brown hair and turned up the collar on his shirt. "That breeze feels good. It's a hot one."

And humid. Torie tucked a loose strand of hair back into her coronet. She could feel his gaze on her as she adjusted the wind damage to her braid, and it wasn't exactly an unpleasant sensation. If only she was sure she could find an ally in him.

Why didn't he want to talk about his job? She knew it had to do with training sea mammals, but that was it. Had Lisbeth ever met him?

"I'm glad you saw me," she said after an awkward pause. "I hate eating alone, and I don't really know any-one yet."

"How'd your first day at work go?"

"Good. I figured out where all the cameras are and found out my duties. I'm just on a dinner break and have to go back. You know Kyle Ballard?" She forced a casual tone she didn't feel. Her boss had unnerved her most of the day.

"Everyone knows him. He hired on about the same time we moved here."

Torie tipped her head to the side. "You don't like him." He glanced her way. "You do?"

She shook her head. "He never looks me in the face."

Realization of what she meant dawned in his green eyes. "I've heard other women complain about that too."

"Lisbeth, the woman who drowned?"

His nod was reluctant. "Among others, but it's impossible to complain to HR when he doesn't say any-thing out of line."

She wondered if anyone had filed a complaint. With small ears listening, she had to be careful what she said about Kyle. And about Lisbeth's death.

She decided to try to probe again. "You said you were on the boat all day."

"Out at the artificial reef. I was working with Simon, my newest sea lion."

He tossed the information out like it was no big deal, but Torie straightened. "Hailey mentioned the sea lions, and I wondered if you were part of the Navy's Marine Mammal Project."

"You've heard of it."

"I saw a documentary not too long ago. It looked fascinating. I thought it was based in San Diego."

"It is. I was there for years, but when Julie—" He broke off and glanced at Hailey, who was playing a game on his phone. "I decided a change was in order so we came here. I leased a building and went freelance with the training. The Navy still wanted the sea lions I trained. Some activists worried the sea lions wouldn't adapt to the Georgia coast, but the winter water temps are nearly the same as San Diego. When training is done, they relax in their enclosures."

"What do you have the sea lions watch for?"

"Hostile divers mostly. They're trained to snap a cuff on the diver's leg so we can haul them up and interrogate them."

"How does that work?"

"The sea lion comes to the boat and signals there's a diver by clapping his flippers. I give him a cuff in his mouth, and it's made to snap as soon as the animal bumps the diver's leg. The metal reinforced tether is attached to the boat, and when the sea lion returns without the cuff, we haul in the diver."

"Have you ever apprehended one?"

He shrugged. "A couple, just harmless divers trying to see how close they could get to the naval base without being detected. The locals know about our work, and you know how brainless teenagers and twentysomethings can be. We give them a stiff warning and turn them loose."

Hailey took a sip of her sweet tea. "Are you going to game night? It starts at seven."

Torie shook her head. "I'll be at the hotel working behind the scenes."

"We always go," Hailey said. "I like charades, but Daddy hates it. I wish you could play with us."

"It sounds like fun. What kinds of games do you play? Anything besides charades?"

"My favorite is the scavenger hunt. I'm really good at finding things. Daddy is the best at it though."

Torie leaned forward and laced her fingers together before her on the tabletop. "I love scavenger hunts. Maybe I can join in sometime."

Talking about the games made Torie pause for a moment. The person who had broken into her cottage had put on the song "Games People Play." Did it mean anything? Was it some kind of clue about what was going to happen tonight?

It seemed too far-fetched to think they could be connected, but she had to consider it. Her gaze met Joe's, and a frown extended from his eyes to his forehead.

"Be careful tonight," he said. "That intruder . . ."

"I was just remembering the song," she said.

"I won't be far away if you need me."

Torie nodded. "I'll remember that."

And the realization she had backup was a comfort. She hadn't thought she'd be in danger by coming here, but she was beginning to think nothing was as it seemed. Her dad was here, too, but she couldn't be seen with him without blowing her cover. This secrecy was already wearing on her, and she'd only been here a few days.

Maybe this was more than she could handle.

==

Guests filled the lobby, and a cacophony of excited chatter rose around Torie as she managed to get through the throng and down the hall to her office. Thankfully, it was empty. Kyle had said he might work tonight, but she'd hoped he didn't see the need. She'd had enough of his gaze crawling all over her.

She just might have to say something if he didn't stop.

She jiggled her mouse and her monitor sprang to life. The sight of her dad brought a lump to her throat. Dressed in his usual gray Armani suit, he mingled with the guests as he made his way around the perimeter of the lobby. His way of putting people at ease was one of the many reasons his resorts were so successful. He'd required that quality in thousands of employees across the globe.

It didn't come so easily for her.

She worked hard at presenting the proper image of a hotel executive with her power suits and heels. Her perfectly coiffed hair and expert makeup. But inside she always felt she was supposed to be doing something else. What that something else could possibly be never came to her. At least not yet.

Her mother's death had taught her to be wary of assuming the best. It caused her to be on the lookout for the dark side of events, and she never completely let her guard down.

Few people tried to get past that reserve, and that was the way she wanted it.

Or so she told herself.

She let her gaze wander until she found Joe's broad shoulders and thick thatch of light-brown hair. He was smiling down at Hailey in a way that brought a lump to Torie's throat. He was a good dad, but even that didn't make him trustworthy in everything.

The door opening behind her jerked her attention away. Her mood plummeted when she saw Kyle's messy mop of red hair. She pressed her lips together and turned back to the screen.

"Just checking to make sure you got here on time." Kyle sidled close enough to envelope her in a cloud of overpowering cologne.

She choked back a cough. "No worries. I'll handle it tonight if you want to go home."

If she didn't look at him, she wouldn't have to see his avid gaze roaming over her. But she could still feel it like a dark slug crawling over her skin. She suppressed a shudder.

How long could she take this before she blew?

A screen flickered and went out. She rose. "We lost a camera. I'm going to go look at it."

"Check your settings first. It's probably not a problem with the camera."

She ignored Kyle and went out the door without slamming it. Following orders had never been her strong suit. Especially when it was someone she regarded with so little respect.

Focus on Lisbeth. It was the only way Torie would be able to get through this.

She had barely exited the office when she bumped into her dad.

He held out his hand to steady her. "There you are. I wondered if you were working."

She wanted to tell him about Kyle, but it wasn't the wise thing to do yet. He'd fire the guy on the spot, and she still hadn't ruled the man out as being behind Lisbeth's death. He seemed to target every attractive woman, and her friend had been a stunner. There was no way Kyle hadn't been attracted to her. HR would hear about Kyle's inappropriate behavior the minute she'd achieved her goals here. The other employees needed to be protected.

She forced a smile. "I'm supposed to be watching the monitors to make sure the guests are safe in all the dark nooks and crannies. I had one go out so I was checking on the camera."

His fingers touched her chin and tipped her head up. "I recognize the fire in your eyes. Someone made you mad."

Her chuckle wouldn't fool her dad, but she tried anyway. "I don't take orders well."

He grinned. "Tell me something I don't know." His hand dropped away, and he leaned forward to brush her cheek with a light kiss. "Hang in there, Torie. Any evidence on Lisbeth yet?"

"Not yet."

"Well, I'd better get back to the scavenger hunt, or my partners will roast me."

"Who are your partners?"

"Joe and Hailey Abbott."

"You know Joe?"

He shook his head. "You sound like you do."

"I've met them."

"Hmm, that's a conversation I'd like to have later." Her dad smiled and went past her to another hallway.

She heard a latch click and turned to see Joe and Hailey standing in an open doorway. He was scowling, and she gulped. How much had he overheard?

His lips were tight. "Hailey, grab us some waters, would you?"

Hailey gave him an uneasy glance. "Sure, Daddy. Stay right here so I don't lose you."

"I'll be right here." He folded his arms over his chest and waited until she disappeared around the corner. "Did Anton Bergstrom ask you to look into Lisbeth Nelson's death?"

She squared her shoulders. "I don't think you have the right to question me."

His gaze hardened. "You knew Lisbeth, didn't you?"

Busted.

She fiddled with a hoop earring and nodded. "She was my best friend. Water terrified her after a near drowning when we were kids. There's no way she would have gone swimming. Zero chance. That means her death was no accident, and I have to find out who killed her. Anton arranged the job here so I could investigate."

"All you'd have to do is tell the state police it couldn't have been an accidental drowning."

"I tried that. The detective practically patted me on the head and said, 'There, there, little lady.' He thought I was refusing to consider any other way she could have drowned. He said she might have been walking in knee-deep water and been swamped by an unexpected wave."

"Possible."

"Not possible. You don't understand how deep her fear was. She never so much as dipped a toe in the ocean. Someone killed her, Joe."

He grasped her forearm when she turned to go. "I believe you. How can I help?"

His quiet acceptance brought tears to her eyes. "Thank you. I need someone to believe me."

"Anton didn't? He could have made a call to the state police too."

"He did and got the same reaction."

Joe frowned and his eyes clouded. "That seems odd. They must have a legitimate reason."

"Yeah, the reason is that the state police are hiding something."

Joe sighed. "Let's talk more tomorrow. Come to the house for dinner. I cook a mean stroganoff."

"Okay." Just knowing she had an ally lifted a boulder off her shoulders. Maybe her quest wasn't a lost cause after all.

CHAPTER 10

JOE MIGHT HAVE BITTEN OFF MORE THAN HE could chew.

The scents of beef and garlic wafted through the kitchen as he stirred the stroganoff. With the added security necessity for all that was happening next weekend, he wasn't sure how much help he'd be to Torie.

But he really wanted to help. The doorbell sounded, and he set down the spoon to answer it. That might be Craig. He'd asked his friend to join them tonight in case he had some real information to shed light about Lisbeth's death. He hoped Torie didn't feel ambushed to have the state trooper here, but Joe trusted Craig.

He opened the door and saw Craig's curious face. "Come in. I hope you're hungry."

"Starving." Craig entered the foyer. "You were very mysterious on the phone, but I did what you asked and brought the information on the Nelson case. Why all the interest?"

His friend still wore his state police uniform, and his face showed his fatigue from the day's work.

"Later," Joe said. "Want a drink? I made sure to get some Dr Pepper. It's in the fridge."

"I'll help myself." Craig shut the door behind him and meandered toward the kitchen, where he opened the fridge and pulled out a can. "Want one?"

Joe had followed him and gave the stroganoff a brisk stir. "Later."

The doorbell rang again. He could only hope and pray Torie would understand why he'd asked Craig here too. She'd take one look at him in his uniform and know something was up.

When Joe opened the door, he nearly took a step back. Her dark-brown hair hung down her shoulders for the first time instead of up in its distinctive crown of braids. She looked softer somehow, more approachable. His fingers itched to test the texture of her hair. The flowing sundress exposed her shoulders and arms before draping gracefully to her knees.

Maybe he shouldn't have invited Craig. Having her to himself would have been much better. But the damage was done.

"You look beautiful." He pressed his lips together, but it was too late to call back the words.

A delicate color swept up her long neck and lodged in her cheeks. "Thanks." She stepped inside and held up a shoebox. "I've got some information in here I wanted you to see."

"Uh, sure."

Her gaze went past him, and her eyes widened when she spotted Craig behind him. Her accusing stare swung back to Joe. "What have you done?"

"He's a good guy, Torie, and he brought all the police know about Lisbeth's death. I thought you'd like to see. He's not actively on the case so he has nothing to hide from you. I haven't told him anything other than I was looking into Lisbeth's death. You can explain your interest in it."

Carrying a Dr Pepper, Craig walked toward them from the kitchen. "Well, hello. I didn't know we had another guest." His quizzical gaze slid from Torie to Joe.

"Torie, this is Craig Hall. He's been a good friend of mine for a while now. Craig, this is Torie Berg. She works in the IT department at the resort."

She heaved a sigh and held out her hand. "Hi, Craig, thanks for coming. Lisbeth Nelson was my best friend, and I've known Anton since I was born. He arranged for the job here so I could look into her death."

Craig glanced at Joe, then back to Torie. "You're the newcomer questioning whether it was suicide?"

"I don't believe her death was suicide or an accident."

Joe heard the note of desperation in her voice and prayed for Craig to really listen. If he discounted her right away, this would be a fiasco.

"I'm listening," Craig said.

"I need to tend to dinner," Joe said. "Let's continue this in the kitchen while I take care of the final prep."

"Where's Hailey?" Torie asked.

Joe spoke over his shoulder as he hurried to stir the stroganoff before it burned. "My parents took her to dinner. I have to pick her up at eight thirty at their house in Brunswick so we have a couple of hours."

Torie settled at the breakfast bar and laced her fingers together. "Nice kitchen. The resort remodeled it?"

"Just before I moved in." Joe gave the meal a brisk stir. "Tell Craig what you told me."

Torie launched into how she was sure Lisbeth's death was not an accident and how the state police had brushed off any concerns. Then she opened the shoebox and withdrew a journal. "I found her journal too. She knew she was in danger." She leafed through the book and found a page before she slid it across the white quartz countertop to Craig. "Look at the June 6 entry."

Joe came around to read it too. He hadn't heard anything about the journal.

June 6

Someone broke into my cottage last night. I didn't know it until I got up this morning and found the back door standing open. There was a note on the dining table that read, "I KNOW WHO YOU ARE. GO AWAY OR FACE THE CONSEQUENCES."

Craig stared at the journal. "Wow, this isn't what I was expecting tonight. I'll help in any way I can. I'm not technically on the case, but I'll poke around and see what I can find out."

Seeing Torie's brown eyes fill with tears geezed up Joe's insides. He clenched his fists together. He didn't have the right to comfort her but sure wanted to.

"Sounds like the guy has had the key to the cottage awhile," Craig said. "Long enough that he terrorized Lisbeth too."

Joe ladled up the food and handed out plates oozing

with the aromas of garlic and sour cream. "Eat up. We've got our work cut out for us."

Julie used to say he had a hero complex and wanted to save everyone, but he'd never admitted to it. Maybe she was right after all.

==

Torie had found it hard to look at Joe while eating dinner. Couldn't he have warned her that he was bringing Craig here? While it appeared the state cop was agreeing to help her, she still felt on edge as she put her plate in the dishwasher.

Craig rinsed his plate and stacked it behind hers. "Let me show you what I've got."

She settled on a seat and watched as he pulled out a file and laid it on the island's countertop. "That's not much evidence. Is that all of it?"

He nodded. "I'd thought only Joe would be looking at it, so I brought everything, even the coroner's report. You might not want to read that or see the pictures. It's graphic."

She suppressed a shudder. "So what do you have then? Why did the detective in charge of the case brush me off when I told him I didn't believe her death was accidental?"

He pulled out a picture of the sand to show her. "There were footsteps along the edge of the water to where she entered the foam at the shoreline. See here—just one set of prints, so she wasn't dragged in by someone else. There was water in her lungs, so she wasn't killed, then dumped in the water."

"Seawater?" Torie asked.

"The results aren't back yet. They should be any time though. There were no bruises on her arms to indicate she'd been roughly handled. And her roommate reported she'd been despondent and had been taking pills for depression. So while we haven't ruled on it yet, the department is leaning toward suicide. It's a dangerous area where she was. There's a sharp drop-off not far offshore and a dangerous riptide."

Torie had to force herself not to leap from her chair. "I don't believe that for a second! Lisbeth was the most optimistic and eternally happy person I've ever met. You say Bella Hansen told you this? I'll talk to her myself. She's wrong."

Craig's eyes shuttered, and she knew her adamant refusal to listen had hurt her case. She bit her lip. "I'm sorry. I have to remember this is evidence that's been collected. It's not a judgment on Lisbeth."

"When did you last talk to her?" Joe asked.

She forced herself to glance his way, and the plea in his green eyes dissolved her sense of betrayal. He was only trying to help. "About a month before she came here we talked for about an hour by phone. And texted nearly every day even after she came."

"So sometime in early May? How much had you been around her in the last few years?"

"Well, she lived in Chicago, and I was in Scottsdale." When she wasn't traveling. "But we got together four times a year or so. And we spoke on the phone every week, sometimes more than once. We emailed and texted nearly every day. Believe me, if she'd been depressed or seeing a doctor for depression, I would have known."

The pity on Craig's face told her he'd heard that kind

of excuse before. People weren't always honest, even with those closest to them.

"Except you hadn't spoken to her in a month by phone, only text," Craig pointed out.

"I tried to call her several times and didn't reach her."

"And she never called back? That was unusual, wasn't it?"

Torie nodded. "I am so mad at myself for not hopping a plane and coming to see her. I thought maybe she was caught up in her new job with odd hours, and I was busy myself." Her dad had sent her to a struggling hotel in The Bahamas, but she couldn't tell them that.

"You didn't find any pills in her belongings, did you? That's because she hated taking pills of any kind. She wouldn't even take aspirin for a headache."

Craig consulted the notes. "There was an unmarked bottle of pills that we tested and found to be Prozac."

"They weren't hers—I'm certain of it." Torie sent a pleading glance Joe's way.

"The bottle could have been planted," Joe put in. "Was it tested for fingerprints?"

Craig frowned and his gaze ran down the page before he shook his head. "Nothing about that. It seemed clear-cut that she'd either been swamped by a rogue wave and carried out to sea or she killed herself."

"Is it too late to check for prints?" Joe asked.

"Maybe not. I can check on it. If her prints are on the bottle, it will be more likely accepted that she was taking the drug."

"What about her doctor? Did you check to see who might have prescribed them?"

Craig shook his head. "There was no prescribing information so we assumed she'd bought them illegally."

"She'd never do that." Torie had to keep reminding herself no one knew Lisbeth like she did. The detectives were making assumptions about the case based on very little evidence.

Her head began to pulse with pain. "Anything else?"

Craig scanned through the pages again, then handed them to her. "I don't see anything, but you can take a look."

At least it wasn't the pictures. Torie read through the pages, and a paragraph jumped out at her. "She was wearing jeans and hiking boots. She loved hiking. Why would she have been walking on the beach in boots? Especially if the waves were coming over her feet. People don't do that."

Joe frowned. "She has a point, Craig. You have to admit that's strange. She was fully dressed when I pulled her out of the surf."

"If she planned to drown herself, maybe she thought the boots would help weigh her down," Craig said. "When someone is in that much despair, they don't always do logical things."

It was clear that Craig thought he had all the answers, so she turned to Joe again with an unspoken plea. His compassionate gaze held her captive for a long moment before he spoke.

"What do you think could explain the evidence?" he asked.

Her thoughts swirled so wildly she had trouble pinning them down. Walking along the water's edge with boots. It didn't make sense. "Could I see the picture of the footprints again?"

Craig plucked a picture off the top of the pile. "Yeah, here you go."

She took the glossy photo and stared at it. Boot prints. She squinted at it. "They look deep. You realize Lisbeth barely weighed a hundred pounds and was only five one?"

Joe reached out his hand. "Let me see that." When she passed the photo over to him, he studied it, then nodded. "She's right, Craig. Those prints are deeper than a tiny woman like Lisbeth would make."

Craig took the print and stared at it. "I'll mention it to the detective, but I think the body has already been released. Unless there's more concrete evidence, I don't think they'll reopen the investigation. The sand could have been extra soft that day."

"Listen to yourself making excuses for headquarters," Joe said. "You've lived here too long to actually believe that. And look at the size of the prints. I'd say that's a man's size ten at least." He turned his attention to Torie. "What size shoe did Lisbeth wear?"

"It was a joke between us that we both had such trouble finding shoes. I wear a twelve, and she wore a four so we both shopped in specialty stores."

"There's no way that's a size four boot," Joe said. "See what you can do, Craig."

Craig tucked the papers and picture away. "Don't hold your breath, but I'll give it a shot."

So much for help. Torie would have to investigate this herself. Her gaze went to Joe, who looked impossibly handsome in his jeans and T-shirt. At least he believed her.

CHAPTER 11

DANGER, DANGER.

Joe watched Torie's dark hair glimmer with red high-lights cast from the pendant lights over the breakfast bar. There hadn't been a woman in his kitchen since Julie had died, and yet somehow he liked watching Torie's tall, elegant figure move around the space, scooping up utensils and loading the dishwasher as if she belonged.

Why would he feel that way about someone he'd just met five days ago? The fact was he'd been intrigued with her from the moment he met her. He wanted to punch through that reserve and see something no one else had noticed. "I can clean up."

"I'm weird. I like cleaning the kitchen, probably because every item has its place and it's easy to make a clean sweep of everything."

"I've never thought of it that way. Cleaning is a continuous chore. It never stays clean, especially with a grazing eight-year-old in the house."

She turned from the sink, and he was struck by the

deep brown of her eyes. In the past three years, he'd never even considered dating someone. Raising Hailey by himself took all his energy and focus. And he wasn't sure how his daughter would receive having another woman around.

He gave a light shake of his head at the way his thoughts were headed. Torie had given no indication she found him attractive so he might as well be swinging for the bleachers in vain.

She rinsed the sink and laid the sponge aside. "All done."

"How about some coffee and popcorn? I've got another hour before I need to pick up Hailey." He could see the *no* forming on her face and rushed on. "I thought we might talk a little more about the case. Maybe even look at that notebook. Are there any other indications Lisbeth felt threatened?"

"Some of the pages had been cut out."

"That sounds suspicious." He took her answer for a yes and poured two cups of coffee before he got out a bag of cheesy popcorn. When she took the popcorn from him without objection, a dose of elation shot up his spine. "Cream in your coffee?"

"You have any heavy whipping cream? And honey?" Her nose wrinkled. "That's a tall order, isn't it? I sound like some kind of diva. Coffee the way I like it is my one vice."

"You're in luck." He got the carton of whipping cream from the fridge and found the bottle of honey in the pantry. "Voilà, your perfect coffee."

"Most people don't have heavy whipping cream on hand."

"My diva daughter likes hot chocolate with heavy whip."

Torie set the bag of popcorn aside and stirred the cream into her coffee. "I knew I liked that kid."

Joe ripped open the top of the popcorn bag and kernels went flying all over the kitchen floor. He was so far out of the practice of trying to impress a woman, he didn't know what to do, and he stood staring at the mess with his mouth slightly open for a long moment.

Torie put down her coffee and knelt to scoop the popcorn together in her hands. "I'm not sure it's Hailey who's the problem in the kitchen."

A laugh bubbled up his throat. "I've got ten thumbs tonight. Let me get a broom."

"I've got it. Open the trash drawer."

He pulled it out, and she dropped the debris into it, then washed her hands while he made more popcorn. With her coffee in hand she followed him into the living room, where he put the popcorn on the coffee table. They settled side by side on the plaid sofa.

"Your cottage is a lot like mine," she said.

He nodded. "The bedrooms are on either end of the open space. We even have the same paint on the walls— Sherwin-Williams's Agreeable Gray."

"I think your floor is darker than mine."

"Maybe." The small talk was killing him. How did he ask about her life, what she liked, and how she'd grown up? Would she be offended if he probed?

He wiped damp palms on his jeans before reaching for a handful of popcorn. "So, you were best friends with Lisbeth. How'd that happen? I mean, what drew you together?"

Her eyes flickered, and she leaned down to pet Lucy, his calico cat who had decided to come out of hiding. At first he didn't think she was going to answer, but she straightened and folded her hands in her lap.

"I traveled a lot as a kid, so I can't exactly say we grew up together, but we knew each other from summers here. When I went to college, she was my roommate. She always made me laugh with the goofiest expressions and her droll way of looking at the world. And she saw the good in everyone. I tend to be more cynical and think people are out to pull one over on me."

He winced inwardly. And wasn't that what he was doing? Masking his romantic interest by talking about Lisbeth's death was just as bad as what other guys had probably pulled with her. When she walked into a room, he could see how she'd command attention from every guy out there with her striking features and gorgeous thick hair. How many people had seen it down like she was wearing it tonight? A stab of jealousy surprised him.

"You ever been married?"

Had he really said that or just thought it? But when her eyes widened, he knew the words had come from his mouth. "Sorry, that's too personal."

"No, it's fine. No, never married. Engaged once but it didn't work out. I'm sorry about your wife. That had to have been hard to lose her. How long was she sick?"

A safe assumption since it was how so many died.

"She died in a freak accident at an amusement park. A car on the Ferris wheel came loose. Julie and I were in the car, and I tried to grab her when she fell out. I missed. Hailey was below with my sister and saw the whole thing. She says she can't remember it, but she has nightmares, and I think deep down she remembers more than she thinks."

Torie put her hand to her mouth. "Oh, Joe, I'm so sorry. That's horrible."

"It was hard, but we've found healing here on the island."

He suddenly didn't want to talk anymore so he stuffed his mouth with popcorn before he said something he'd regret even more.

$$==$$

After work on Wednesday, Torie biked along Old Plantation Road past the turn-of-the-century buildings lined with oak trees, their twisted limbs dripping with hanging moss. Magnolia branches displayed their shiny leaves and fought with pine trees for a share of the sunshine. Shrimp boats motored past in the distance as the birds sang overhead.

She saw Island Sweets Shoppe and couldn't resist heading that way. She stopped and leaned her bike into a stand. The scents of ice cream, fudge, and waffle cones greeted her when she stepped inside, and the aroma took her back eighteen years to when she was ten.

The little girl in front of the counter turned to face her. "Torie!" Hailey's face lit up. "I told Daddy we should have stopped by to see if you wanted to come with us."

Torie's gaze met Joe's. "Great minds think alike. What's the best flavor of ice cream?"

"Sea turtle," they both said in unison.

"What's in it?" she asked.

"Sea turtle–shaped chocolate chips in caramel ice cream," Joe said.

That was a no-brainer. "Sea turtle cone, please," Torie told the girl behind the counter.

Joe ordered two of the same, but Hailey shook her head. "I think I'll have rocky road today. I want to be different."

Joe gave her a sidelong glance but changed the order.

The surge in Torie's spirit at seeing them took her aback, but Hailey had an engaging way about her that blew down her defenses. Joe was another story. Being with him last night had been a little uncomfortable.

"Dessert instead of dinner seemed a good way to avoid another Mexican meal tonight," Joe said. "I don't think I can look another fish taco in the eye for a few days."

Torie chuckled. "I'm with Hailey. I could eat Mexican every meal."

"You have plans tonight?" Joe asked.

She accepted her cone and shook her head. "Just getting the lay of the land while I have some time off. I'll be working all next weekend."

"Me too. Walk with us?"

"Sure. Where are we headed?" She followed them back into the sunshine.

"Daddy promised me a glass sea turtle necklace." Hailey pointed down Pier Road. "It's supposed to be ready."

They turned toward more small shops, and a splash of color in one of the windows drew her attention. Rogers Glass. Wasn't that the artisan Aunt Genevieve had mentioned—the one making the glass globes for the scavenger hunt?

"This is the place." Joe held open the door to the small building.

The interior was full of light reflecting off a kaleidoscope of glass colors. A woman behind the counter looked up with a smile. "Hailey, I thought I might see you this week. I've got your sea turtle done." She reached behind her into an old quartersawn oak cupboard and pulled out a small box.

"It's all she's talked about, Amelia," Joe said.

The shop owner opened the small white box and withdrew a green sea turtle that sparkled in the light. Hailey squealed with delight when Amelia fastened it around her neck.

"It's amazing," Joe said. "Thank you."

Torie studied Amelia Rogers and tried to recall if they'd ever met. She didn't remember her if they had. Amelia was in her fifties with a trim figure and smooth skin. Her hair was that reddish-brown color that had been enhanced with a bottle, but it suited her coloring. Her ready smile encompassed all three of them, and Torie instantly liked her.

Something about being back on the island had stripped away some of Torie's defenses. Maybe it was coming home, back to her roots and the life she'd led before she'd learned most people only wanted to be friends because of her money and family connections. She didn't know if she wanted it to last or if she wanted to don the mantle of reserve again.

Maybe she had no choice. Once she left here, she'd likely be right back where she was with constant travel and never getting a chance to know someone better than the preliminary niceties.

But what else could she do? Going against her father's expectations wasn't something she knew how to do.

Amelia directed a smile at Torie. "Hello, I don't think we've met."

Torie returned the smile. "Torie Berg. I'm working at the hotel in the IT department."

"Oh good, so you'll be around for the upcoming glass globe event."

"I just heard about it this week from Ms. Hallston. It sounds intriguing. Do you have some of the globes here?"

"They're all ready. I'll show you." Amelia beckoned them to a door on the other side of the counter.

They followed her into a work space in the back that smelled of dust and left a metallic taste in the air. A man at a workbench looked up from his task of stringing glass items together in a wind chime.

His interested gaze settled on Torie. "Hello."

She returned his smile. "Hi." He was attractive enough—about five eleven with brown hair and hazel eyes above a neatly trimmed beard. She judged him to be about thirty.

"This is my son, Noah," Amelia said.

"I'm Torie Berg. I'm new here."

"Good to meet you. I'm an aide to Senator Richardson

who is attending the meeting here next week, so I came early to spend a little time with Mom."

Torie noticed the copy of *The Creature from Jekyll Island* on the table by him. "Is that yours? I've just been reading it. Interesting stuff."

He glanced at it. "Yeah. I've been trying to get the senator to read this. He might be able to do something about it."

Amelia pointed to a glass furnace on the outside wall. "There's my glory hole."

There were Y-shaped benches in front of the furnace and other metal stands around the room. Torie recognized some blow pipes, but the other equipment in the room wasn't familiar. A set of shelves along the back held various glass globes with such delicate workmanship and exquisite colors they took her breath away. Smaller globes of other colors melded into the interior of the larger globe.

Torie stepped closer. "You're giving these away? They're beautiful! I love the lapis lazuli one."

Amelia reached past her and took it from the shelf. "It's yours as a welcome gift to the island."

"Oh I couldn't take it! It has to be worth a lot of money."

Amelia pressed it into her hand. "I have a feeling you belong here on the island, and I want you to have it. I won't take no for an answer."

Once her fingertips touched the cool glass of the glass float, Torie didn't have the strength to say no. The swirling blue colors drew her in and held her captive. "Your art is amazing. The scavenger hunt is going to be a huge success with our guests. They truly get to keep a float?"

"Oh yes. I've been working on them for months. They're some of my finest pieces, but it's not totally altruistic. These executives have the clout to mention my art to other people who will buy it. It's a win-win situation."

Noah wandered over to stand beside her. "Her work is selling like hotcakes in my online store. Business is booming."

Torie smiled at the pride in his voice and touched the globe to her cheek. "Thank you, Amelia. I'll treasure it." And once she slipped back into her real life, she could direct people here as well.

They left the workroom and went out front, where Torie perused some of the other items. If only she had a real home so she could buy some of these things. Her gaze lingered on a lapis lazuli mermaid.

When she moved on, while trying to decide if she should buy it, she made the circuit around the interior and came back to the counter, where Amelia was wrapping up something in brown paper. She handed it to Joe, and he passed it over to Torie.

"What on earth?"

"It's the mermaid. Consider it a welcome gift."

Torie was seldom speechless, but every thought in her head flew away at the kindness in his green eyes. When had someone other than her father given her a gift just because he wanted to? Maybe only Lisbeth.

CHAPTER 12

WHAT HAD POSSESSED HIM TO BUY THAT MERMAID?
The sunset lit Torie's hair with orange and gold as they walked back toward the parking lot. Torie carried both her treasures as if they were the most precious things she'd ever owned, and Joe didn't regret his impulse, even if he didn't understand it.

He'd seen the longing in her brown eyes and hadn't been able to stop himself.

"Let's take Torie on a tour," Hailey said. "I don't want to go home yet."

Joe poked her in the ribs. "I'll bet a little girl wants her dad to buy her a stuffed animal in the gift shop."

She gave him a cheeky grin. "They're supposed to have new stuffed baby turtles."

"I wouldn't say no either," Torie said. "I've been wanting to take a tour. Let me drop my treasures off in your truck if you don't mind, and I'll grab my bike." She retrieved it from the bike rack and wheeled it along with them.

They reached the parking lot at the hotel, and he unlocked his truck for her to place the wrapped glass items behind the seat before he locked it again.

"I'll put your bike in the bed and you can ride home with us." Without waiting for an answer, he lifted it into the bed, and they turned toward the museum.

Excursions and shrimp boats were coming in, and the *putt-putt* of motors mingled with the tinkle of silverware as they walked to the long building.

"The museum is housed in the historic stables of the original compound," Joe said.

They skirted the line of red trolleys and went inside. Hailey hurried to the gift shop and began to sort through the stuffed animals while Torie wandered over to the history exhibit. He'd spent many hours in here with his daughter.

It didn't take long for Hailey to pick out a stuffed turtle, and he paid for it along with the tour tickets. He wanted to let Torie browse through the history exhibit longer, but they had to hurry if they wanted to catch the departing tour trolley.

Every minute he spent with her seemed more and more special, and he couldn't put his finger on the reason why he was becoming so intrigued. Was it the way she held her shoulders and head high and proud as if being tall was the best thing in the world? Was it the hint of uncertainty in her eyes as she looked out on the world? She seemed to always be waiting for a blow to fall, and he wanted to dig under the surface and see what had caused that shadow in her eyes.

Whatever it was, he was caught in her net as firmly as the shrimp in the nets pulling up to the pier right now.

It felt terrifying when he'd evaded any attraction to a woman all these years. Especially when she still held that wall around her, a wall he might never break through.

They stepped out into the fading sunshine, and Hailey's eyes widened. "There's Emily and her parents. Can we ride in the same trolley, Daddy?"

"As long as you sit with us."

She drew herself up to her full height. "I'm *eight*, Daddy. I'm big enough to sit with my friend."

She stared him down, and he shrugged. Sometimes it was hard figuring out the changing goalposts with kids. "Okay, but I'll be right behind you so don't get out of line."

His daughter scampered over to join her friend on the front bench seat while he and Torie found a spot a couple of rows behind. Truth be told, he relished the idea of having Torie to himself for a few minutes. Not that he knew how to approach her without making himself look like an idiot, but he could try while the trolley filled with tourists.

He cleared his throat. "So are you ready for next week with all the bigwigs? I will be swamped myself. We're deploying our sea mammals all along the Eastern Seaboard as the Navy's new Trident sub comes into port for war games."

"Are the subs always armed?"

"They always carry nuclear missiles, yes."

She hugged herself and shivered. "That sounds scary."

"The Navy has only launched them as tests, and we pray we never have to use them in a war. But with all the terrorism, they're always on high alert with them. The subs are impressive to see."

"I'd love to see one someday."

"I could arrange that if you like when this one comes in."

Her perfectly shaped brows winged up. "Really? I'd love that."

A small victory but he'd take it. "It's coming next week, Wednesday. I'll let you know what time."

"How long have you been training sea lions?"

"About thirteen years. I enlisted in the Navy at twenty-one when I got out of college with a degree in marine biology. Julie and I were married that same year and moved to San Diego when I was picked for the program. After a few years, I got out of the Navy and started my own training center. Then Julie died. Well, you know the rest of that story. Do you dive?"

She blinked at his out-of-the-blue question. "I do, actually. I was certified at twelve and have been on dives in the Maldives, Hawaii, Belize, all over really. I love it, but I haven't had a chance to dive here yet."

With her close association with Anton and this litany of everywhere she'd traveled, he assumed her expensive clothing had been purchased new. Maybe her family moved in the same circles as the Bergstroms. "Did you bring your gear?"

"I shipped it and it's arriving Friday. I-I didn't send all my belongings since I wasn't sure how long I'd be here. But I knew I had to dive while I was here."

His spirits sagged at the thought that she had an end date in sight to her job here. "You're planning on leaving as soon as you find out what happened to Lisbeth?"

"That's the plan." Her gaze focused across the road to the hotel. "Though this place feels like home already. It might not be as easy to leave as I'd once thought. My life is elsewhere though."

"What's your life usually like when you're not tracking down a murderer?"

Her smile emerged then and lifted him out of the pit. He loved the way it lit her eyes.

"My life is pretty boring. I work for Anton, and he often sends me to hotels to fix underlying problems."

So that explained how she knew Anton. "All that travel makes for a lonely life."

She nodded. "That's why losing Lisbeth was so devastating to me. She was my one constant, the best friend I'd had since grade school. She understood me without long explanations. We were always able to pick up right where we left off."

Her brown eyes glistened with moisture, and he wished he could change things for her. Julie's death had been hard, and he knew how it felt to lose a piece of his soul. For the past three years he hadn't thought he'd ever be able to move on and discover any kind of new life without her. He'd sometimes worried about what he'd do when Hailey grew up and left the nest.

But since he'd met Torie, he began to think of what it might be like not to wake up alone. To share his life with a woman again. That may have been a pipe dream with Torie, but if her arrival accomplished nothing else, at least it had opened his eyes to the possibilities.

==

The hanging moss on the oak trees cast weird shadows in the twilight by the time Torie returned from the tour with Joe and Hailey. The breeze, laden with the scents of the sea, blew in off the Intracoastal Waterway and made her shiver.

"Cold?" Joe asked.

"A little. Walking will warm me up." She stopped as she stepped off the sidewalk and tried to get her bearings in the darkness.

"This way." He took her hand and led her onto the walkway.

The warm clasp of his hand made her pull away and take Hailey's hand instead. The little girl was safe. Once they broke the cover of trees lining the road, she saw the lights of the hotel. "I have the worst sense of direction in the world. Is that south?"

His chuckle was without a hint of mockery. "It's northeast."

"You just know that kind of thing?"

"It's almost impossible to get Daddy lost. It's like he has a compass in his head. I'm pretty good at it too."

"I can get lost in a parking lot," Torie said. "Right now I can't even remember where to find your truck."

"We're in the lot behind the hotel."

"Of course. I remember now."

They turned left on North Riverview Drive, then made a right on the small road leading to the hotel. It was grand at night with the lights shining out the windows. Her gaze always went to the tower where her mother had fallen. From this distance it didn't look tall enough to kill someone, but her mother's neck had broken. People had speculated that she dove headfirst off the tower to make sure the impact was fatal, but Torie couldn't see any woman doing something that would damage her face so severely.

It made no sense and never would.

"You okay?" Joe asked.

Had she gasped or something? "I'm fine."

"There's the truck."

She glanced in the direction he'd pointed and frowned. "The interior light is on, but I'm sure you locked it after I shut the door."

"I did. Wait here with Hailey while I check it out." He positioned them under a bright streetlight before he approached his pickup.

He stooped and peered in the driver's window before going around to the other side of the vehicle. She lost sight of him when he leaned inside the truck.

Hailey's small hand crept into hers. "Is Daddy okay?"

Torie pulled the little girl into the circle of her arms. "I'm sure he's fine. See, there he is now. He's coming back." But Joe's grim expression made her breath catch in her chest.

He reached them. "Someone broke into my truck and took your glass pieces. Your bike is gone too."

"Oh no! Both of the glass pieces?"

He nodded. "I'm sorry. The passenger window is busted out. There's glass everywhere. We need to call the state police and report it."

"Do we have to do it tonight? I'm tired, and it will take forever to make the report."

"I'll call Craig and ask him to stop by your cottage to talk to us. We'll leave the truck here for him to check out and run for prints. We can have the hotel shuttle take us home."

"Okay."

Joe placed the call, and she listened to him explain what had happened. Reporting it was still more than she wanted to do, but it was the right thing to do. To make a claim to his insurance, they'd have to file a report. All she wanted to do was crawl under a quilt with a good book and forget this had happened. Maybe she'd call her dad and see if he wanted to come by. He could use the back door so no one would see him. Sneaking around to see her own father wasn't fair, especially when she needed him.

"My beautiful glass pieces," she lamented when she got in the shuttle.

Joe waited until Hailey mounted the steps into the shuttle and he sat across the aisle from them. "My insurance should cover it, and we can see if Amelia has another mermaid and globe you like."

"But it won't be the same."

The sting of tears in her eyes took her by surprise, and she turned her head to stare unseeingly out at the dark landscape. She didn't want to admit no other gift could replicate the rush of pleasure she'd felt when he bought the mermaid for her. She'd felt so special in that moment, so *seen*.

Every glass piece was unique, too, and even if she tried, Amelia would never fully duplicate it. Torie swallowed down the lump of despair in her throat. Was she some kind of child that she'd cry over the loss of a gift? Growing up, her dad had always taught her to straighten her shoulders and face adversity square on. And she'd done just that, so why did such an inconsequential theft strip away her courage?

"You feel violated," Joe said. "There's something so personal about a theft like that."

She gave a jerky nod. "Maybe that's it. I don't think anyone has ever stolen from me before. It's much more shocking than I expected."

Beside her, Hailey clasped Torie's hand. "I'll give you my turtle necklace." Her voice quavered.

"Oh honey, that's so sweet of you, but I'll be okay. Like your dad said, insurance will pay for it, and I can buy another mermaid and globe."

"You're sure?" Hailey's voice settled into a more usual cadence. "I'd give it to you so you don't cry."

"You're the sweetest little girl I ever met, but you keep your special necklace. Your daddy got it for you."

"Okay."

The shuttle driver pulled up at Torie's cottage and let them out. Joe tipped the driver. Torie gaped when she spied the front of her cottage. Her front door stood open, and it looked like every light in the house was on. Her bike leaned against the front.

Joe turned toward a car stopping in front.

"Here comes Craig now." Joe intercepted the state police officer. "It appears someone has broken into her house. The thief took her bike, but it's here now."

Craig's hand went to the butt of his gun. "I'll check it out."

Torie didn't want to stay behind, but Hailey needed someone with her while the men advanced to the front door and went inside.

It seemed forever until Joe reappeared from inside the

cottage. "No one's inside, but the mermaid and globe are on the coffee table, Torie."

"What?" She rushed past him into her cottage and spied the glass items.

That same detestable song was playing on her Apple TV. If she ever heard "Games People Play" again, it would be too soon.

CHAPTER 13

JOE WANTED TO SMASH THE BOX PLAYING THAT
stupid song. What was this guy's problem and why was he
tormenting Torie? Had he picked her for a reason, or did
he get his kicks by terrorizing women? The whole thing
steamed him.

Craig exited the bedroom to the right of the living
space. "All clear there. Doesn't look like anything was
disturbed, but you'll have to check for yourself, Torie."

She looked a little pale sitting on the sofa, where
she held the glass mermaid on her lap. Hailey had fallen
asleep beside her. "I'm a neat freak, so I'll know if any of
my things have been disturbed."

"The other bedroom is okay too," Joe said. "Whoever
it was came in to set the glass items and turn on the music."

Craig took out a notebook and pen. "Tell me everything that happened tonight."

It was over an hour later by the time they'd gone
through all their movements, and Craig dusted the door

for fingerprints. Joe noticed Torie's slow movements and her lids at half-mast. She had to be exhausted.

"That it, Craig? My truck's in the hotel parking lot and you can dust it. Torie needs to get to bed."

Craig nodded. "I think I have enough for now. I'll dust the truck for prints, but I doubt our perp left anything, and I suspect any prints from the door or your truck will belong to one of you."

"You know what this means, don't you?" Torie asked. "The person behind this has to be following me."

Joe had hoped she wouldn't land on that conclusion, but it was obvious. "Agreed. You need to be careful. In fact, I'm not sure you should be staying alone."

"So far there hasn't been any direct threat," Craig said.

Joe gave him a withering glance. "You know as well as I do that stalkers often progress to violence. You could move into a room at the hotel instead of staying here alone."

She chewed on her lower lip. "I really like this cottage, but I'll admit I'm jumpy. I see every shadow and hear every creak."

Joe picked up the globe and examined it. It seemed unharmed. "Anton would arrange for a room for you."

She nodded. "I suppose you're right. I'll see what I can do tomorrow. It's already ten, and I'm exhausted. I have to be at work at seven tomorrow, and I don't want to pack tonight. It seems overwhelming."

"I don't think you should stay here alone tonight," Joe said. "I'll stay in the spare room with Hailey. I don't think anyone would dare break in with a man here."

"Probably not," Craig agreed. "That's a good idea."

"I hate to put you out," Torie said. "Hailey should be in her own bed."

"Once she's asleep, she's dead to the world. There's a king bed in the spare room, plenty of space for us. We can go home first thing in the morning to get cleaned up."

"*Amicus certus in re incerta cernitur,*" Torie said.

Joe blinked, then grinned. "I took Latin too. 'One's friends are known in the hour of need.'"

A pleasant warmth spread from his midsection at the realization she considered him a friend. It was a start.

He put down the globe and went to lift his daughter from the sofa. She didn't stir, and her head lolled onto his chest. Her mutter didn't make sense, and he knew she wasn't awake.

Torie sprang up and went ahead of him to the bedroom door. "I'll turn down the covers. The bedding is clean."

She stepped into the room and yanked back the quilt and the pink top sheet edged in lace. "Not exactly the sheets a guy would want to sleep on. You can sleep in my room if you like. At least the sheets are navy."

He lowered his daughter and gently set her on the bed. "Color doesn't bother me."

If he even slept at all. He always carried his SIG Sauer M11, and he planned to rest with one eye open just in case. He pulled the covers over Hailey and backed out of the room, then eased the door closed behind him. He walked Craig out to the porch.

The porch light came on and pushed back the shadows around the cottage. "Thanks for coming, buddy."

"You bet. It's very peculiar for sure. I'm still not convinced the guy is out to get her."

"He's bold—someone could have seen him breaking into my truck. The hotel is right there, and a guest could have seen him."

"It's not well lit because of the sea turtles."

True enough. "Okay, you got me there. But still, staff and workers would have been moving around the grounds. The shop employees are all close too. Someone could have seen something."

"I'll poke around and ask questions. Maybe we'll get lucky. I need to go. We're finalizing plans to close the bridge during the conference." Craig headed for his vehicle.

The whole evening felt surreal. Joe walked around the yard in the darkness and checked the windows. They all appeared locked and secure, and he couldn't see in any window except the living room. He spent a moment gazing at Torie. She'd picked up the mermaid again and stared at it as if it held the answer to what had happened tonight.

If only the mermaid could tell the tale. He shook his head and went back inside, pausing long enough to lock both the doorknob and the dead bolt.

"I thought you'd be in bed by now," he said.

"I'm so tired, but I'm not sure I can sleep."

He held out his hand, and she let him help her up. "I'll make sure we're all safe tonight. You sleep. If you get scared, just call my name and I'll come running."

She gave his hand a light squeeze before she pulled away. "You're a good man, Joe Abbott."

He dropped his gaze to her lips, then took a step back. Too soon for anything like that. He was here to protect her, not hit on her. "Good night."

"Good night," she echoed before going to her bedroom and shutting the door.

He sighed and stared at the closed door.

==

Joe held a spatula aloft as Torie entered her kitchen, and the aroma of bacon and eggs filled the room. "Sleep okay?"

She yawned and went to perch on a bar stool beside Hailey. "Like a baby. You look tired though. Did you get any rest?"

"I catnapped."

Hailey yanked on her arm. "Torie, can I sleep over again? I love that room! It was so fun to stay here."

Torie glanced at Joe. "If it's okay with your dad, you can stay anytime. Well, at least when I'm not working."

"We'll see." Joe stirred the scrambled eggs. "I hope this is how you like them."

"I like them any way I can get them when someone else is cooking. What a treat. I usually opt for cereal or toast in the morning because it's easy. Or yogurt and granola."

"Daddy says I have to eat protein in the morning."

"I'm sure it's a very good idea." She smiled at Joe. "Are you going to be late for work?"

"A little, but I'm the boss. Hailey is late for her camp too. Pack up what you need today. I already called the hotel shuttle, and it will drop you at the hotel before delivering me and Hailey where we need to go."

"I already have a suitcase packed. Enough for about a week. Maybe by then we'll figure out who is behind this."

She wasn't sure she believed her own assurances. While the intruder seemed bold, he hadn't slipped up enough yet to figure out his identity. "What about putting some cameras in here? We might be able to catch him in the act."

Joe nodded. "I thought about that too. I'll pick up some and install them. We should have them by the doors and one in the living room. Did you call Anton?"

She shook her head. "Not yet, but I will."

Telling her dad would be hard. He'd be apt to ask her to leave, and she couldn't do that. The intruder felt threatened or he wouldn't be terrorizing her like this. He was trying to drive her out, and she refused to let him. She might be closer than she realized.

Joe prayed over the food, then handed her a plate piled high with eggs and bacon.

"I can't eat all that," she protested.

"Give it a try."

She wrinkled her nose, then dug in. "I want to talk to Bella today about her claim that Lisbeth was depressed. I don't believe it."

"And if she lied, maybe there's a reason."

She picked up a piece of crispy bacon. "Do you know her?"

"I know who she is—that's it though. She came to the beach minutes after I discovered Lisbeth."

"I hadn't heard that. Did she say why she was out by the water right then? It was very early, right?"

"Six in the morning. She said she was supposed to go for a morning hike with Lisbeth, but she'd overslept."

"A hike? But why meet on the beach?"

Joe frowned. "I didn't think to ask her that. It was a chaotic scene, and she was clearly distraught."

Torie couldn't wait to talk to her. She stuffed a final piece of bacon in her mouth as she went to grab her suitcase. By the time she came out, Joe had loaded the dishwasher and turned it on. The kitchen was as neat as if she'd cleaned it herself, which was saying a lot. She didn't think any guy cared about that kind of thing.

It was only a two-minute ride to the hotel. Joe tried to take her suitcase, but she had the porter grab it. "Put it in storage for now," she told him. "Thanks, Joe, for everything."

"Um, you want to have dinner with us tonight, get away from the hotel awhile?"

Her pulse kicked at the hopeful tone in his voice. "I'll text you and let you know later, okay? I'm not sure what the day will bring." She'd already spent more time with him than was wise.

"Sounds good." He waved to her as the shuttle drove off to deliver Hailey to camp.

Torie made a beeline for the check-in desk, but Bella wasn't on duty, so she asked one of the bellhops about her and discovered she was in the break room. As Torie hurried back to find Bella, she rehearsed how she planned to start the conversation. She didn't want to be accusatory and back Bella into a corner where she refused to answer questions.

Bella was the only one in the break room when Torie entered. "Good morning," Torie said.

The large room held tables and chairs as well as an array of sweet-smelling pastries and breakfast items for the staff. The aroma from the coffee bar made her mouth water, and she spied small tubs of half-and-half on the table. It would do.

Bella tucked a strand of blonde hair behind her ear. "Hi. Coffee's fresh."

Was she watching Torie warily, or was it her imagination? Torie poured a cup of java and added plenty of half-and-half. Bella sat at a table and ate fresh fruit, and she barely looked up when Torie joined her.

"Um, I met Craig Hall this week." Torie took a sip of coffee and grimaced at the weak brew.

"Our state trooper? Nice guy." Bella twirled her engagement ring on her finger.

"He is. He said something I hadn't heard before—that you mentioned Lisbeth was on antidepressants."

Bella's eyes widened, and she choked on her fruit. "I'm late. We'll have to talk another time. Sorry."

She practically ran from the room, and Torie leaned back in her chair with her heart still pounding. What on earth had just happened?

CHAPTER 14

TODAY WAS A PERFECT DAY FOR BEING OUT ON
the open water—or at least it would have been if Joe
weren't so exhausted. He'd downplayed his fatigue to
Torie this morning, but as the day wore on, his movements were getting slower, his reflexes turning almost
nonexistent.

The sea lion had alerted them to a possible target,
and Simon had been gone about five minutes. There
was a tug on the line at the bow of the boat. Adrenaline
washed away Joe's exhaustion. He moved to the line
and touched it. Taut and strained. "I think Simon has
deployed the cuff."

"Let's hope it's not a piece of driftwood," Danielle said.

Joe began reeling in the line, and the load made the
boat slew in the water. "I don't think it's driftwood."

Simon's head popped above the waves, and he gave
an excited vocalization that sounded like a trumpet as he
clapped his flippers.

"Throw him a fish," Joe said. "He thinks he deserves it."

The winch groaned from the strain, but the line kept winding up until a dark shape could be seen just under the blue water.

"It's a swimmer!" Tyrone drew his weapon and moved to the starboard side.

Joe saw the flash of a knife. "The guy's armed with a blade!"

"I see it." Tyrone pulled out handcuffs.

A hand with a knife in it arced above the waves, but Tyrone reached over and wrestled it out of the man's grip, then snapped a cuff on that arm. In short order the big guy had the swimmer trussed up and lying on the boat deck.

The guy wore black from head to toe, even his snorkel and fins. Joe reached over and yanked the mask off the guy's face. A blond male stared up at them. If looks could kill, his green eyes would have sliced Joe's guts open.

"What's your name and what are you doing here?" Joe demanded.

The man pressed his lips together and didn't answer. Not good. This looked like an actual hostile swimmer, not a war game or a diver who accidentally wandered into Simon's watch.

"Check him for ID," Joe told Tyrone.

"You got it." Tyrone leaned over and patted down the guy's wet suit, then showed his teammates what he'd retrieved. "Looky here. Caps for plastic explosives."

"But no explosives," Danielle said.

"Could be he ditched them down below when Simon nailed him," Tyrone said.

"Call it in," Joe said. "We need divers down there to see if we can figure out what he was doing."

Danielle nodded and went to the radio. Joe squatted beside the diver. "What's your name? Why are you here?"

The man sneered, then spat in Joe's face. Joe clenched his fists and struggled to keep his cool. Somehow he managed not to put his fist in the guy's contemptuous face. Without so much as a word spoken by the swimmer, it was impossible to tell his nationality.

"No ID?" he asked Tyrone.

"Nothing I found." Tyrone picked up the mask and snorkel. "High-end equipment though, and it's made in China."

"That doesn't tell us much since so many things are made in China," Joe said. He didn't want to jump to conclusions, but his unease was at DEFCON 1. "You get Ajax?"

"I did," Danielle said. "Here come reinforcements now."

The diver they'd apprehended made a choking sound, and all three of them turned toward him. His hands were on his neck and he gagged before toppling to the bottom of the boat. Joe and Tyrone stood back while Danielle moved in to check him.

She pressed her fingers to the swimmer's neck. "No pulse." She eased off his oxygen tank and backpack before laying him out on his back to perform CPR.

She drew back and looked up at Joe. "I smell almonds. I think it's cyanide. I don't dare perform mouth-to-mouth." She began chest compressions. "Grab the air bag."

Tyrone sprang to get it out of the medical kit, and he

knelt by the man's head and put the mask over his face to inflate his lungs.

Joe's pulse kicked. "Poison?" This didn't make sense, but he relayed the information. "That swimmer we caught doesn't have a pulse. Maybe cyanide poisoning. We're administering chest compressions."

The guy told him a medic with the team was on its way. Joe hung up and stood back while Danielle and Tyrone worked on the diver. The guy was already blue, so Joe didn't think their efforts would be successful.

His gaze fell on the backpack, and he squatted beside it. Inside was a conglomeration of wires and explosives. "This was the real deal, guys. There's a bomb in here."

Tyrone paused. "Is it activated?"

Joe examined more closely. "I don't think so. There's a detonator in here too." He gingerly moved it to the other side of the boat, away from his team, then went back to the radio.

"Hey, this guy isn't Navy. He's got a bomb with him, so he meant business."

There was a long pause on the radio before the guy answered. "Did the diver survive?"

Joe looked back at his team, who had finally stood and moved away from the swimmer. "No. We were unable to revive him."

Which meant his identity and purpose would be hard to decipher.

Two boats zipped toward them. One held four master-at-arms sailors, and the other boat carried divers. The two boats anchored off the starboard side, then tied up to Joe's boat. The security officers were the first to board. Two of them flanked the prisoner, and one of the men knelt to check him out. "He's dead." The men loaded the body onto their boat.

The divers wasted no time and disappeared into the water without any chitchat. Danielle had already sent in Simon's last coordinates, and Joe waited to see what they'd find. He could only pray whatever was down there was easily disarmed. If there *was* anything.

Maybe he was overreacting, but he didn't think so.

Simon swam around the boat, and Danielle fed him fish every time he came close so he wouldn't swim off into danger. The boat that had taken the prisoner off disappeared to the south, and the sound of its engine faded into the roar of the surf.

The divers surfaced, and their underwater transport held several items that looked suspiciously like bombs.

Joe shaded his eyes with his hand. "You disarm those things?"

"Didn't have to," the diver closest to him said. "He didn't have a chance to finish up and ditched this on the bottom. Simon needs a whole cooler full of fish."

Joe whistled. "What could he be doing here?"

"Hard to say. We'll get more divers out here to make sure we're not missing anything. And the Navy needs to have all the sea mammals out patrolling the area. This might not be over. This guy meant business."

The divers loaded their loot onto the boat and headed off. Joe threw fish to Simon until the food was gone, then sent him back down.

This job just got a whole lot more real.

Why hadn't Dad answered her text?

Alone at her desk, Torie checked her phone. Three hours since she'd texted him. Surely he was still on the island. It wasn't like she and her dad were always in each other's pockets, but he usually answered her immediately.

The hotel felt creepy today, or maybe it was her own jumpiness playing tricks on her. As she made the rounds checking the cameras, she kept thinking people were staring at her. Which was silly. No one knew her. She was just a faceless worker bee here to help the guests.

She'd been glad to finish up so she could hole up in her office. These four walls made her feel cocooned and protected. And Kyle wasn't here either, which helped.

She needed to get her living situation squared away. Maybe she should talk directly to her aunt. That's what she would expect anyway, now that Torie thought about it. Having her father intervene would be a sure way to send up red flags when Aunt Genevieve didn't know they were acquainted.

She checked the time again. Two. Not sure why she was agreeing, she fired off a text to Joe telling him she'd love to have dinner, then went in search of her aunt. Torie found her standing outside the coffee shop. The Pantry served sandwiches, salads, pastries, and surprisingly good coffee. While her aunt spoke with another employee, Torie got a breve, then stood a few feet away waiting for her turn with Aunt Genevieve.

Her aunt turned toward her as the employee left. "Is there a problem, Torie?"

"Not with the hotel, Ms. Hallston. An intruder has broken into my cottage several times, and someone stole some of my things out of Joe Abbott's truck last night. When I got back to my cottage, the thief had broken in and left the stolen items inside. The state trooper thinks I shouldn't stay there alone for a few days while he investigates, and I wondered if there might be a room at the hotel where I could stay in the meantime?"

Her aunt frowned. "That's most inconvenient, Torie. We have a full house right now."

It took all of Torie's resolve to bite her tongue. "Should I stay at one of the other hotels?"

She'd known her aunt wouldn't want club business spread to other hotels. "I'll see what I can do. There might be a storeroom where we can put a bed."

A storeroom. What was the woman thinking? The hotel was busy but not that busy. "Thank you, Ms. Hallston. I'll go home as soon as the state police says it's safe."

"Broken into?" Her aunt's hazel eyes raked Torie from head to toe. "What were they after? You hardly are the type to be harboring crown jewels or anything of value."

Did her aunt think money was all that mattered? Torie wasn't sure she'd be around by the time everything came out, but she hoped she was nearby when Aunt Genevieve realized she'd been dissing her own niece all this time.

"Do I have your cell?"

"Yes, ma'am, it's in the system."

"I'll text you what I discover."

"I appreciate it." Torie forced a smile, then backed away.

Her phone broke into song—her father's ringtone of "Daddy's Hands." She glanced back to make sure her aunt was out of earshot, then answered it. "Hey, Dad, what's going on with you? You didn't answer earlier."

"I was out diving. Just got to the boat. What's up, honey?"

He was actually acting like this was a real vacation. When was the last time she'd seen him do anything just for fun? Ages.

"You're not going to like it." She explained what had happened in the past twenty-four hours and could almost hear the steam spewing around her father's head.

"Who would dare attack you?"

"It wasn't an attack. More of a warning. Like don't forget I'm watching you." Put like that it sounded even creepier. "I mean, the guy hasn't tried to hurt me or anything."

"You need to go back to Scottsdale, Torie. I won't have you in danger. I'm here now. I can poke around Lisbeth's death."

"I'm not leaving. This guy must be worried about what I'll find out. If I leave now, he's won. I can't let that happen. I love you, Dad, but I have to do this. I really called to ask if you can arrange for a room at the hotel for me for a few days, but I already took care of it. Well, at least I think so. Aunt Genevieve says she can have a bed put in one of the storerooms."

"She what?" he yelled.

Torie held the phone out from her ear and chuckled. "I doubt she'll really do that. It was all bluster."

"I'll make sure she gives you a good room. The connecting room next to mine is empty."

"That's a suite. She won't let me have that."

"Oh yes she will," he said grimly.

"If you intervene she'll know something is up."

"I'll tell her I heard there was an employee with a problem, and as caring employers, we should take good care of that person. I'll mention I think you should get that room. Or I'll just arrange it and tell her. That's a better idea. Then she can't try an end run to bypass me."

"Are you sure? It might make her angrier."

"Like I've ever been afraid of her. She brought your mom a lot of grief, and she and Lily were nothing alike."

"I didn't know there was bad blood between them."

"Maybe not bad blood but wariness. I dated Genevieve first, and she was livid when I dropped her and dated your mother."

"Dad! You never told me that. You heartbreaker, you."

He laughed. "There was no great love lost between us. All she ever wanted was my money. Your mom never cared about that kind of thing. After we were married, I made sure Genevieve had a respectable position in the company to compensate. I don't think she ever saw it as anything less than her due."

Torie felt the first stirrings of pity for her aunt. Maybe there was a reason she was so bitter.

CHAPTER 15

"DAD, COME QUICK, THE GULLS ARE AFTER THE hatchlings!"

The sun was already sinking, leaving shadows and casting the sky in magenta and purple hues. Torie would be here at the picnic area on St. Andrews Beach any minute. He didn't have time for turtle rescue right now, but his daughter would never forgive him if a gull made off with one of her little ones.

The soft sand slowed his run toward the line of sea grass and rocks where the latest sea turtle nest lay hidden. Hailey waved her arms and shouted at the screeching gulls with their black heads as they dive-bombed the hatchlings. The scent of the sea blended with the aroma of the steaks grilling near the picnic table, and he glanced at his watch. He had about five minutes before he needed to flip them.

"Shoo, shoo!" He waved his hands, then grabbed a palm frond nearby and chased off the gulls.

Protecting the march of the turtles with the frond, he

walked with them to where the foam rolled onto the sand until each one disappeared into the surf.

Hailey hovered anxiously nearby until she was sure they were all safe. "Thanks, Daddy."

"You're welcome. I could use your help with the food now. I'll flip the steaks if you get everything out of the truck." He'd been able to pick up his vandalized truck earlier this afternoon.

"Okay. I hope she likes the brownies I made." Hailey loved to bake, and though she was only eight, she had a talent for it.

She skipped along beside him back to their picnic spot. "I like Torie. She is never in a hurry and always listens to me."

"I've noticed. She seems to like you a lot."

How hard would it be to bring a new relationship into their lives? He and Hailey had been managing on their own for three years, and they had everyday life down to a science where everything worked. What if meeting Torie changed everything in a bad way? He'd never want Hailey to think she'd lost her place in his heart.

All this was new territory, and he wasn't sure how to navigate the tangle. But maybe he was jumping the gun anyway. The feelings stirring for Torie might not be anything. Or they might not be reciprocated. It was too early to be thinking of those kinds of what-ifs.

He reached the grill, then grabbed the tongs and lifted the lid. He flipped the steaks and smiled. Perfect. He wanted everything to go well tonight. Hailey went past him to the truck and got out the basket with utensils and food. She set it on the picnic table, then vanished into the bathroom. She was still wiping her hands with a damp paper towel when she exited. She looked like a small adult as she pulled out the bags of veggies to arrange in a salad. She snuck a few cherry tomatoes to eat as she worked. The girl was lucky she hadn't turned into a tomato with how much she loved them.

He could hear her banging around and talking to herself, though he couldn't make out any words. The sound of tires crunching on gravel made him turn, and his pulse ratcheted to high speed when he saw Torie get off a bike.

Torie carried a six-pack of boxed apple juice, and he eyed the drinks. "Thirsty?"

She smiled. "Hailey mentioned she loves boxed apple juice. I hope this brand is okay. It's organic."

"It's her favorite."

She passed the juice boxes to him and followed him to the picnic table. "I put them in a bag to ride my bike over."

"I told you I would have been glad to pick you up."

"I know, but it's a perfect day for biking, and it only took ten minutes." She gazed past him. "Hi, Hailey!" She waved, and his little girl turned from her salad prep and waved back.

"I made brownies," Hailey called.

"I love brownies," Torie said.

"Any problem getting a room at the hotel?"

"Ms. Hallston offered me a storeroom with a cot, but Anton arranged for a suite. She might not be too happy with me when she learns about it."

He set the juice boxes on the picnic table. "You can always call Anton if she gets mean about it."

"Apple juice! Can I have one now? It's hot work making salad."

"If you name the verse." Joe grinned. "'For He has satisfied the thirsty soul, and He has filled the hungry soul with what is good.'"

Hailey frowned. "I think it's in Psalms."

"Good guess. Psalm 107, verse 9." He opened the cooler and peered inside. "I have iced tea and several different Cokes. What would you like?"

"I'll have iced tea." Torie settled on the picnic table. "I tried to talk to Bella about Lisbeth, but she went white when I asked about the antidepressants and rushed off. I think she was scared."

"Of who or what?" He pulled out bottles of iced tea and handed her one.

She uncapped her bottle and took a long swig. "I don't know yet, but I'm going to pin her down tomorrow. Maybe she's ashamed that she lied and doesn't want to continue it."

"Did you talk to Anton about it?"

"Not yet. I suppose I should. He might be able to get her to talk if I can't. I don't understand why she would lie about this. It's strange."

"You're certain it's not true? People are often embarrassed about that kind of thing."

"Not Lisbeth. This isn't possible. Not in any way. I'm as certain of that as I know she didn't go in the water. Knowing Bella was on the scene right away seems suspicious. It might account for the fear she showed when I started questioning her. I think she knows more than she's telling. And I need to find out what she knows."

Maybe Torie was right. Someone didn't want her poking into things, but at least she'd be safe at the hotel.

══

The smile Torie had carried since the picnic died as she looked at the closed door to her suite. Did she really want to sleep on the same floor where her mother died?

Torie paused another long moment before she unlocked the door and stepped into the dark suite. Moonlight streamed through the open French doors, illuminating the white sofa and gray armchair. A clean scent welcomed her, and she switched on the light, then dropped her purse onto a table beside a fruit basket before glancing around the small living room. Her suitcase sat by the closet where a bellhop had left it.

A gleam drew her to the balcony, and she stood looking down on the swimming pool, and then farther out, the glimmer of the Intracoastal Waterway.

She retraced her steps and found the door to the bedroom. An odd odor hit her when she stepped into the space, and she turned on the light. A bare foot protruded from one end of the bed on the far side near the window.

Torie gasped and took a step back as she identified the odor as the coppery stench of blood. Her knees shook as she approached the person on the floor. The slender foot and ankle appeared to be that of a woman who was lying on her side. When she reached the prone figure, her gaze traveled up the shapely legs to land on the blonde hair matted with blood.

Bella!

Torie knelt beside the young woman and pressed her fingers to her neck. No pulse. She gasped and jumped to her feet. Her dad would know what to do. She fumbled with the connecting doorknob and found he'd already unlocked his side.

"Dad!" She practically fell into the room. "Daddy!"

He leaped from the sofa where he'd been watching TV in his pajamas. "Torie, what's happened?"

She pointed a shaking hand toward her room. "It's Bella. I think she's dead. There's blood all over her hair." Her voice quivered, and she struggled not to cry.

Had Bella come to her suite to tell her what she knew about Lisbeth's death? Or had someone placed her there as a warning? But no. Blood soaked the carpet too. Had she been killed there?

Her dad picked up his phone from the table. "I'll call security while you call the state police. Tell them we might be dealing with a homicide."

She nodded and went to retrieve her purse in her living room. After digging out her phone, she first called 911. Maybe she was wrong, and Bella was still alive. After giving the dispatcher the information, she found the entry for Craig.

He answered on the first ring. "Officer Craig Hall."

"C-Craig, I think there's been a murder in my room at the hotel. This is Torie Berg. I just got here and found Bella Hansen's body. I think she's dead, though the paramedics aren't here yet."

"Room number?"

She gave him the details on how to find her room.

"Be right there."

Her dad let in security, and they stood back as two guards swept her suite as well as her dad's. It wasn't until one of them gave her a sidelong glance that she realized how it probably looked. Like she and the older man beside her were having an affair or something. They had no idea he was her father. But she clamped her mouth shut and let him speculate.

"All clear," the oldest one said.

The faint wail of a siren approached. "The ambulance is here."

Her dad gave a curt nod. "It's too late."

"I know. I-I was hopeful at first." She went to let in the paramedics.

After a quick examination, the female paramedic shook her head. "I'm sorry. Do you know the woman's name?"

"Bella Hansen. She worked as a desk clerk here," Torie said.

"We'll wait for the police," a security guard said. "You called them, right?"

"Yes."

"They'll need the room cleared so they can sweep it for evidence."

Her father took her arm. "Let's go to my suite."

She let him guide her through the door and into his living room. She sank into the armchair and tried to control the way her insides trembled. She had to squash a deep longing to call Joe. His quiet strength would bolster her courage. But they were probably in the middle of baths and bedtime routine by now.

The door to her suite stood open as various people

thronged the space. Craig entered as the paramedics finished. He was out of uniform, and he went straight to the body where he began to take pictures.

Torie rose and stood in the connecting doorway. "I'm in here when you need to talk to me."

"Forensics will be here in about an hour." He turned away from the body and came toward her. "You discovered Ms. Hansen?"

Torie hugged herself. "I did." She described her movements when she first came in and how she'd noticed the odor before seeing Bella's foot. "I touched her neck to check for a pulse."

"Weren't you afraid the intruder was still in your room?"

"I-I was only concerned about Bella. I hoped she might still be alive."

"What time did you get here?"

"Joe dropped me off a little after eight. By the time I got the key to the room and arrived here, it was probably close to eight thirty."

"And you found her within five minutes or so?"

She nodded. "About that."

"What did you do next?"

"I called for help from Mr. Bergstrom. He's in the suite next door."

Craig's gaze went to the connecting door before he turned to talk to her dad. "What did you do when she summoned you?"

"I checked for a pulse too. Then I called security while Torie phoned 911 and you. I wanted to make sure the killer wasn't still around."

Craig nodded. "They found nothing?"

"Both rooms were clear. I suspect the killer hit her with the lamp. I noticed blood on it."

Torie hadn't been able to look anywhere except at the body. She shuddered at the mental picture of someone taking Bella's life in such a violent way.

Joe. She longed to see him and hear his deep, steady voice. "Am I free to go now?"

Craig put away his pen and pad. "Yeah. Clearly you won't be sleeping here tonight."

And she couldn't cause more gossip by staying with her dad. She slung her purse over her shoulder and bolted for the door. If nothing else, she could stay at her cottage. It would be as safe as here.

CHAPTER 16

WHAT WAS TORIE DOING RIGHT NOW?

Lucy's aggrieved meow brought Joe out of his thoughts. He needed to get over this obsession with Torie. It was ridiculous for a grown man to be mooning over a woman he barely knew.

He filled Lucy's dish with food and refreshed her water bowl, then turned on the ten o'clock news. It was the usual political news until a special broadcast cut in.

An animated female reporter stood in front of the Club Resort. "We've received a tip about a death here a few hours ago. The police are not yet releasing the name of the victim, pending notification of next of kin, but sources inside tell us the young woman who was on staff at the hotel was brutally bludgeoned to death. Stay tuned for more on this breaking story."

Nausea roiled in his belly. It couldn't be Torie, could it? Surely not. Craig would have called him. He snatched his phone and started to call Craig, but the doorbell sounded. Still carrying his phone, he raced to the door and threw it open.

Torie.

The relief of seeing her face nearly buckled his knees. He didn't stop to think about his actions or how she would view them, but he took a step forward and folded her in his arms. "Torie, you're all right."

She wrapped her arms around his waist and rested her head on his chest. "Bella's dead, Joe. I found her in my suite."

He held her close. "*Your* suite?" His gaze swept the darkness behind her, and he steered her off the porch and into the house. Even once he locked the door, he didn't feel they were safe so he moved her away from the window.

She settled on the sofa with him and shifted a foot away. Strands of dark-brown hair had escaped her braided updo, and her brown eyes held a sheen.

Her body trembled as she recounted the events.

He kept his arm around her. "Did Craig think you might be the target?"

"He didn't mention it. And we don't really look alike. She has—had blonde hair."

"But it makes sense after what's happened so far. The killer would have expected you to be in that room, not Bella. The lights were probably off. What was she doing there?"

"I thought she might have sneaked in so she could talk to me about Lisbeth. Maybe she rushed off when I asked her about the antidepressants because she didn't want to be overheard." She pressed her fingers to her temple. "It's so hard to think. D–Anton came right over."

"He didn't hear a struggle or a crash when she fell?"
She stilled. "He didn't mention it."

Odd. "Did he say how long he'd been in his suite?"

"He was watching TV in his pajamas so he'd been there awhile."

"The television could have drowned out any noise."

She nodded. "It was kind of loud and there were gunshots. He likes thrillers."

She sure knew a lot about the older man. Joe wasn't the suspicious sort, but he had to wonder about their relationship. "Have you checked the cameras on the floor?"

She shook her head. "I should have, but I was so shook up. All I wanted was to get to you. I know that sounds weird, but I knew everything would be all right once I got here."

A jolt of warmth spread to his chest. "I'm glad you came." He gestured to the TV. "The news had a clip about her death, and my first thought was that you were the victim. I'd grabbed my phone to call when I heard the doorbell."

"I can't stay in my suite, and you should have seen the way people looked at Anton and me. Like they thought we were having an affair or something because the connecting door was open between the rooms by the time they arrived. I knew he was in the next room because he mentioned it was empty and he'd assigned it to me. So I went to him when I found Bella."

He exhaled at the welcome revelation. "The rumors will die down."

She pulled away and hugged herself. "It's really late.

I'd better go. I'm going to stay at my cottage. Clearly the hotel isn't any safer than my place."

He took her hand. "No, you're not. You can have my room, and I'll sleep on the sofa. For all you know, the killer suspects you'll go back to the cottage and is waiting there. It's not safe."

She chewed on her lip, then nodded. "You're right. I so hate to be a burden."

"You're never a burden. Hailey will be thrilled when she wakes up. And I'll even fix bacon and eggs again." Her smile was lopsided and didn't reach her eyes, but it was a start, so he gave her hand a quick squeeze. "You look exhausted. Let me show you the room. Did you bring your things?"

She shook her head. "Everything in there was evidence for now. I can sleep in my clothes."

"I've got some pajama bottoms with a drawstring and a T-shirt. They'd be more comfortable than sleeping in your jeans."

"Okay."

He rose and pulled her up with him. "My room is down that hall. I'll grab the clothes and let you change."

He squeezed her hand again, then went to his bedroom where he pulled out plaid pajama bottoms and a red Tiger Woods T-shirt. He handed them to her and shut the door behind him. At least the sheets were clean. He'd changed them this morning. Before making up the sofa with a sheet and pillow, he checked on Hailey, who was sound asleep.

He had a feeling he would find rest hard to come by again tonight, even though he hadn't slept last night either. The danger was far from past.

Torie shut the door behind Joe and got ready for bed. His pj's held the faint whiff of his cologne, as if he'd folded them after applying it. The scent comforted her almost as much as his embrace.

Her so-called fiancé, Matthew Cunningham, had never brought her a sense of security when she was with him. She'd been aware, as he had, that their engagement was what their parents wanted. He never looked at her like Joe did. When Joe's green eyes focused on her, she saw a deep thirst for something more, something only she could provide. She wasn't yet sure what that something was, but she wasn't ready to find out either. The comfort Joe brought was probably because he was in security.

She climbed into the soft cotton sheets smelling of fabric softener, but sleep eluded her. She lay there with her eyes open, listening to the clicking of the alarm clock on the bedside table as each minute flipped by. At midnight, she sat up and turned on the light, then slipped her legs out from under the sheet and sighed. Maybe she could find a book to read.

The small bookcase on the other side of the room held hardbacks, and nearly all were by Lisa Gardner. She selected *The Perfect Husband* and turned back toward the bed, but a picture on top of the bookcase caught her attention. She picked it up and studied it. A beautiful redhead in a green sundress stood on a beach beside a guy with windblown light-brown hair dressed in shorts and a tropical shirt.

Joe and Julie. Maybe on their honeymoon since the backdrop appeared to be Hawaii.

Torie stared at the woman's face. Julie gazed up at Joe with clear adoration, and Joe's smile held total joy. Torie drank in their expressions. This was what love looked like.

She whirled at a tap on the door. "Come in."

Joe poked his head in, and his gaze swept over her. "That outfit looks a lot better on you than on me." He grinned and leaned against the doorjamb. "The light was shining under the door. Are you okay? I hoped you'd be able to sleep." His smile faltered when he saw the picture in her hand.

She settled the frame back where she'd found it. "I'm sorry. I didn't mean to pry. Julie was very beautiful."

"She was. Hailey looks a lot like her." He opened the door wider and stepped inside the room. "That was on our honeymoon on Kauai."

"On Shipwreck Beach. Did you jump off the sea cliff there? I wasn't brave enough."

"We did." He smiled at the memory. "Julie was a daredevil."

"I wish I'd known her. About the only daredevil thing I do is scuba."

"You would have liked her. Other people flocked around her, and she had a ton of friends. I never thought I'd get over losing her." His gaze locked with hers.

Her breath hitched. Was he trying to tell her something? She gave a slight shake of her head. Fatigue was doing a number on her emotions.

"Did your dive gear get here?"

"It did."

"Want to go diving on Saturday?"

"Sure."

He was close enough to touch now. "Weren't you engaged once?"

She nodded. "It was what our parents expected. I don't think either of us held any feelings beyond fondness. I certainly didn't. And then I found him in bed with one of my friends. The betrayal made me wary of ever trusting a man again."

"Not every man is like that. There are plenty of us one-woman men around."

"Maybe." She looked away.

His hands came down on her shoulders, and she looked up at him as he stared deep into her eyes, almost like he was searching into her soul. Like he could read her thoughts, dreams, and hopes. No subterfuge, no pretense. He accepted her, warts and all.

She took a step back, and his hands dropped away. Did she want to lower her defenses? Did she have the courage?

She gave a shaky laugh. "We're probably moving a little too fast."

His green eyes darkened. "Not for me."

"Maybe for me. I don't know what to think."

"I can be patient."

But could he be patient when it was time for her to leave? Would any of these unfamiliar feelings last when distance intervened? She was lost at sea with no landmarks on the horizon. All she could do was take one day at a time and see what happened. This might all be a mirage that vanished as quickly as a building storm that blew itself out. What was infatuation and what was budding love? How did someone tell the difference?

It was way too soon to even be thinking of the L-word. She had to be sensible and slam on the brakes. Obsessing over Joe could get in the way of why she was here. Justice for Lisbeth was her goal, and nothing could be allowed to get in the way of that.

CHAPTER 17

JOE HAD PROBABLY SHOT HIMSELF IN THE FOOT.
In fact, the way Torie had left this morning while he was
showering was a sure indication he'd been a little too bold.

The boat barely moved on the glassy water just offshore the base. Joe stared out at the sea, mirror-smooth
this morning as it reflected back the perfect blue of a
cloudless sky. The wind blew in his face and carried the
salty air with it. Nothing was as relaxing as smelling the
ocean and listening to its calming waves. And he needed
to ditch this agitation.

She'd come here for justice for her friend, and she had
no plans of staying. He knew that, and it had made him
try to press too fast.

She liked him, and that should be enough for now. But
it wasn't. He had nightmares of waking up one morning
and finding a text from her telling him good-bye. That
was the whole crux of the matter. He didn't think he
would have enough time to show her what could develop
between them.

Tyrone's gravelly voice interrupted Joe's thoughts. "Here comes Simon."

The sea lion's dark form zipped through the clear water, and his head broke the waves. He swam back and forth on the starboard side, and Joe frowned. "He's agitated."

"I see that." Danielle tossed a fish into the water, and the sea lion ignored it.

She and Joe exchanged a perplexed glance. "He never turns down fish," Joe said.

"Maybe he got hurt." Tyrone patted the side of the boat to call Simon over.

Simon swam near, then darted away. "Something's wrong," Joe said. "I'm going in."

He shrugged on his tank and donned a mask, then dropped into the water. The ocean enveloped him in a warm embrace, and he dove down to follow Simon, but the sea lion swam in circles near the top of the water and all around the boat.

What could be wrong? His eyesight adjusted to the lower light levels, and he searched around the anchorage. Nothing appeared out of place. Just fish, coral, and sand. He dove a little deeper and examined a bit of artificial reef made from tires. Nothing.

He gave up and swam back to the boat, where he climbed the ladder and dropped into a chair. He yanked out his mouthpiece. "I don't know why he's upset. I didn't find anything down there."

"I've been watching him," Tyrone said. "He keeps touching the starboard side of the boat. Did you look on the hull to see if anything's there?"

"No." Joe leaned over the side of the boat and ran his hand down as far as he could, but it wasn't far enough. "I'll go back down." He fitted his mouthpiece back into place and adjusted his mask, then dropped back into the water.

Under the boat it was darker, so he pulled out his flashlight and turned it on to make a careful examination of the boat's hull. For good measure he ran his hand along the surface too. His fingers touched something stuck to the hull, and he focused the beam for a closer look.

A small bomb had been strapped to the starboard side near the stern.

Without waiting to see if there was a timer, he shot to the surface. "Get off the boat now! Bomb!"

Tyrone's eyes went wide, and he dove overboard. Danielle dove off the other side, and all three of them swam away from the boat.

He felt the explosion before he heard it. A wave lifted him and a second later, the *boom* blasted. Debris rained down on his head, and he ducked under the water. Something struck the back of his head, his vision started to go black, and he sank deeper into the water.

He felt a hard nudge at his cheek and reached out blindly. His fingers found Simon's sleek, muscular body, and he grabbed hold while the sea lion towed him to the surface, where he drank in the sweetest air on earth.

He gasped and floated in the water for a moment until he found the strength to call out for his team. "Tyrone, Danielle!" He saw no other heads bobbing amid the scattered debris of the boat, but he yelled again.

He still had on his dive gear, so he put his mouthpiece on and prepared to dive to look for them.

"Here!" Tyrone's deep voice came from his right.

Joe turned that way and found Tyrone clinging to a wooden piece of what used to be a cabinet. Joe swam to his side. Blood matted Tyrone's hair from a scalp wound.

"I haven't seen Danielle," Tyrone said, panting from the exertion.

His slurred voice alarmed Joe, and he spat out his mouthpiece. "We need to get you some medical attention."

But how? He had no way of calling for anyone, but he prayed someone on the base had seen the explosion and would send out help.

He cupped his hands to his mouth. "Danielle!"

He had to find her. She had a husband and two little girls waiting for her at home. "Simon, find Danielle."

The sea lion barked, then dove under the water. Joe grabbed the mouthpiece and put it on, then followed Simon. The animal zoomed down to the artificial coral reef, and Joe saw her floating in the water. He kicked harder and prayed she was still alive. He grabbed her arm and turned her over, then slid his octopus mouthpiece in her mouth.

Breathe.

Even as he waited for her to take a breath, he kicked with her to the surface. His head broke the waves, and he lifted her up so her face was above the water. She still wasn't breathing, so he turned her so he could give her mouth-to-mouth, but the movement caused her head to roll, and she gasped and coughed.

Her eyes opened, and she vomited up seawater.

"That's it," he said. "Get it up."

They'd all survived but just barely. Who had targeted

them—and why? Could the diver who had ditched bomb materials yesterday have been planning to do this?

== ==

If news about last night's murder got to Aunt Genevieve, there'd be trouble.

Torie sat with her father in a quiet corner of the Grand Dining Room near the fireplace. White plantation shutters blocked the bright sunlight, and this corner by a large tree was in shadow. The double-clothed tables muffled the tinkle of silverware, and the thick patterned carpet allowed the servers to walk noiselessly from table to table.

There weren't many people here this early, and she could only pray no one mentioned seeing her with Anton Bergstrom. Torie knew hotel gossip well enough to be certain staff would talk about how her father had been there and had comforted her. They'd all take it in the sleaziest way possible, and she wasn't sure how to handle the inevitable questions.

She took a sip of her coffee laced with cream. "I think I should stay at my cottage tonight."

"Absolutely not. Whoever is stalking you is brazen, Torie. I went to my room after dinner at seven, and I didn't hear a peep from your room. Whoever killed Bella waltzed right in there without a thought for being caught."

Her dad wore a tropical shirt and khaki pants again today, and she liked seeing him dressed so casually. Did he plan to stay on vacation this whole trip? She suspected once the bank board meeting started, he'd be in a gray pinstripe Armani suit again, just to make sure the other members took note of his opinions. He was representing the service industry on the board, and his reputation was important.

She put down her coffee cup. "Maybe they were dressed as an employee."

"It doesn't matter how they dressed! The fact is he managed to get inside that room and kill Bella without any sound of a struggle. I think you need to go back to Scottsdale, Torie. I don't want you in danger."

"I'm not going to leave, Dad." She folded her arms over her chest. He would *not* change her mind. "You were watching TV, and it was loud when I heard it. Maybe there was more noise than you realized."

"I'd only turned it on half an hour before you came in."

"We don't know when Bella died."

"True enough."

She stared at him for a long minute and took in the lines around his eyes and mouth. When had he aged like that? He was sixty, but he'd always looked younger than his years. Today he seemed older, tired and defeated. Worry for her probably. He was slim and rather unimpressive with his paler coloring and mild manner. Except in a boardroom where he had legendary negotiating skills. An opponent could agree to something he'd never intended, then the next day wonder how it happened.

She forked up a bit of her omelet and ate it. "You realize what people are saying now, don't you?"

"About what?"

"The door between our rooms was open. They're assuming we're having an affair."

His eyes widened. "I'm thirty years older than you!"

"You're a rich and powerful man. Lots of guys your age take up with younger women."

"I'm not the sort of man who needs a bauble on my arm."

She stared into his blue eyes. "Why did you never remarry, Dad? You must have had plenty of opportunity over the years. Mom's been gone eighteen years."

He moved restlessly. "I've always been wary of anyone with an agenda. And too many women who flirt only want what my money and position will bring. They never look past the name to really see me."

"That's exactly how I feel! I didn't know you had the same fears. Matthew and I didn't have any real emotion between us. He wanted to be part of the Bergstrom family."

His gaze went past her shoulder, and he straightened. "Speak of the devil."

Which devil? Her aunt?

Before she could turn to look, her dad rose and said, "Hello, Matthew."

Matthew? She turned and looked up to see her former fiancé. She felt light-headed at the sight of his blond hair and blue eyes. His surfer tan was gone, replaced with the pallor that came from days on end spent in a boardroom. His hair was trimmed close to his head and no longer curled over his ears. He was a paler replica of her father.

"W-What are you doing here?" She was either going to have to throw herself on his mercy and beg him to keep quiet about her identity, or she'd have to confess to her aunt. Neither choice seemed good.

Her father shook hands with Matthew, then gestured to an empty chair. "Have a seat."

Was he crazy? She'd just told him how she felt about Matthew. If he was going to start pushing the man on her again, she would have a firm talk with him.

She pressed her lips together as their server brought Matthew a cup of coffee and took his order. Surely he didn't know she'd come here? She hadn't seen him in five years, and even now, remembering his betrayal stung. But it was only her pride, not her heart.

"What are you doing here?" she asked in a soft voice.

"I came to see your dad. We had some issues at the hotel in Sarasota, and I thought it would be better to discuss them in person. I had no idea you were here."

"She's not," her father said in a stern voice. "And if you blow her cover, Matthew, we won't be discussing anything because you'll no longer be employed by Bergstrom Hotels and Resorts."

Matthew paled. "What are you talking about?"

"Torie is here on the q.t. No one knows she's my daughter, and it needs to remain that way. Do you understand?"

"Not really, but I'll honor your wishes." He didn't look at Torie.

She sagged back in her chair. "Thank you." She rose. "I'll leave the two of you to talk business."

As she walked away, she marveled at how different he was from Joe. And he'd never even apologized for cheating on her. Not that it would have mattered, but the man had no morals.

CHAPTER 18

JOE KNEW IT WAS TROUBLE WHEN THE BASE
commander met the boat at the wharf. A passing shrimp
boat had picked them up, and he'd directed them to call
Ajax, who must have called the commander. In the meantime Ajax had retrieved Simon and gotten him back to
headquarters.

Commander Elijah Chen had worked with the sea
mammals the longest of anyone at the base. In his fifties,
his dark eyes took in every bit of data and processed it
before he spoke. His slow Texas drawl was in keeping
with the measured way he sifted what he knew and made
a decision.

Joe had never seen the man look worried, but today a
frown creased his forehead, and he paced the dock as he
waited for Joe to disembark. Not a good sign.

Joe nodded. "Commander." He had to raise his voice
as tourists disembarked from an excursion cruise and
flowed past them.

Chen beckoned for Joe to follow him to a secluded

spot where they wouldn't be overheard. "What happened out there, Joe?"

Joe started with Simon's agitation and ended with the boat exploding. "It's unknown if we went out with the bomb on us or if Simon missed a hostile swimmer."

"Any sign of a break-in at your facility?"

"No."

"As agitated as he became, I would suspect he tried to apprehend the swimmer and missed." The commander glanced around and lowered his voice. "We're getting chatter about a terrorist attack on the base. The new submarine coming to port is particularly vulnerable as it passes along the Eastern Seaboard. We're putting a lot of security on this, but I don't want any slipups."

"Yes, sir. Maybe your team will recover enough of the bomb to identify where the raw material came from. Do we have any idea of where the threat is originating?"

"Maybe Russia. At least that's what Homeland Security is telling us. They've been monitoring transmissions, and the threat seems credible."

"I'll be on alert, sir."

"Thank you."

Joe watched him stalk off. This was big, bigger than he'd thought. A terrorist plot to take out a nuclear sub seemed unbelievable. Yet somehow against all odds, a bomb had found its way onto the hull of his boat.

He glanced at his watch. He was going to be late getting Hailey from camp. Not having his phone left him feeling crippled. He couldn't even call and let the camp know he would be late. He didn't take time to shower and change at the lab but dug his keys out of his desk and headed for his truck. The camp director would be livid, but there wasn't anything he could do about it.

He drove as fast as he could to the camp and arrived just as the gates were being locked.

Hailey was outside with the director. Tears tracked down her cheeks, and he grimaced at the fear on her face. He'd never been so late, especially without a call. No wonder she was upset.

He tapped the horn, and she and the director whirled to look his way. The director was in her sixties and had never had kids. Her drill sergeant manner came to the fore as she marched to the truck. He rolled down his window to hear her recriminations.

"I don't think we'll be able to have Hailey back, Joe. Not after this kind of irresponsible behavior."

"My boat blew up," he said in a soft voice. He kept his gaze on Hailey as she knelt to grab her bag. "My phone went down with it. Don't say anything to Hailey. I don't want to scare her. I want to break it to her easy."

The director blinked. "You expect me to believe that? It's a far-fetched tale."

"It's the truth. You'll likely see it on the evening news." He gestured down to his clothing. "Look at me. I'm still in dive gear. I was rescued by a shrimp boat and didn't take time to change after I got to shore."

She blinked. "I see."

Hailey came his direction, and he pasted on a smile. "Hi, honey, sorry I'm late."

"Daddy, you scared me! It's way past time for you to be here."

"I know, and I'm sorry. Hop in, and I'll tell you what

happened later." He sent a pleading glance toward the director who sniffed, then gave a jerky nod. "Thank you," he said softly.

He ran up the window, then turned around in the parking lot and headed for the road. "I need a quick shower before we meet up with Grammy and Grandpa. Five minutes, okay? You can change too. I'm supposed to have dinner with Torie tonight. Since I don't have my phone with her number, we'll need to run by the hotel and take our chances on finding her. I'll call Grammy and have her meet us there."

Hailey looked him over. "Did you fall overboard?"

"Something like that." He reached over and took her hand. "It's probably going to be on the news, but as you can see, I'm fine. There was an accident with my boat. But we're all okay. Simon is fine too. I had to wait for a boat to pick us up, and then the commander had to talk to me. My phone went into the water, too, so I couldn't call."

Her gaze took in the condition of his wet suit, and her face went pale. "You have to be careful, Daddy. I only have you and Gram and Grandpa."

"And God," he reminded her. "He was with me today like he always is. I don't like you to worry."

Her green eyes clouded. "God wasn't with Mommy."

"He was, honey. He was right there with her and took her in his arms."

This was the first time she'd voiced the questions he'd seen in her eyes lately. How did he explain the unexplainable? Joe didn't even understand why God had taken Julie, so how did he tell Hailey?

Had she even eaten today? Judging from the empty feel in her stomach, Torie didn't think she'd put anything in it since breakfast with her dad that morning, and it was nearly seven. Thankfully, she hadn't run into Matthew all day either. Of course she'd been holed up in her office all day.

She stretched out the kinks in her back and stood. It was past time to figure out where she was sleeping. For all her bravado with Joe last night, the thought of spending the night alone in her cottage made her chest squeeze. So that idea was clearly out. She supposed she'd have to beg a storeroom from her aunt. The suite was still off-limits until the police were done and it had been cleaned.

The police had taken the recordings from the security cameras all over the hotel before she had a chance to review them, so she still had no idea who had been in her hotel room. Being in the dark like this didn't bring much assurance of her safety. Was this how Lisbeth had felt as things closed in on her? According to her journal, she had been aware she was in danger.

The journal.

Those missing pages gnawed at her. Where could her friend have hidden them? Or maybe someone else had taken them.

The phone on her desk rang, and she sighed before answering it. "IT, Torie here."

"There's a gentleman here to see you, Torie. Joe Abbott."

Her pulse gave a kick at his name. "I'll be right there."

She replaced the phone and grabbed her purse, then locked the door behind her. Kyle hadn't been around at all today so that had been a huge blessing.

Joe was waiting with Hailey in comfortable armchairs in front of the fireplace. He rose when he saw her. "I hope you don't mind me stopping in here."

"Why didn't you text me or call?"

Hailey jumped up and came to Torie's side. "Daddy's boat sank today. It took his phone down with it."

"Sank? What happened?"

He put his finger to his lips. "Later. Hailey is spending the night with my parents. They should be here any minute, and we can grab some dinner. Where do you want to go?"

She smiled. "Tortuga Jack's."

He groaned. "You're as bad as Hailey. I need to stop by the cellular store and get a new phone."

Torie slipped her arm around the little girl. "I looked at their menu today to see what I needed to try next."

"I'm doomed," Joe said in a tragic voice. "Two women with insatiable appetites for fish tacos."

Hailey giggled. "You're funny, Daddy."

The brooding mood Torie had been in vanished, and she felt better than she had since finding Bella's body. While everything seemed murky right now, she was going to find her way through this. She had friends here already—good friends. People she could count on when things got hard. Joe wasn't the kind to cut and run when faced with trouble.

She held Hailey's hand as they walked toward the seating area to wait on her grandparents. The little girl was prattling on about the Jurassic World exhibit in Jacksonville the next day, and Joe promised he'd take her in the afternoon following the dive excursion.

He nudged Torie. "You want to go too?"

"Where?"

"Jurassic World after diving tomorrow morning."

"Sure."

A TV was airing the evening news, and she stared at the headline of a boat explosion. Was that Joe's boat in the picture?

Hailey pulled her hand from Torie's. "Daddy, that's your boat, isn't it? Did it *blow up?*"

Joe's smile faded. "I don't want you to worry, Peanut, but yes."

"You didn't tell me! You just said it sank. Did someone try to hurt you?"

His gaze met Torie's before he squatted in front of Hailey and cupped her face in his hands. "We don't know what happened yet. The Navy is investigating. You know I work with a lot of very important defense ships and submarines. No one was trying to hurt us deliberately, but someone could want to get to one of the subs or a Trident missile."

Hailey blinked back tears. "I don't want you to work with Simon anymore. You need to stay home with me where it's safe."

"Life isn't always safe, Hailey. It's an adventure God gives us, and we never know exactly what will happen. But what do we know for sure?"

"That God is in control," she parroted. "But I don't want him to be in control! I don't want him to let bad things happen like he did with Mommy. I want to be safe, and he's not always safe."

"That's because he can see things we can't. What do we do when we're afraid?"

"We trust God." She yanked her face away from his hands and folded her arms over her chest. "But I don't trust him! I can't. Not when he let Mommy die."

His helpless gaze met Torie's, and she wanted to throw her hands up and agree with Hailey, but she forced a smile. "I'll spare you the Latin since it's long, but one of my favorite St. Augustine quotes is, 'God judged it better to bring good out of evil than to suffer no evil to exist.'"

"I don't know what that means," Hailey said.

"It's hard to understand even for adults. But evil things happen to all of us, honey. Hard things, bad things. We don't understand, and a lot of the time, we can't understand because we aren't God. When those times come—and they come to everyone—all we can do is trust that God loves us."

Hailey absorbed the words. "Okay."

That was it—okay? Oh to be like a child and be able to accept. Torie wasn't good at it. Maybe she never would be.

Hailey waved wildly toward a blonde entering the hotel. "Grammy!" She darted off to throw her arms around the woman.

Joe's mother's smile faltered as she came toward them. "Well, hello." Her gaze took in her son. "I heard the news. You're okay?"

He nodded. "I'm fine, Mom. Hailey can't wait for the sleepover."

"Your dad is parked outside." Her quizzical look

landed back on Torie, and she held out her hand. "I'm Joe's mom, Carol."

Torie took her hand. "Torie Berg. I work here at the hotel, and your son has been kind enough to befriend me."

The older woman's smile widened. "Nice to meet you, Torie. I hope we see more of you." She released Torie's hand, then turned her granddaughter toward the door. "Let's go, kiddo. See you tomorrow, Joe. I'll have her back around noon."

Joe grinned as his mother walked away. "See that spring in her step? She's been nagging me to date for over a year."

Torie tucked her hand into the crook of Joe's arm. "Let's get some dinner. I'm starved."

She should have made it clear she and Joe were just friends.

CHAPTER 19

SHE DIDN'T WANT TO GO IN.

Torie stared at the door and then at the key in her shaking hand.

Joe took the key from her. "Let me check it out first."

She let him open the door and step inside while she waited in the hall. At dinner she'd gotten a text from her dad that the suite had been cleared by the police and cleaned. She knew he had lit a fire under some people to get it done. She should have known her dad would make sure she wasn't tempted to stay at the cottage tonight.

Lights came on in the suite, and she heard Joe opening doors and rummaging through the two rooms before he reappeared in the doorway. "All clear."

"Thank you. Want to come in? I can order up dessert."

Joe glanced at his feet for a moment. "After the day I had, I'm about asleep on my feet so I'd better get home."

The pang of disappointment surprised her. "I understand. We're still on for diving?"

"Yeah. I thought we'd go to the HLHA."

She'd heard of the artificial reef. It was supposed to be awesome diving. "Sounds great. I'll see you in the morning." She gave him a nod good-bye, then slipped into her room.

She locked the dead bolt and the chain, then checked out the suite for herself. All clear. The scent of new carpet erased the memory of the smell of blood from the night before. She went to the connecting door and opened it, but her dad's side was closed.

She tapped on it. "Hello?" When he didn't answer, she tapped again. Were there voices on the other side? She probably should have texted him first. Maybe Matthew was there, and he was the last person she wanted to talk to again.

The door swung open, and Torie took a step back when she saw her aunt's angry face. The voices had been the television. Her dad was nowhere to be found. Had Aunt Genevieve waited for her to show up like a spider lurking in its own web?

It was all going to come out now. It had to.

"You're fired. I suspected it last night after I heard about this door being open. I won't have Anton being taken advantage of by some little twit who fancies herself as the next Bergstrom."

"I don't think so. You don't have the authority to fire me."

Her aunt's eyes widened. "If you think Anton will be able to save your job, you're quite mistaken. He lets me run this hotel as I see fit. Once you're gone, he'll forget all about you. Pack your things and get out."

"I'm already a Bergstrom. I'm Victoria, Anton's

daughter. I'm surprised you didn't recognize your own niece, Aunt Genevieve."

Her aunt went white and swayed. Torie grabbed her arm to steady her, but she shook it off.

"You're lying," her aunt whispered.

"Look at me. Do you honestly not see the family resemblance? I look so much like Mom, at least that's what Dad says. And do you really think my father is so weak that he'd be dallying with a woman my age? You don't think much of him, do you?"

Her aunt brushed past her and went to drop into the armchair by the fireplace. "This is an outrage! Why are you here under false pretenses?" She picked up a travel magazine and fanned herself with it. Her color still hadn't come back.

How much of the truth should she spill? Torie followed her aunt and sat across from her on the love seat. "Lisbeth Nelson."

"I don't understand."

"She was my best friend. If you think back hard enough, you would recognize her name. We played together every summer, and she was my roommate at boarding school and later at college. Her death rocked me, and I wanted to find out what happened."

Her aunt's hazel eyes narrowed. "She drowned herself. Everyone knows it, so I fail to see how it was worth all this subterfuge. All this *lying* to your own aunt!"

Torie should have known her aunt would react this way. "I've never known Lisbeth to be depressed, and I know for sure she would never go in the water. She was terrified of the ocean. I have to find out the truth."

She didn't want her aunt to know that Lisbeth was

here to find out what happened to Torie's mother, though it might come to that eventually. Torie would need to ask her aunt questions at some point. But not tonight when she was already tired and upset from Bella's death.

"Do you have any idea why Bella would have been in my suite last night?"

Her aunt's mouth gaped. "You think Bella's death had something to do with your ridiculous quest? It was nothing of the kind. I sent her up here to leave a fruit basket. Anton made me feel guilty about the way I'd treated you, and I wanted to make amends. How ridiculous now that I know. Why didn't you tell me straight up who you were? This spy stuff makes no sense."

Torie could hardly tell her she trusted no one who worked here—not even her aunt. "The fewer people who knew, the more I thought I'd be able to get answers. If employees knew I was a Bergstrom, they might clam up and not tell me any suspicions they had."

"I see." Her aunt heaved a sigh. "That makes sense, I suppose." She looked around the room. "Now I understand why Anton insisted you have this room."

"Where is he?"

"Eating a late dinner with Matthew Cunningham." Her eyes narrowed. "Is Matthew here to see you too?"

"No. He had no idea I was here."

Her aunt rose and went past her, leaving a lingering scent of lavender. "I'll have to digest all this. I must say I'm disappointed in you, Victoria. Good night."

Not half as disappointed as Torie was at knowing her cover was blown and it would be doubly hard to get to the bottom of Lisbeth's death.

The last thing Torie wanted to do after the confrontation with her aunt was go to sleep.

She smacked her pillow into a better shape and lay staring at the dark ceiling. Her mind spun like lights from a disco ball. Her aunt would never keep this quiet, and everything would change. By this time tomorrow all of the hotel staff would know she was Victoria Bergstrom, heir to the massive Bergstrom Hospitality empire. They'd wonder why she was here under false pretenses, and she wouldn't be able to tell them, not really. It was something much too private to bandy around in a gossip session.

And Joe. He didn't know she'd been lying to him all this time either.

She rolled to her side and thumped the pillow again.

Her dad had tried to tell her this had been a stupid idea in the first place. She was no detective and her computer knowledge wasn't enough to get to the bottom of Lisbeth's death. Now she'd messed up her friendship with Joe. He wouldn't take kindly to the fact she'd hidden her identity from him.

She glanced at the bedside clock. The numbers flipped to just after two, and she still wasn't the least bit sleepy. It was much too late to call and talk to him too.

She threw off the covers and slid her feet to the floor. There was unlikely to be anyone roaming the hallways this late. What if she went into her family's former living quarters at the other end of the hall?

Before she could talk herself out of it, she slid her feet into slippers and donned the robe at the foot of her bed. She had a master key that would let her in, and she rummaged in her handbag for it, then headed to the door.

She paused at the sound of someone moving around in the next room. Her dad was up too? She pushed open the unlocked connecting door and poked her head into the living room. "Dad?"

Fully clothed, he sat on the sofa. "What are you doing up?"

"I was about to ask you the same thing." She told him about the run-in with her aunt.

"I'll talk to her in the morning and tell her not to repeat it."

"I doubt she'll listen." She took a step into the room. "You mentioned our old living quarters are unoccupied. I'm going to go see them."

His blue eyes went wide. "For what purpose?"

"I want to remember Mom. I want to find some closure. Eighteen years is long enough."

"Very well. I'll go with you."

Torie wasn't sure if she was relieved or disappointed. The thought of going in there made the air stall in her lungs.

Her dad didn't give her a chance to refuse. He opened the door for her, and they stepped out into an empty hall. It was only when they were outside the door that she realized she should have gotten dressed in case her dad was successful in convincing Aunt Genevieve to keep quiet. It was too late now though. Security cameras would have captured her running the halls in her nightgown and robe with hotel owner Anton Bergstrom.

Her slippers sank into the thick hall carpet, and she

slowed her steps as the big wood door to the apartment neared. This had been her idea, but now her heart wanted to jump out of her chest. There was no reason for her claustrophobia to be acting up. The hall was well lit, and she didn't feel trapped. But her lungs labored, and she wanted to run.

She forced her lips to move. "I have a master key."

Her dad stood back while she unlocked the door. When she didn't move forward, he reached past her and flipped on the light switches. With the shadows gone, she moved into the space. The bright illumination pushed back the darkness, revealing a room where nothing had changed in eighteen years. The same white sofa stood in the same spot near the fireplace. The gold armchairs showed no signs of wear. Even the vases with artificial flowers were in their spots on the mantel.

"It's like a time warp," she whispered. "I can almost see Mom out on the balcony with a glass of wine. Why have you never updated it and rented it out?"

"I couldn't bring myself to have her things thrown out like so much flotsam." Her dad's voice sounded strained and off. "I could have rented it for two thousand a night, but the thought of someone living where we'd had so much happiness was more than I could stand." He wandered across the thick white carpet to the fireplace to pick up a silver framed photograph of Torie playing Monopoly with him and her mom.

She trailed after him and stared at the picture in his hand. They all looked impossibly happy. Her gap-toothed smile and innocent eyes had been a lifetime ago.

Her dad put it back on the mantel. "This was taken the week before your mom died."

"I remember."

Her dad stared at her. "How much do you remember of that night?"

"I was being a brat. I wanted her to take me swimming, and she had a headache. I stomped out into the hall." She hadn't talked about this in years. Those memories were too painful.

"I-I heard a scream and ran back in. I couldn't find her, and I went out onto the balcony. People were yelling, and I looked over the side. I recognized her red dress on the concrete below, and I hid in a closet. I don't remember which one."

He touched her shoulder. "I'm sorry, Torie."

Her cheeks were wet, though she didn't remember crying. She swiped her face. "Lisbeth always said if I'd talk about it, I could get over it."

"The closet was in our room."

Her dad started in that direction, and she had no choice but to follow even though she wasn't ready. Her feet felt wooden as she forced herself to step into the bedroom. A blue silk bedspread still covered the king bed, at least what you could see beneath the mound of pillows. She'd forgotten that detail—her mom loved pillows. The more the better. Torie had often made forts with them and hid from her parents.

Her gaze went to the walk-in closet door, and she forced herself to step to it and turn the doorknob.

She gasped at the scent of her mother's perfume. The

blouse she touched was silk. "What was the perfume she loved? I remember the smell but not the name."

"Clive Christian No. 1. She loved the jasmine and pineapple tones in it."

She caught the note of suffering in his voice, but a picture began to form in her head. A little girl crouched on the right side of the closet near all her mother's shoes. She'd tried to hide in the shoeboxes.

She tried to turn her attention back to her father, but it was a struggle. "I shouldn't have let you come with me. This is hard for you."

"Cathartic too. And I've wanted to tell you that I've finally met someone. A lovely woman I think you'll like. When we get back to Scottsdale, I'll introduce you."

Her dad was finally moving on. Now if only Torie could.

CHAPTER 20

THE SCENT OF A STORM IN THE AIR MADE JOE'S
nose twitch, but the blue sky held only puffy clouds.

The storm forecast wasn't until midafternoon. Long
enough to get down to the reef and enjoy a two-tank dive.
The rental boat banged along on the choppy waves, but
Joe knew where he was going and made a beeline for the
yellow buoy. Once they were down there, the choppiness
wouldn't be a problem. It would be smooth going.

He had to focus on the sea foam to avoid staring at
Torie in her cute one-piece turquoise suit. Diving was his
favorite pastime, and being able to share it with her was
a dream come true. For just a moment last night when he
was saying good-bye, he'd thought he saw a flash of longing in her eyes. Unless it was his imagination. He wouldn't
rule out that possibility.

He throttled back the engine, then turned it off.
"We're here." His text message notification went off, and
he picked up his phone. "Oh no, Danielle says Simon got
out of his enclosure."

"Do we need to go back?"

The sea lion had gotten out a few times before, but he always came back. He'd been born in an enclosure so it was home.

He shook his head. "He'll come back on his own. I don't want to miss our dive."

She moved to toss over the anchor. "I haven't been diving in a year. I can't wait."

"Need a refresher course?"

She shook her head. "I've gone a million times. Or something like that."

Gosh, she was pretty with the sunlight gleaming on her dark-brown hair. She had her hair in a tighter braid than usual, which hung down her back. Her brown eyes glowed with anticipation. He'd like to think being with him had brought at least one little sparkle.

After she stuffed her hair in her cap, he held out her buoyancy compensation device and helped her put it on. He might have taken his time just so he could smell her light scent a little while longer, but he wouldn't admit it if she asked.

While she adjusted her mask and mouthpiece, he donned his own equipment. "I assume you usually dive with a buddy?"

"Always. I wouldn't want to be trapped down there without help. You use a buddy, don't you?"

"Yep." He'd met a few hotshots who wouldn't stay with their buddy, and it was way too dangerous. He gestured for her to get in, and once she fell back into the water, he did the same.

The sea enveloped him in its warm embrace, and he took a moment to get his bearings before kicking down with her to the reef. The water was clear today, but it wouldn't be after the storm. They were directly above the reef formed from the Jacksonville stadium, and the rubble from the structure had made the most natural-looking area of the HLHA. They spent their first tank examining the sea life. He found an octopus and played with it for a few minutes before she got up the courage to let him hand it to her. Its velvety texture made her smile.

Her eyes were wide behind her mask, and bubbles escaped in a flurry when the octopus squirted ink. She let it go, and it zoomed off to its hiding space again.

He pointed to the *Edwin Nettleton*, a WWII Liberty ship that formed part of the reef. She swam beside him, and he admired her kicks and strokes. She was a natural in the water. Maybe he could relax. He kept expecting her to have a problem, but she was a pro like she'd said.

They reached the ship and swam around it for several minutes until she pointed to another area of the reef. The sunken sailboat was clearly outlined with coral, and it was one of his favorite places to dive. While she explored the colorful reef, he poked his head into the sailboat and looked around to get his bearings for when he needed to exit. Coral encrusted the interior of the boat as well, and he spotted the remains of the galley and head that beckoned for a closer inspection. He swam into the boat.

Who had owned this old craft and allowed her to be scuttled for the reef? He'd likely never know. He touched the side of the window and saw a shape jet toward him. A man dressed in a black wet suit and wearing a black mask slapped a small device against the hull of the boat, then kicked away as a sleek sea lion barreled toward him.

Simon.

The sea lion chased after the diver just as something lifted Joe in the air and slammed him against the side. Disoriented, he shook his head.

A small bomb had gone off.

His vision cleared, and he saw that the hull had collapsed and crumbled where the window used to be.

He struggled to stay conscious from the blow to his head. Hailey. He had to get back to his daughter. The darkness disoriented him, and he remembered his flashlight. He fumbled for it, then flicked it on. The beam cast shadows and made the interior of the boat look green and eerie, but his panic began to subside. He had to think logically through this. Torie would have seen him go in here, and she'd be looking for a way to help him.

He swam to the hull and banged on it with his light. The metal didn't make much sound against the coral so he searched for a spot that was mostly fiberglass. There. He pounded on it with the base of this flashlight and heard a satisfying *thunk*. After a moment, he heard an answering thump from outside the sailboat. Torie knew he was in here.

But how could she get him out? He checked his regulator. Only fifteen minutes of oxygen left. She wouldn't have time to get to the rental boat, call for help, then break into the sailboat's hull. She'd likely have more air left than him because she was lighter, but would she think about that? Her reg might read thirty or forty minutes.

He prayed she thought this through and figured out how to break through the hull. Maybe there was something in here he could use to bust a hole in the side himself.

He shone the light around the space. Nothing but coral. No rocks, no leftover toilet tank or anything he might use as a battering ram.

It was going to be up to Torie to figure it out.

==

Joe was trapped in there.

Torie pounded on the hull again to let him know she realized the danger. She forced her breathing to calm, and the bubbles escaping her regulator slowed to a steady pace. Panic wouldn't save him, only clear thinking and a plan. She checked her air. Forty-five minutes, but that didn't mean anything, not really. Joe was six four with big muscles. He'd use up air faster than she would. She prayed he had half an hour, but there wasn't a guarantee of that either. She should plan to have him out within fifteen minutes.

She swam through a large school of fish and checked the integrity of the sunken sailboat all around the hull. The heavy incrustations of coral would make it hard to batter through, even if she had something to use. And she didn't.

She glanced overhead, but they'd swum away from their boat far enough that its shadow couldn't be seen. No time to go back there for a tool.

Her chest compressed, and she fought her breathing again. How did she get him out? If only she had a crowbar or something to pry away the coral and fiberglass. She banged the butt of her flashlight on the hull and heard another answering knock from inside.

He was still alive—for now.

But he wouldn't be for long. She tried not to imagine the sensation of being unable to breathe. That couldn't happen. Not to wonderful Joe with his kind green eyes and easy manner. He was Hailey's whole world.

With new determination, she swam down along the ocean floor where various artifacts poked up through the coral. Joe had said the artificial reef was comprised of old subway cars and tugboats. All kinds of things. There had to be something she could use.

She reached a coral outcropping that rose higher. From its vague shape, she thought it might have been an old subway car. It might be the best chance of finding a piece of sturdy metal she could use. She swam along the perimeter. Frequent windows let her look inside where more debris lay scattered. Swimming inside was out of the question. Her claustrophobia would get the better of her. She'd never taken a course on wreck diving because it was something she'd never be tempted to do.

She used her flashlight to prod the various rocks and coral along the bottom. She reached the end of the subway car without finding any kind of tool, then checked her air. Five minutes had passed.

Time might be running out for Joe.

She swam down the other side of the car, and a long metal piece caught her eye. But it was *inside*. Maybe she could reach it without going all the way in. Holding the flashlight, she extended her arm through the window and tried to scrape the metal toward her. It refused to budge.

She closed her eyes and tried to push past the panic bubbling in her chest. She had to go in there and grab it.

There was no other way to save Joe. And as she stared at the all-important metal bar, she realized she'd been fooling herself about him. Joe wasn't someone she would be able to fly away from and forget. He wasn't a vacation romance never to be thought of again.

He was special. And as much as she might say she was happy with her life the way it was, she recognized the hole there. She'd told Lisbeth she didn't care about marriage and children, but faced with the threat of losing Joe, she knew she'd been wrong.

She cared too much.

A flurry of bubbles escaped in a flood as she forced herself through the window and into the murky depths of the subway car's interior. The gloom added to her panic, but she worked on measured breathing and kicked toward the metal piece.

It was stuck to coral, and she had to use her flashlight to help pry it up. With a final twist of the end, she freed it.

She turned to swim back out, but a dark shadow swam past the window. A shark. It wasn't large, only about eight feet long, but it was a tiger shark. Fast and dangerous. She glanced at her air again. Another five minutes had eked away. She had to go out there and hope to chase it off. Staying in here would mean Joe could be drowning right this minute.

Holding the metal at the ready like a baseball bat, she swam back through the opening into the sea. The shark's tail was toward her, and it hadn't noticed she was nearby. She prayed it would keep on swimming away.

She gazed past it to the sunken sailboat. If she stayed on the other side, maybe the shark wouldn't notice her.

The closest path to the other side was through the windows, so she forced herself back into the subway car, swam to the other side, and wiggled out of a tighter window. Kicking her fins with all her strength, she swam as fast as she could back to the sailboat.

The shark hadn't reappeared, and she prayed feverishly it wouldn't as she used the metal to pry at the coral and fiberglass. It resisted her efforts, but she gritted her teeth and went at it even harder.

It sank into the fiberglass and she gave a mighty yank on it. It splintered away a large hole, big enough for her to put her arm through. With a hole to work on, she chipped away a larger and larger area until she thought it was big enough for Joe to get out.

Why wasn't he coming?

She cautiously poked her head into the hull and saw him floating a few feet away. No bubbles emanated from his reg, and his eyes were wide. She kicked her fins and got inside, then zoomed to him. She grabbed the spare octopus from her BCD and yanked out his mouthpiece, then put her octopus in his mouth.

He took several breaths, and his color began to improve. He gave her a thumbs-up and a shaky smile.

Swimming close together, they reached the escape hole, but one of them would have to go first. Joe let go of the octopus and gestured for her to get out. She quickly wiggled through the hole and held the octopus at the ready for him. He was right behind her, but the hole was a bit small for him, and he had to wiggle hard to get through. A thin line of blood on his shoulder seeped where he'd scraped it. He reached her and grabbed for more air.

After two breaths, his gaze went past her, and a flurry of bubbles floated around his face as he pointed. She turned to look.

The shark. It was coming for them like a gray bullet.

CHAPTER 21

THE TIGER SHARK MUST HAVE GOTTEN A WHIFF of the blood oozing from Joe's shoulder.

The shark darted toward them, then veered away at the last minute. Joe slapped his hand over the scrape, but that wouldn't deter the shark. He dragged in more air, and his strength began to return after his near miss with death.

Torie's eyes were wide behind her mask, and he gestured for her to back up as far as the octopus apparatus that connected them would let her. She shook her head and brandished the metal she'd used to pry him free.

He grabbed it, taking comfort in its sturdiness, as he waited for the shark's next attack. It wasn't long in coming, and this time the gray form stayed zoned in on him. When the fish was in jabbing distance, he thrust the sharpest point of the metal at its gill on Joe's right side, then jabbed again at its eye. It veered off, leaving a trail of blood in its wake.

Knowing that might not deter it for long, Joe jabbed upward with his thumb. She nodded, and they began to ascend to the surface. He kept a wary eye out for another attack from the shark, but there was no sign of it when his head finally broke water.

He pulled out his mouthpiece and drew in the most wonderful salty air. "There's the boat." He pointed a hundred feet away. "We'll never see the shark coming from up here. Let's get aboard as fast as we can."

Something bumped his leg and he jerked, expecting to feel shark teeth, but Simon's sleek head peeked up out of the water. "Stick with me, buddy."

She removed her mouthpiece. "Maybe Simon will protect us from the shark. You tow me while I breathe through the snorkel and watch for the shark."

A surge of adrenaline shot through him. "Good idea."

She slid on her snorkel and put her mask in the water, then took the metal in one hand and grabbed his ankle in the other. He pulled her through the waves as fast as he could. Her grip on him didn't falter so he assumed she saw no sign of their toothy attacker.

They had almost reached the boat's ladder when her grip went rigid, and she came up sputtering. "It's coming! Simon is swimming toward it."

He took the metal from her, then slid on his snorkel. "Get aboard the boat!" He submerged and watched the shark slice toward them as if it was determined for revenge. The sea lion zoomed to drive it off, but the shark swam past.

Joe's heart thumped against his rib cage as he waited for its next strike. Its eye was a little squinty, but he clearly hadn't done enough damage. He held the metal like a javelin. His strength had surged back the more air he'd taken in, and he was ready to fend it off this time. To kill it if he could.

The shark's formidable serrated teeth came at him, but he thrust the metal squarely in the tiger's eye. Blood spurted from the wound and fanned out in a red haze around the shark. It would be sure to attract more predators. It went limp and begin to sink toward the bottom. Without waiting for another bullet shape to appear, he kicked for the surface, then swam for all he was worth to the boat.

Aboard the boat, Torie urged him on, "Hurry! There's blood in the water."

His legs were tired from kicking, but he unleashed an extra spurt of speed as she screamed, "I see fins!"

His hand slapped against the metal of the ladder, and he hauled himself aboard as something bumped his thigh from under the water. He scrambled up the rungs and fell onto the deck, then ripped off his mask and snorkel to draw in the freshest breath he'd ever had.

Torie was beside him in the next moment. "Are you all right?"

"I think so." He touched the spot on his leg where he'd been hit. No cuts. "Something tested my leg to see if it wanted to take a bite, but I got up the ladder in time. Someone planted a small explosive on the hull of the sailboat. The collapse was no accident."

Her mouth trembled, and she bit down on her lower lip. "You saw a diver?"

"Yeah. Simon took off after him just as it exploded. This doesn't make any sense."

She leaned down and pulled his head over and cradled him in her arms. She pressed her cool lips against his in a fierce kiss that was much too short. He wrapped his arms around her, but she pulled away before he had a chance to really respond.

Her braid was coming loose around her face, and she pushed a loose strand out of her eyes. "When I thought you might die, I realized how wrong I was to try to protect myself from feeling anything for you. It was too late anyway."

Too late? Was she saying what he thought she was saying?

Her brown eyes searched his. "I have told myself for years it's better to be alone, better to be footloose and free to do what I wanted. Better to be in control of my own destiny. I tried to believe I wasn't lonely—that a life like that was exactly what I wanted. But when I imagined you taking your last breath trapped in the hull, I couldn't stand it."

Tears pooled in her eyes and rolled down her cheeks. "It's funny how we deceive ourselves. Talking to Hailey yesterday made me realize I have a problem with lack of trust. Ever since my mom died, I don't trust anyone to stay with me. I don't trust God. I don't even believe my dad won't ever leave. But what kind of life is that?"

He cupped her cheek in his hand. "It's not life. By its very nature, life involves loss. If we stop taking chances, stop living our lives, we might as well crawl in the grave and let someone kick the dirt over us. Real life is worth the risk."

She nodded. "I know that now. But just know even though I realize my thinking is wrong, I might take one step toward you and two steps back."

"I have more patience than you give me credit for." He

pulled her head down for a proper kiss, and she seemed happy to oblige.

==

Dinosaurs loomed everywhere she looked.

Torie watched Hailey, who grinned widely as she dashed from exhibit to exhibit inside the big tent of the Jurassic World show. They'd made the hour drive to Jacksonville right after reporting the attack to the Navy and the state police. Joe had made sure Simon returned to the enclosure, and they'd grabbed lunch on the way.

Torie hadn't expected such fun animatronics. Children of all ages flocked around the T-Rex exhibit. Joe kept being drawn to the real bones and teeth in glass cabinets, but Hailey couldn't be bothered with anything that mundane. She wanted to see the raptors.

"They don't look anything like in the movies," Hailey said. "They're so small, and they have feathers. I had nightmares after watching the movie, but these guys don't seem all that scary."

Joe frowned. "When did you watch the movie? The violence isn't appropriate for your age."

Hailey rolled her eyes. "Dad, I'm eight years old. I'm not a kid. I just hid my eyes when they ate a guy."

"You didn't answer the question."

"I don't remember. A playdate sometime." Hailey waved madly, then dashed to join a friend and her family at the display of megalodon and prehistoric ocean creatures. "Millie!" The two little girls embraced and chattered excitedly.

"That kid will be the death of me," Joe muttered.

Torie could hardly take her gaze off the megalodon's triangular serrated teeth. "Glad we don't see sharks like that anymore. Especially today. Our flimsy piece of metal wouldn't have dented its hide."

Joe, looking impossibly handsome in shorts and a red tee, handed her an iced tea. "I was thinking the same thing. You doing okay? You've been quiet. I know this morning was terrifying."

It was now or never. She didn't want him to hear about her identity from a rumor. "I . . . um. Well, I have something I need to tell you, and I'm not sure how."

His green-eyed gaze sharpened. "What is it? Have you found out something about Lisbeth's death?"

"No, it's not that." She wet her lips and forced herself to hold his gaze. She wanted to track every flicker of his eyelids and every turn of his mouth for clues to how he took her news. "It's about my name."

His forehead furrowed. "Your name? I don't understand."

"My full name is Victoria. Victoria Bergstrom. I'm Anton's daughter."

His jaw sagged. "You're not serious." She held his gaze. "You *are* serious. Why would you show up here pretending to be an employee?"

"I thought I could learn more about Lisbeth's death if no one knew I was a Bergstrom." She clenched her hands together. "You don't know what it's like to grow up with a famous name. People watch what they say. They make assumptions about you based on nothing more than something they read in a magazine or watched on TV. I knew everyone would clam up if they thought they were talking out of school, and I didn't want that."

"So even though I was helping you try to discover the truth, you didn't think I needed to know your real identity?"

"I was afraid it would get out to everyone."

He folded his arms across his chest. "So not only did you not trust me enough with your real name, but you thought I was a gossip."

This was quickly going south. She touched his forearm. "I didn't know you well enough to make that kind of judgment. I don't open up easily to people. I'm awkward and inept in relationships. I'm sorry I didn't tell you right away. I didn't *know* you, Joe. Surely you can understand that."

"I took you at face value."

"No you didn't. You were suspicious right from the beginning. You know you were."

He exhaled. "Maybe so. But we've come a ways in the past few days." His mouth softened. "Is that why you're telling me now?"

She wished she could tell him it was true, but another lie would make things worse. "No. I had to tell my aunt last night, and she's already blabbed it to the world."

He took a step back. "So you're only telling me because you got caught and knew I'd hear about it somewhere else?"

"I wanted to tell you before this, but there hasn't been a good time."

"You could have told me after we got on the boat this morning. There have been plenty of opportunities to open up and be honest."

"I know. I wish I could do things differently, but I can't."

His lips flattened, and she could see him physically pull away from her in his stance and the way he avoided her gaze. She had expected this, but she'd hoped it would go better.

To distance herself from the confrontation, she glanced over to see what Hailey was doing, but there was no sign of her red hair. The girl she'd run over to talk to was listening to the audio exhibit about ancient sea life.

"Where's Hailey?"

Joe turned to look too. "She was right here a minute ago."

Torie wasn't worried, not yet. She turned and searched through the groups of children in case Hailey had found another friend, but she didn't see the little girl.

Joe strode to Millie and her family with Torie on his heels. "Did you see where Hailey went?"

Millie, a cute blonde in a blue-and-white sundress, shook her head. "One of the employees told her she'd won a megalodon tooth, and she went with him. The employee was dressed like a dinosaur so I couldn't tell you if it was a man or a woman."

Torie gasped and clutched at Joe's arm. "Which direction?" she asked the girl.

The mother answered and pointed to the exit. "They went out of the tent."

Dread curled through Torie's spine, and she couldn't breathe. It might be nothing, but her gut said little Hailey was in danger.

CHAPTER 22

SHE HAD TO BE HERE SOMEWHERE.

Calling Hailey's name, Joe ran outside with Torie behind him and looked around the tents and buildings scattered across the fairgrounds. People strolled the various walkways, gazing at the dinosaur exhibits. Still shouting her name, he searched for his little girl among the patrons and the staff dressed like dinosaurs. Nothing.

His chest compressed. *Stay calm. Panic won't help you find Hailey.* He needed a clear head.

Torie touched his arm. "The sign points to information. Maybe that's where they went if she won something."

He hurried toward the building. "Maybe it's a teenager inside the costume who didn't realize how problematic it would be to take a child away without the parent's knowledge."

"Maybe."

Her long legs kept up with his fast stride. He wanted to believe he was overreacting, but the grim line of Torie's lips was a reminder she felt how wrong this all was too.

He yanked open the door and followed her through to the information desk.

A girl of about seventeen looked up with a smile from behind the desk. "Can I help you?"

"My daughter was told she won a megalodon tooth. Is this where she would get that prize? She's eight and has red hair."

The girl's smile faltered. "We aren't giving away megalodon teeth. They are much too valuable. And we have no fake ones either, so that's odd. You're sure she was told she won something?"

Dread took a firmer hold on his gut. "Positive. Someone dressed in a dinosaur costume led her away. I didn't see it, and a friend told me what was said. Why would an employee or volunteer take a kid without talking to the parents?" He drew in a deep breath when he realized he was nearly shouting. "I'm sorry. I'm a little upset and worried."

"I understand that, but I don't believe any of our employees would have done this. Maybe I should call the police." She reached for a phone.

The police.

His terror ramped up. This wasn't sanctioned by the exhibitors. "You call them while I keep looking. And call your supervisor. We need to lock down the fairgrounds and not let anyone out."

He started to walk through the rest of the building, but Torie tugged at his arm. "She's not in here. Let's look elsewhere. There are other buildings." Her phone went off, and she glanced at it.

Her gasp stopped him dead in his tracks. "What is it?"

Her hand shook when she held out her phone for him to see the message.

Tag, you're it.

He froze. "He has her."

"They have to be here somewhere."

"I've taught Hailey to scream for help if she's being abducted. To fight and do whatever she has to. She would have caused a commotion." He thought it through. "But she might not have been afraid if she couldn't see who had her. She might have thought it was all part of a game."

The phone dinged again, and they peered together at the message.

Livestock can make quite a stink.
But you'll find me here before you can blink.

He turned the other direction. "One of the barns!"

They ran down the path to the two barns, neither of which were being used by the Jurassic exhibit. The first barn was locked.

Torie headed past him. "I'll try the other one."

He looked around for another point of entry into the barn—a window, another door.

"It's open!" Torie disappeared inside the other barn, and he ran to catch up with her.

The place was a cave inside. No lights, no sign of life. Just the stink of manure, dust, and old hay.

"Hailey!" he shouted.

"I found the lights," Torie said.

A moment later, the overhead lamps came on and illuminated the cavernous interior. He saw no movement in the open area and no indication anyone had been here recently. But it *was* unlocked. That had to mean something.

Unless the guy was leading them on a chase to torment them.

He cupped his hands to his mouth. "Hailey!"

"Daddy?"

He whirled at the tiny voice. "Hailey, where are you?"

"H-Here." A door opened to his right, and Hailey peeked out of it.

He shot forward and pulled her into his arms. Tears struggled for dominance, and he breathed in the sweet aroma of her hair, vaguely aware Torie was right there too.

After a fierce hug, he gripped her shoulders and checked her over. "Are you all right?"

Please, God, don't let her have been harmed.

Her clothing was all intact. She still wore her shoes. Even her hair looked in order.

Torie caressed Hailey's hair. "It's all right now, honey. You're safe."

He should have reassured his daughter like that so he hugged her again. "We've got you. Did he put you in the bathroom or did you get away?"

"The T-Rex told me to go inside and wait for you. He said if I came out, I'd be sorry." Hailey sniffled. "I messed up, Daddy. I knew better than to go off with someone without telling you. B-But I thought I won a tooth!" She began to cry in earnest.

He held her close and let her sob on his shirt. "You're okay, Peanut. He can't hurt you."

In the distance the sound of a siren wailed toward them. This ordeal wouldn't be over for Hailey for hours.

If he got his hands on the guy who had terrorized her, he'd be the one going to jail.

==

He'd spare his little girl if he could.

Joe wanted to reply to every question the police asked Hailey, but only she knew the answers to so much of what had happened today. The problem was, even she didn't know the identity of the man who had taken her.

The female officer gave Hailey a reassuring smile. "Since you don't know what he looked like, how tall was he?"

Hailey glanced at her dad sitting next to Torie by a wall outside. "Not as tall as Daddy or Torie. Taller than me."

Which meant exactly nothing since they were both six feet tall and over.

"How about his voice? Was it deep? Did he have an accent?"

Did Hailey even know what an accent was? Joe didn't want to sit here wasting time when he should be scouring the place for the guy.

"He talked funny. Like this." She did a falsetto imitation. "He kind of sounded like Donald Duck."

Joe exchanged a glance with Torie. The guy had changed his voice, hidden his face, and could basically be one of these detectives and Hailey would never know. They'd been outsmarted in every way.

The female officer put away her pad. "Thanks for helping us, Hailey." She handed a card to Torie. "Could you forward the texts you got from the kidnapper? We'll start with your phone number, too, and see if we can trace the messages. Our tech guys might want your phone to try to get to the perp."

Torie held out her phone. "You want it now? We need to find this guy. I can get a new one on the way home."

"It might speed things up," the detective said.

"That's fine. I'm due an upgrade anyway. Nothing is more important than keeping Hailey safe."

Joe set his hand on her knee. "Thank you."

He would have offered to buy her a phone, but that was ridiculous now that he knew who she was. She could buy a cellular company all by herself. His shock over that revelation had been pushed aside by the trauma of nearly losing Hailey, but the knowledge festered in the background.

The detective took the phone and bagged it as evidence. "Thank you. I have your contact info, and we'll be in touch."

"That's it?" Joe asked. "We just go home now not knowing if this guy is still watching?"

"I'd assume he is," the detective said. "Take precautions and be alert."

He wouldn't want to go to work and let her out of his sight. Maybe he could take a leave of absence, but he was badly needed to work this next week, especially knowing someone had planted an explosive and tried to kill him. The thought of bringing her into the office crossed his mind, but she'd be bored silly. It would take some thought to figure out what to do. His parents both worked so they couldn't really take her either.

When the police officers left, he rose and pulled Hailey to his side. "Let's go home, Peanut."

"I didn't get to see all the dinosaurs." Her voice took on a whine.

That guy could still be here, watching them, waiting for another chance. He glanced at Torie, and she shrugged and nodded. Hailey might sense his fear if he rushed her home and didn't let her out of the house. The last thing he wanted was to turn her into a kid afraid of every shadow.

"Okay, one hour. We should be able to let you ride the T-Rex and get your face painted. Deal?"

"Deal!" Hailey started to run ahead.

"Hailey, stay right by us," he ordered. "Don't run off to talk to anyone else and don't run ahead."

She slowed. "Okay."

Her crestfallen expression pierced his heart, but there were too many people and too many ways she could disappear.

Torie stepped close to his other side and whispered, "I don't want us to be foolhardy, but we have to realize whoever did this wanted to traumatize me. He wasn't really trying to hurt Hailey."

The words stopped him short. Of course, she was right. It had been a ploy to terrify Torie. And him. But it had been scary for his daughter too. The person who had done this hadn't cared who was hurt as long as Torie realized someone dangerous lurked in the shadows ready to harm her. The guy who had done this was still trying to scare her off and make her quit looking into Lisbeth's death.

"I wanted to help before today, but this makes me all the more determined," he said. "This guy means business. He will do anything, dare any outrageous behavior it takes to drive you off. Who does that?"

"Well, he doesn't want to go to jail for murder," Torie said.

"I think it's more than that. I mean, he took a *kid* to get your attention. It's like he's taunting you. Why is it so personal? He didn't even tell you to leave or he'd harm her. I just don't get it."

"I don't either." She inhaled and her voice went husky. "But maybe you should back off and let me do this alone. I couldn't bear it if anything happened to Hailey. Or to you."

He shook his head before she finished speaking. "He's got me mad now. No one messes with my daughter and gets away with it. I *will* find him and make sure he never does anything like this to anyone else."

She chewed her lip. "I can't believe I'm saying this, but maybe I should just go. I could hire a private investigator. I'm not getting any closer to this guy's identity."

"I don't think an investigator could do much. We wouldn't know for sure Lisbeth was murdered if the guy hadn't made the move to try to drive you away. You're a catalyst somehow. I think if you leave, we'll never know his identity."

CHAPTER 23

THE STARTLED LOOKS AND WIDE EYES FROM THE staff told Torie they knew exactly who she was.

She ignored the speculative stares and whispered comments as she moved down the center aisle of the historic Faith Chapel. The rich hardwood pews contrasted with the red carpet, and the Tiffany and Armstrong stained glass glowed in the Sunday morning sunlight. She hadn't been inside the historical building in years, and she'd forgotten the wood-clad cathedral ceilings and the peaceful vibe of the small A-frame chapel.

She might as well sit by her dad in the front row since her aunt had blabbed about her identity to everyone in the hotel by now. She shouldn't have been disappointed in Aunt Genevieve, but she struggled to hold back tears. Her aunt had never been the warmest person, but Torie had held out a thin streak of hope she might want to help get justice for Lisbeth. Her aunt didn't care about much of anything though—certainly not a young woman without any standing or rich family.

Torie settled beside her dad, and he squeezed her hand, then released it. "You doing okay?"

"Yes." Her throat constricted and she sniffled. "No, I guess not. I don't really know how I should feel. Seeing the casket makes it all so real. Lisbeth really is gone from this life."

The closed casket at the front of the church was the focal point of Torie's attention. Her dad had paid for the coffin, and it was a handsome copper Lisbeth would have loved. Masses of flowers covered the casket, but the scent of roses and lilies was cloying and suffocating. Other flowers lined the sides as well as a few other gifts, like a set of wind chimes, potted plants, and a Bible with artificial flowers.

The church capacity was limited to 110, but Torie doubted there were even half that many here now. Lisbeth had been a new employee, and she had no siblings. Her parents had died in a small plane crash when she was eighteen, which was why Torie's dad had become her benefactor. Torie doubted anyone on the island knew Lisbeth from her grade school days.

A movement to her left drew her attention, and her pulse kicked when she saw Joe's tall figure slide into the pew beside her. She'd never seen him in a suit, and the navy fabric accentuated his broad shoulders.

"You look handsome." Torie took his hand, but he pulled it away so she clasped her hands together in her lap. "Thanks for coming. Where's Hailey?"

"With Danielle and her kids. I didn't want to bring her in case it was too upsetting for her. She hasn't been to a funeral since Julie's."

Though his voice was cold, at least he'd come. She hadn't been sure what to expect after his reaction to the truth of her identity. He was clearly still mad though.

She inclined her head to the left. "I see Craig is here. I've heard the killer often comes to the funeral. Do you think the killer is here?"

"I scanned the mourners as I came in. I can't say for sure anyone suspicious is here, but I didn't see anyone who seemed like a suspect to me. Employees and a few people I didn't know. Some business owners who are here out of respect for your dad."

"Is Aunt Genevieve coming today?" Torie asked her dad.

"I don't think so. She claims she's got some issues to deal with at the hotel, but I think she wants to avoid me." Her dad leaned in to whisper in her ear. "I let her know I was unhappy with her gossip." Her dad reached over and gripped Joe's hand. "Thank you for saving Torie yesterday."

"She rescued me first."

"I heard she went inside the subway car. You might not know she is claustrophobic, and it took a lot of courage for her to get past her fear."

Torie's cheeks heated, and she waved her hand between the two of them. "Hey, I'm right here. You don't need to talk about me like I'm absent. Anyone would have done what I did. There wasn't an option."

She wasn't yet ready to talk to her dad about her epiphany when she thought she was going to die down there. It was too new, and she hadn't yet thought through what it meant to life as she knew it. For one thing, she wouldn't be traveling all over the world for Bergstrom Hospitality.

She'd realized she was unable to be truly present in her life with the way she was expected to flit from place to place every three or four days.

So what was her purpose in life? What did she want to do? The holy sense of this place enveloped her. She liked the hospitality industry, and if she could stay in one place, it would be better. She'd have to think about that.

She was her dad's only heir, and she knew in her gut he would not understand her decision. Eighteen years since her mother's death, and he'd only moved on recently. She didn't want to walk in his lonely footsteps. He'd deny he'd felt alone all those years, but she recognized it now.

Her gaze wandered to Joe. Even if he never forgave her and this budding relationship died on the vine, she knew her life was going to change forever. Now that the scales were gone from her eyes, she could never return to holding back and hiding behind the shields she'd erected. The ordeal under the sea had ripped away every pretense.

But she prayed he could forgive her. Time would tell.

Simon barked at Joe from his saltwater enclosure inside the metal structure housing Joe's headquarters. The place stank of fish and stale water. A gull that had gotten inside swooped down to land on the concrete beside him. It stepped closer and stared at Joe with beady black eyes as if to dare him to leave the crab unattended for a minute.

Joe sat with his feet dangling over the edge of the enclosure and threw crab to Simon. "You were a big help yesterday, buddy."

Danielle dropped to the concrete beside him and swung her legs over. "I just talked to Pete. Hailey and the twins are splashing around on the waterslide he put up for them."

"Any sign of someone lurking around?"

"Nope. Pete called one of his Marine buddies over, and he's sitting out front with a magazine and a beer pretending to be enjoying the day. All is quiet."

"I'll thank him with a lobster dinner."

Her husband, Pete, was a burly guy and a Marine Embassy Guard. He was used to guarding ambassadors and heads of state. He was home for the next month, and Hailey was safe with him. Danielle had suggested it once she had heard about Hailey's abduction.

Danielle splashed her feet in the water. "I don't get why anyone would try to take you out, Joe. What's the end game?"

"I wish I knew. This is the second explosion that's been set. I think someone is targeting our research with the sea lions, but I can't figure out why. It's not like the three we have here are the only ones protecting the area. The Navy has more, and they're fully trained."

"The new sub is coming. We'd thought it had something to do with that, but why target here? King's Bay is nineteen nautical miles away. If they're going to send in a hostile swimmer, it won't be up here."

"True enough."

Could it have anything to do with Torie's investigation? That seemed even more far-fetched. What could be on Jekyll Island that would attract a hostile swimmer? It's not like the place swarmed with millionaires or hidden treasure.

Simon swam to the side of the pool and bumped Joe's leg as if to say, *Hey, give me more food.* Joe touched the sea lion's nose. "Sorry, big guy. All gone." He held up his empty hands to demonstrate.

Simon barked again and dove down to the bottom to snare a plastic ring he liked to play with. He tossed it in the air, then caught it on his nose. Joe could almost see him smile.

"Did you hear from the Navy about any evidence they retrieved from the site of the explosion?" Danielle asked.

"Yeah, I talked to Chen. They found a few bits of wire and traces of the explosive but nothing that would provide any certainty on who tried to kill me. A common explosive and wire. They didn't find the detonator or any sign of the swimmer."

"Too bad Simon escaped without the cuffs. We could have nabbed him."

"Though he might have drowned by the time help arrived."

"You have any enemies, Joe? Someone you ticked off when you started your own research lab?"

He started to shake his head, then reconsidered long enough to think about it. "Owen Hamilton probably doesn't hold me in high regard. He was supposed to be my partner but couldn't come up with his half of the money, so I went with Ajax instead. He hasn't spoken to me since. But he's in San Diego, and I hardly think he'd send an assassin to take me out. What would be the point? He wouldn't gain anything."

"What would your failure do to the Navy? Anything?"

He had to chew on that for a few minutes because he'd

always had an excellent relationship with them. "They'd have to get their sea lions from San Diego, but that would be no big hardship."

"When is Simon supposed to be transferred to the Navy?"

"In a couple of weeks. He's nearly ready."

"And the war games will be going on there. Is it possible some place like Russia would want to whittle down the numbers of sea mammals out there working the area?"

He straightened and looked at her. "You might have something there. One of the sea lions they have is getting old and too infirm to patrol for more than an hour at a time. Chen has been pushing me to get Simon up to speed because he needs him."

Joe reached for his phone. "I'd better call Chen and mention it. I could go ahead and let him take Simon. He's my buddy, but he proved his worth today. He's ready to protect the country."

CHAPTER 24

SHE SHOULD BE IN BED, NOT SNEAKING AROUND her office at midnight.

Torie suppressed a yawn and clicked on another security camera file. The police had released the files back to the hotel, and this was her first chance to review them. After the scare with Hailey yesterday, Torie had a fresh urgency to track down what happened to Lisbeth. It would kill her if something happened to another person she cared about—especially sweet Hailey. Or Joe.

Joe had distanced himself from her. The pain of that still gripped her heart, but she had to hope he would understand. In the meantime, she had to focus on her purpose here.

Was Joe right and the guy had something personal against her? If so, why? She was a stranger to most people here except for her aunt. But all this had started well before her identity had become known. None of it made sense.

When she'd told her dad about the incident with

Hailey, he wanted Torie to abandon her quest as well. And she'd nearly succumbed to his pleas until she ran across a picture of Lisbeth and her at Poipu Beach on Kauai. Someone had snuffed out her friend's smile and the joy of life in her eyes. That person couldn't get away with it. Not while Torie lived.

With one eye on the screen, she pulled a pad of paper toward her and jotted down things to research.

- Look for the missing journal pages.
- Talk to friends of Bella's. Someone has to know something.
- Talk to Kyle.
- Question my aunt.

That third bullet point made her stomach clench. The guy was just plain weird, and she didn't like being around him. But she couldn't let her distaste stand in the way of getting at the truth.

A movement on the screen caught her eye, and she gave the file her full attention. This file was of the night Bella died, and the camera focused on the side door by the laundry room. She gasped when she recognized Bella slinking out the door. She paused and glanced around as if she was making sure the coast was clear before she stepped around the landscape bushes and walked toward a waiting car.

The interior light in the vehicle came on, but the person's head was turned away from the camera, and the picture was too fuzzy to make out much. She thought it was a man with longish hair, but it could have been a woman with short hair. And what was the make of the car? It was a sedan, but there wasn't enough light to discern the color. Maybe light green or blue but it could be gray. She wasn't good at determining make and model, but Joe might be. Or she could look it up.

She took a snapshot of the frame and printed it out. As the vehicle pulled away, she got another shot and sent it over to the printer too. It had been much earlier than when Torie had discovered Bella's body so it might or might not be pertinent. At this point, everything mattered though.

Seeing Bella in the video strengthened Torie's resolve even more. Just three days ago, the young woman had been alive and well. It wasn't fair.

She scrolled through the files on the computer and found the one of her hotel floor the night Bella died. It might show the killer entering Torie's room. She fast-forwarded it to eight o'clock and watched various couples walk the floors. At eight thirty, the picture went out. Just—nothing. She let it play, but the rest of the file was blank. Had someone done something to the camera or the file?

The door opened behind her, and she whirled toward the sound. Her stomach clenched when she recognized Kyle's hunched shoulders and wild red hair. What was he doing up so late?

He put his big hands in the pockets of his khaki shorts. "What are you doing here so late, Ms. *Bergstrom*?" His voice held a sneer. "And why are you even working? What are you doing in my department—trying to get me fired?"

So at least her aunt hadn't revealed the reason for the

deception. And what right did he have to be upset about it? His attitude could get him fired, and she'd be glad to do it. She'd never met a more distasteful person.

She fixed him with a stern stare in keeping with her true identity. "There have been some irregularities at the hotel, and I'm trying to track them down. Those things don't involve you."

His brown eyes lost a bit of their suspicion. "You don't say. What kind of irregularities? Maybe I can help you."

"They involve Lisbeth Nelson."

"You think she stole money or something?"

That reason could play as well as anything for making inquiries about Lisbeth. "We're not sure. Was she dating anyone?"

"Maybe. She didn't seem interested in seeing me, at least. I asked her out several times."

Her friend would never have been interested in Kyle in a million years. At least now that he knew who she was, he kept his gaze on her face and didn't let it roam any lower. But he was still going to have to face HR when she was done here.

"Did you ever see her with a man?"

"Not that I recall. She and Bella hung out a lot. Of course, they were roommates so that makes sense."

"Did you know Bella well?"

He shrugged. "We went out a couple of times. She wasn't my type though, even before she got engaged."

"Was she seeing anyone other than her fiancé? Someone who might have wanted to harm her? Was her fiancé the jealous type?"

"Bella ran through men like water through a hose.

I overheard her arguing with her fiancé several times. I expected her to take off that big rock on her hand any day."

"What about her female friends? Anyone besides Lisbeth?"

"Well, she and Felicia were tight. At least for a while. When Lisbeth moved in, they had some kind of tiff."

This Felicia was someone Torie needed to talk to. "Where can I find her?"

"She works as a hostess in the dining room."

Torie would have breakfast there tomorrow and see if the woman would talk.

==

Torie still hadn't heard from Joe even though she'd sent him a *good morning* message. But then, it was only six.

She stood at the entrance to the dining room and waited for the hostess. Now that everyone knew who she was, she'd donned her usual attire—linen slacks and a red silk blouse under a matching linen blazer. But somehow the elegant apparel felt wrong for the new Torie.

Habit was hard to break, and it would be even more difficult to throw off the shackles of expectation and privilege. It would take her constant focus to do it.

An attractive brunette of about thirty approached. "Good morning, Ms. Bergstrom. Table for one?"

It was early, and there were no other diners yet. "Actually make it a table for two and join me for a few minutes." She let an imperious tone creep into her words. "You're Felicia, right?"

The woman colored and ducked her head. "Yes."

"You're not in trouble. I just wanted to talk to you for a moment. Can you call someone else to take your place for fifteen minutes? I won't keep you long."

Felicia gave her a level look from her brown eyes and nodded. "Just a minute." She walked over to a server and spoke a few words, then rejoined Torie. "She can help out a few minutes. This way." She picked up a menu and led Torie to a table in a corner. "I told her to bring you coffee."

Torie smiled. "The word is out that I like my java."

"Yes, Ms. Bergstrom."

Torie debated on whether to tell her to call her by her first name, then decided against it. Maybe if she feared her a little, she'd be forthcoming.

Torie settled in a chair and pointed to the one across the table. "Have a seat. I hear you were good friends with Bella."

Felicia eased onto the chair and nodded. "I still can't believe someone would kill her." Her voice trembled, and she adjusted a wrinkle in the white tablecloth.

The server brought a steaming pot of coffee with a deliciously strong aroma and filled Torie's cup. Torie thanked her and added cream.

She took a sip. "Did she say anything to you about Lisbeth Nelson?"

Felicia's gaze shot to Torie, and her eyes widened. "You're here about Lisbeth?" She rose and turned.

"Wait! Sit down."

Felicia's mouth was tight as she turned and sank back into the chair. "This has nothing to do with my job. You have no right to fire me for refusing to discuss something personal."

"I'm not going to fire you. Lisbeth was my best friend. I believe she was murdered, and I think Bella knew something about it. Maybe the same person who killed Lisbeth killed Bella."

Felicia's gaze searched hers, and the anger in her eyes ebbed. "Bella never believed she killed herself, even though she said—" Her gaze fell away to the hands she'd clenched in her lap.

"Even though she lied about her being on antidepressants because she was depressed?"

Felicia bit her lip and cautiously raised her gaze again. "You know about that? Bella didn't want to put the pills in her things."

I was right. Torie tried to keep the elation from her voice. "Then why did she plant evidence? Why did she lie about the depression?"

"She was talked into it."

"By whom?"

Felicia hesitated. "I don't know for sure, but I thought it was Jason Graham, her fiancé, though she never admitted it. He held way too much influence over her. I never liked him. He's the controlling type, even though nearly everyone else thinks he's this great guy. She just said it was necessary for her to do it to stay out of trouble herself."

"Did someone blackmail her into planting the bottle of pills?"

"I never thought about blackmail. I thought she did it because she was talked into it."

"What exactly did she say?"

"She said something big depended on her. That if she

didn't do it, the plans would fail. She would never tell me what plans she was talking about."

It made no sense to Torie. Lisbeth was poking into her mom's death, but even if it hadn't been an accident, an eighteen-year-old murder couldn't upset any kind of current plans she could think of.

Had Lisbeth stumbled into something unrelated to Torie's mother's death?

"Her reference to plans seems odd."

"Especially here where nothing ever happens. But she wouldn't budge when I asked her."

"Did she ever mention a hiding place in the cottage where she lived with Lisbeth?"

Felicia glanced back at the hostess stand as a couple entered. "I'll have to go in a minute. Bella never mentioned a hiding place, but I've lived in some of the cottages. In most of them there is a hidden safe in the back of the closet in the spare room. You might check there."

"Thank you for your help, Felicia. I really appreciate it."

Felicia rose and hesitated. "I hope you find out what happened. Lisbeth was so sweet. Everyone who met her loved her. She asked some questions about your mom. Was that her real reason for coming here? She talked Bella into letting her look around the abandoned apartment."

Felicia hurried off with a pasted-on smile to greet the guests. Torie took another sip of coffee. What kind of plan could be happening here? A big drug run? It would be easy for boats to dock and transport them. Bella's fiancé could be into something illegal.

Torie ordered an omelet and pulled out her phone to

make notes of things to check. Talking to Jason Graham would be first on her list, and she wanted to check on the hidden safe. She'd either missed it or it hadn't been installed. She had only done a cursory check of the closets, looking for a shoebox or something.

A male voice jerked her out of her thoughts. "Hello, Torie."

She looked up and her heart dropped. "Matthew."

"I was hoping I'd run into you again by yourself. I never did apologize for treating you so badly."

"No, you didn't, and it's a little late now. I heard you married Mary."

He twisted his wedding ring on his finger. "I did, but it was a mistake. I should never have let you get away."

She shrugged. "Only because you think you'd be running Bergstrom Hospitality by now. You never loved me. And let's face it, I never loved you. I'm worth more than my money, Matthew. And I'm glad I didn't settle for something less."

Leaving her omelet, she rose and walked away. It felt good to tell him the truth. Glancing at her phone, she saw there was still no message from Joe. She could either let this awkwardness stand or she could march over there after breakfast and demand he deal with the situation.

Empowered by telling Matthew the truth, she decided this was a good time to do it.

CHAPTER 25

HOLDING A GRUDGE WOULD GET HIM NOWHERE.

Joe downed coffee and looked at the clock. Seven in the morning. Torie would still be in her room, but he didn't know what to do with Hailey while he went over there and cleared the air with Torie.

Her lie had shaken his belief in her. If she'd hidden who she was from him, what else hadn't she told him? He'd always prided himself on being a good judge of character, but this had blindsided him.

And where did that leave those deeper feelings he had swirling in his gut?

And she was a *Bergstrom*. A future with her seemed a ridiculous notion now. He'd worked his way through college. He and Julie had lived on a shoestring in the early days. Most of the baby things they had for Hailey had been secondhand. The idea of a romance between him and Torie washed away like seaweed on the tide.

The doorbell rang, and he checked his watch again to make sure he hadn't looked at it wrong. Nope. Five minutes past seven. Who would be here this early? Maybe the police had caught the guy who took Hailey.

But as he neared the window, he recognized Torie's elegant updo and the proud way she carried herself. Her manner and bearing all made way too much sense now.

He unlocked the door and opened it. "You're out early."

"I didn't get much sleep."

And the dark circles under her eyes spoke to the truth of her statement. Her braid looked a little messy, but she wore a power suit that proclaimed her true identity.

He stepped out of the way for her to enter, then shut the door behind her. "Coffee?"

"I'd like a whole pot."

Her wan smile stopped the recriminations on his tongue. There would be time to talk about it after they'd both had some coffee and breakfast.

She followed him to the kitchen, and he poured her a large mug of java. She wrapped her fingers around it and took a sip. "Heavenly. Just what I needed. How's Hailey?"

"Still sleeping, thank goodness. I took the day off. My boss wasn't happy, but he understood after I explained what had happened on Saturday."

"Was she upset last night? We didn't really talk after Lisbeth's service."

"She prattled nonstop about the twins after she got home from Danielle's, which was good. I don't want her to be afraid and develop some kind of problem because of it."

"Maybe she should talk to a counselor, just to be sure she's okay after all this."

"I'll make an appointment with hers today. She hasn't seen her in a while, not once she accepted what had happened to her mother, but she's got a good one."

Torie took another sip of her coffee. "That's good." She set her mug on the counter. "I wanted a chance to clear the air between us. We didn't have time to talk about who I am. What are you thinking?"

"You should have told me the truth, Torie, right from the start."

She gave an exasperated huff. "Listen to yourself, Joe. Would you have gone into an investigation not knowing if the person you were talking to was involved? You *found* Lisbeth! Of course I suspected you. I didn't know you at all. Even criminals have cute kids, so Hailey's presence didn't clear you."

Her eyes were as stormy as the Intracoastal Waterway in a hurricane, and he bristled. "One thing you should know about me is that I detest liars. Fabrication and evasion of truth have caused more heartache than just about anything in our world. I try to make sure I speak truth to the people I care about, and to find out everyone else on the island knew who you were before I did stings. More than stings. It is downright painful."

Her eyes filled with tears and she stared down at her feet. "I'm sorry for that. It all spiraled down so fast. It was late when my aunt found out, and there was no time to talk to you. I meant to do it Saturday, but we nearly died and I was dealing with all of that. I couldn't face one more traumatic event. I hope you can forgive me. I was wrong."

Her humble apology extinguished the heat of his anger. And he was a sucker for tears. Julie hadn't cried often, but when she did, it was buckshot to his gut. Torie didn't seem the type to resort to tears to get out of trouble either.

Right after that kiss on the boat would have been the perfect time to tell him the truth. If she trusted him enough to kiss him, she should have been able to tell him the truth.

Sometimes he thought he'd never understand women—and he had a small one to raise, so it was going to be a tough road ahead.

He sighed. "I forgive you."

She swiped at her tears. "Thank you. I hate tears. Too many women use them to manipulate the men they care about. I'm not like that, and I'm sorry I couldn't control myself. I care about you and Hailey. To know I hurt you tears me up inside. I didn't mean to. I'm doing the best I can in a situation that's spinning in crazy ways that make me feel out of control. In case you haven't figured it out yet, I like things to be neat and tidy in life. And this situation is anything but."

"No, it's not."

She stared across the breakfast bar at him. "Can we put this behind us? Or have I ruined everything?"

The tremulous smile she lifted his way tore at his heart. "Even though I forgive you, it's hard to get past the differences in our social status, Torie. You're a *Bergstrom*, and I'm just a marine researcher. I probably couldn't afford your shoes."

"I can buy my own shoes. A relationship is a partnership, isn't it?"

"Well, yes. But a man likes to feel he's needed."

"You have something way more important than money that I need."

His pulse jumped at the tenderness in her eyes. "And what's that?"

"Courage. Stability. Honor. Steadfast support. You're a lot of things, Joe, but the bedrock in your character holds me up."

He swallowed hard. "I'm not sure I can live up to that pedestal you have me on."

"You climbed there all by yourself."

She took a step closer, and he opened his arms. Her cheek nestled on his chest, and she fit as if she'd been made for him. Maybe she had.

==

Joe seemed to have put her duplicity behind him and had pulled out a skillet to fix breakfast. She wanted him to know the real her. The Torie few people saw.

She took another sip of coffee. "People have always wanted something from me because I'm a Bergstrom. Very few people have gotten past the walls I've had to erect. Lisbeth was one of those. But since meeting you and Hailey, I have realized it's really lonely inside this thorny prison."

He stopped stirring the eggs for a moment, and their gazes met. He looked good this morning with his brown hair still wet from his shower. His broad chest and arms strained his T-shirt, and his tan made his eyes look all the greener.

He gave another brisk stir with the spatula. "Not everyone wants something from other people."

"They seem to when you have more money than Midas. When you have the power to offer jobs and influence. Until someone has walked in my shoes, they don't understand what that's like. Some people take to using that power without a thought. I never did. I don't want power over people. I thought if people didn't see the real me, they couldn't hurt me."

She fell silent, not sure how to make him understand when it was something as natural to her as breathing. That second skin she wore to present to the world was a shell that shielded her.

He piled her plate with eggs, bacon, and toast, then slid it over to her. "Eat up."

She'd ordered an omelet from the restaurant this morning, but didn't take one bite and she was suddenly ravenous. She forked some eggs and deposited them onto her tongue. "Delicious."

Could she change for Joe and Hailey? The reserve she'd donned all her life had made ruts through her soul, tracks she followed like a mule plodding a well-worn trail. It wasn't a pretty thought to realize those patterns she'd allowed had shaped her when she should have been brave. She should have been forging her own path. Nothing said she had to be a traditional Bergstrom.

What did a nontraditional Bergstrom look like?

He refilled her coffee. "I think I kind of get it. Probably no one really can, but as a parent, I have certain expectations of Hailey's behavior. Lately I've noticed she wants to go her own way. If I say I like red, she likes blue. If I want chocolate ice cream, she wants strawberry. I would never want her to become a carbon copy of me. She has to make her own way. And there's a girl at school who picks on her, and it's made her self-conscious about what clothes she wears. Trying to fit into a mold isn't what God wants for her either. She's unique."

His gaze held her in place, probing places inside her heart. She swallowed the suddenly tasteless bite of egg.

"And you're unique, Torie. I understand why you would feel the need to fight hard against being used for your name when someone doesn't even get to know you. That would be a painful thing. It would make anyone wary."

At his affirming words, moisture burned her eyes and she sniffled, then took a sip of coffee to hide her emotion. Maybe she could be herself with him. She prayed so. It helped that he'd liked her before he knew her identity.

She pulled out her red plastic file and withdrew the two pictures of the vehicle Bella had gotten into. "What kind of car is this, and do you recognize the driver?"

Joe took the pictures and studied them one at a time. "Looks to be a Chevy Impala, maybe a 2018. I can't tell the color, but it's a common vehicle. The outline of the driver's head seems vaguely familiar, but I can't place who it reminds me of. Honestly, I can't tell if it's a man or a woman." He handed them back to her.

She put them back in her folder. "I couldn't tell either. I was in my office at midnight, and Kyle came in. He'd heard who I was and was a little aggrieved. He told me he went out with Bella a few times, but she wasn't his type. I'd guess she ditched him though. He made it sound like she dated one guy after another, even though she was engaged. I'd love to be able to talk to someone she went out with a few times. Her fiancé too. And I talked to another of Bella's friends this morning. She claims Bella planted the bottle of pills because she was pressured to in order to save some kind of plan." She told him everything Felicia had said.

He frowned. "A plan. That sounds ominous. No idea what it could be?"

She shook her head. "I need to talk to more of Bella's friends."

"Talk to Amelia Rogers. She and Bella were friends. Bella worked for her part-time during busy times. She was learning all about glassblowing. I saw her there a few times. The two were working together on plans for the banking summit."

She glanced at the clock above the sink. "It's seven thirty, and I have to be at work at eight. Do you know what time she opens?"

"I think she's there early working on her glass, but the shop doesn't open until ten. But why would you continue to go to work in the IT department now that your cover is blown? You can look at the files all you want while you pursue any leads."

She nodded. "Good point. I hadn't thought it through. Lack of sleep does a number on the brain synapses. I could run over there right now and knock on the back door where she has her furnace."

"That area is called a hot shop," Joe said. "It's an interesting process to watch. She might let you hang around if you don't get in her way. Go on ahead, and once Hailey gets up, we'll join you. We have an open invitation to watch her work anytime. The kid should be up any minute."

"Sounds good." She rose and picked up her file. "I'm praying I find some kind of lead. I feel like I'm shooting at the moon and not hitting anything. This guy is so slick."

"But you're smart. You'll nail him."

A warmth radiated through her at the confidence in his words. Maybe she would.

CHAPTER 26

TORIE SLAMMED ON HER BIKE'S BRAKES, AND
the vehicle behind her blared the horn. The car in her
pictures was there—right there.

She sent an apologetic wave in the direction of the
black SUV that zoomed around her, then stopped her bike
and rolled it into a rack behind the hot shop next to the
Chevy. The car had to belong to Amelia. So that meant
the glass artisan had been with Bella just hours before her
death. She might know something she didn't realize was
pertinent.

Torie went to the back door. It stood ajar a couple of
inches, and she saw a red glow from inside. She rapped her
knuckles against the door and pushed it open a few more
inches. Something inside smelled hot and dusty.

Amelia was manipulating a long metal stick of some
kind that had a glob of glowing glass on the end, which
extended into the glory hole. It looked terrifying to Torie.
One little fling of melted glass off the end could do serious
damage to skin.

She stood by the door and waited for the woman to notice her. It didn't take long until Amelia saw her from the corner of her eye and turned with an irritated expression that vanished when recognition lit her eyes.

She held up a finger to indicate Torie should wait a minute, then moved to the bigger furnace to knock the glass off the end of the stick and set down the tool.

She wiped her hands on her jeans, peppered with burn holes. "Torie, isn't it? How nice to see you again."

Had she heard talk of Torie's true identity? Torie didn't see any evidence of irritation in her face, other than that first glance before Amelia had recognized her. She might as well be honest now. It might get her further if she used her name and position.

"Yes, it's Torie, um, Torie Bergstrom."

"Bergstrom?"

"Yes, Anton's daughter. I'm sorry I wasn't more upfront when we first met. I didn't want people to treat me differently like they always do when they hear I'm a Bergstrom."

Amelia blinked, then gave a slow nod. "I'm honored you're taking such an interest in the glass globes yourself."

"They're beautiful, but I'm here for another reason. It's about Bella Hansen."

Amelia winced. "I still can't believe someone killed her."

"When did you see her last?"

"The night she died. I picked her up, and we went to dinner together. She had just been promoted to events coordinator at the hotel, and we discussed the upcoming bank summit."

"What time did you take her back to the hotel?"

"About eight, I think. We ate dinner, then came back here to take a look at the globes I had done."

"Did she seem on edge at all? Upset about anything?"

Amelia pursed her lips. "She got a call from a guy. He was yelling at her, and I could hear how mad he was, though I couldn't make out what he said. She cried and told him she was sorry, but when she hung up, she didn't want to talk about it."

"Any idea who it was?"

"Not really. It sounded like a love affair gone wrong because she said something to him about being sorry and that he was overreacting."

"Did you ever see her with a man?"

Amelia went to the fridge in a back corner and pulled out two cans of iced tea. She handed one to Torie and popped the top of the one she kept. "Sure, she was engaged. Jason Graham. He runs a nonprofit."

"Maybe her fiancé was the man who called and argued with her."

"I don't think so. Jason hasn't been around for about a month. He's been in Washington, DC."

"So you suspect she was cheating on him?"

"It would be my guess, though I'm making no assumptions or judgments. She was a bit of a flirt and even went out with Noah a few times. She hated being alone, and she liked male attention."

"You're sure Jason hasn't been around?"

"Positive. He's been on TV a few times as part of an investigation where he had to testify."

That seemed definitive. Maybe this mysterious man

wanted Bella to break her engagement. Or maybe she was seeing more than one. Surface impressions could be misleading, but Torie hadn't taken Bella for that kind of person.

"I wish we could find out who called her that night."

"I told the police about it. I'm sure they checked her phone to see who it was. A victim usually knows their killer." Amelia smiled. "At least that's what all the TV shows say."

"That's what I hear."

A knock came at the back door, and Torie turned to see Joe and Hailey standing there.

Joe pushed the door all the way open. "We hoped you were blowing today, Amelia. We wanted to watch if we won't annoy you."

Hailey gave an excited wave in Torie's direction, and the little girl's obvious joy at seeing her gave Torie a boost.

"I'd love to see it too," Torie said. "I know nothing about it, but it looks so interesting."

"Sure." Amelia gestured with her hand toward the exterior wall to her left. "Pull up a chair and stay back. I'll explain what I'm doing as I do it."

Joe grabbed three chairs, and Hailey sat between Torie and him.

Amelia took up that strange stick thing again. "This is my blowpipe. Inside the furnace is a crucible, which is another name for a pot that holds the batch, which is what the melted glass ingredient is called. I get a glob of batch on my blowpipe and bring it to this table, which is known as the marvel. It's thick metal so I can roll and shape the hot glass."

Torie watched as Amelia rolled the blob on the table, then grabbed what looked like newspaper out of a bowl of water. She rotated the hot glass against the wet newspaper. The next tool was a metal set of something similar to tongs that the artisan called jacks.

Torie was struck by how hot glass could be formed and molded by so many outside forces.

Joe leaned over to Hailey. "Look at how beautiful that glass is in spite of being manipulated and worked on by so many outside forces. God uses all the bad things in our lives to make us more beautiful too. Nothing is wasted—it all serves a purpose."

"Even Mommy dying?" Hailey asked.

"Even losing Mommy can make you a better person."

Torie saw the parallel to her own losses and heartaches. Maybe God was working her character in the same way with the stressors he'd brought her way. Would she be as beautiful inside someday because of it?

==

The globe Amelia had finished glowed with vibrant color on its metal stand, and Joe touched it with a finger. It was still warm from the fire.

He turned back to where Amelia stood putting away her tools. Torie rose and joined them while Hailey played a game on his phone.

"You have time to answer a few questions?" he asked Amelia.

It wasn't ideal to have Hailey here, but he wasn't about to let her out of his sight. He still felt traumatized by nearly losing her Saturday. Julie's death had nearly destroyed him, and his daughter was everything to him.

"If you make it fast. I have to open the shop in fifteen minutes." She glanced at Torie. "Ms. Bergstrom already asked me questions about when I last saw Bella, and I told her we had a business dinner a few hours before she died."

Her stiff "Ms. Bergstrom" told him she hadn't taken kindly to Torie's deception, and he suspected Torie hadn't told Amelia why she was really here. They would have to start asking pointed questions if they hoped to get to the bottom of Lisbeth's death.

"How about we go into the shop? We can ask our questions there while you open things up," Torie suggested.

Amelia nodded and opened the middle door that led into her shop. Sunlight poured into the space and revealed the glorious colors of the various glass pieces. She lit the candle on the counter, and the scent of vanilla grew stronger.

Still looking at the game playing on Joe's phone, Hailey followed them into the shop and settled on a chair in the corner where Joe could keep an eye on her.

"Did Bella ever talk about Lisbeth?" Joe asked.

Amelia wrinkled her nose and opened the register to load the trays with change and one-dollar bills. "I'd rather not talk about Lisbeth."

"You didn't like her?" Torie asked.

Torie's tone was prickly, and Joe put a calming hand on her forearm. "It's important. She was Torie's best friend, and we believe she didn't kill herself." Torie shot him a glance with a question in her eyes, and he gave her a quick nod.

"She was a troublemaker, always questioning how things were done at the resort and trying to get Bella to break up with Jason. She had Bella buy her antidepressants on the street. I was with Bella when she bought them. I didn't like her influence. Bella and I were the best of friends until Lisbeth came along."

Amelia glared at Torie. "You should evaluate your choice of friends. It didn't surprise me to learn she'd killed herself. She was always threatening to do it, and it kept Bella on edge every minute. She'd cancel out on dinners we'd planned because she was afraid of what she'd find when she got back to the cottage."

Torie raised her chin and stared Amelia down. "I think Bella was lying to you. Lisbeth and I were friends for twenty years. I would have known if she was suicidal. She was the most cheerful, optimistic person I have ever known. And I heard from another source just this morning that Bella planted those pills. Lisbeth had never used them."

Amelia blinked and braced her hands on her hips. "So Bella lied to me? That's hard to hear. I will say that Lisbeth seemed to want Bella all to herself. At least according to Bella."

"Then you're making statements based on hearsay," Joe said.

Amelia put an order pad on the counter with more force than necessary. "I'll admit that much, but I knew Bella very well."

"Did she ever talk to you about helping with some kind of plan?" Joe asked.

"What kind of plan?"

"We don't know. According to the other source, Bella admitted she planted the pills to save some kind of plan. We have no other information."

"Sketchy. I have no idea."

Torie touched a suncatcher with one finger. "Did Bella tell you I wanted to talk to her about her claim Lisbeth was suicidal? She seemed very upset, almost scared, when I first asked to talk to her."

"No, she didn't. When was this?"

"The morning of the day she died. Right after I heard about her claims of Lisbeth's mental state. I didn't believe it then, and I don't believe it now. There had to be some reason she would lie about it. Maybe it had something to do with the argument with the guy on the phone." Torie glanced at Joe and told him about the phone call.

"What exactly did you hear Bella say?" he asked.

"Just that she was sorry, and he was overreacting," Amelia said.

"The state police probably know who she was talking to. I'm sure they took her phone," he said.

"I told them about the argument as soon as I heard she'd been murdered. I knew they'd want to talk to me anyway since I saw her just before her death."

Torie turned from her perusal of a row of glass paperweights. "Any idea why she would have been in my hotel room? I thought maybe she wanted to talk to me in private about Lisbeth."

"She didn't mention you at all so I don't know." Amelia went to the door and threw the dead bolt, then turned on the glass *Open* sign in the window. "I see some customers coming this way, so that's all the time I can spare. And I don't know anything more anyway."

At her terse voice, Joe took Torie's elbow and moved toward the door into the workroom. "We'll get out of your hair. Thanks for your time, Amelia. Appreciate it."

Bella's death was seeming even more strange. And who was right about Lisbeth—Bella or Torie?

CHAPTER 27

"IT'S CRAIG." HAILEY HANDED JOE'S PHONE back when it rang as they left the glass shop.

Torie waited with Hailey and shamelessly listened in while Joe talked to the state trooper.

Joe ended the call and handed the phone back to Hailey. "Craig wants to meet up at the marina."

Torie nodded and reversed direction. The marina was in the other direction, and she could already smell the water and hear the gulls.

It was going to be a beautiful day with lower than usual humidity. Puffy white clouds drifted across the blue sky, and the scent of flowers drifted their way along the walk to the wharf. She spotted the state trooper seated on a bench outside the boat excursions office.

Craig waved when he saw them and rose. "So you're a Bergstrom."

She bit her lip. "So you heard. I'm sorry, but I wanted to investigate without anyone knowing who I was."

Hailey moved to the side of the wharf to dangle her

feet over with her dad's phone in her hand, and the adults moved away to talk.

"I'm the police, Torie. It was safe to tell me."

"I thought about it, but once one person knows, it gets around. An innocent remark here or there, and the whole island knows."

"I'm not a squealer."

"I didn't think you were. Look, I said I'm sorry."

He gave an exasperated sigh. "Just don't lie to me again. I won't let it go so easily next time."

She nodded and studied the trooper's face. Why had he wanted to see them?

He answered the question without being asked. "So, you wondered about the bottle of antidepressants. The fingerprinting came back, and there are unknown fingerprints on the bottle. None of them are Lisbeth's."

"Bella?" Torie asked.

He lifted a brow. "Why would you think it was Bella?"

"Amelia claims Bella got the drugs for her on the street. And I have another source who claims Bella planted them." She told him about her conversation with Felicia.

"But the prints don't belong to Bella. We don't know whose they are."

"Maybe Bella picked up the bag with the bottle in it and never handled it," Joe put in.

"How will you find out whose prints those are?" Torie asked.

"We're running them through a database, but if the person has never committed a crime, we might not discover anything."

"Could you talk to known drug dealers and see if

anyone sold the drugs to Bella?" Joe asked. "I'm sure you've got some informants out on the street. And what about checking her phone? We heard she was arguing with someone too."

"We have some informants, and we're looking, but it's a long shot," Craig said. "I'll request a list of her calls too."

"Any surprises on Lisbeth's autopsy?" Joe asked. "I know the preliminary seemed to indicate drowning, but is there anything new?"

"Actually, yes," Craig said. "There was both seawater and fresh water in her lungs. We're not sure what to make of that, but it does look like she might have been drowned in fresh water and put in the ocean."

Torie frowned. "So she could have been partially drowned, then thrown in the ocean?"

"It's possible she was assumed dead before she was put into the ocean."

"So the state police is leaning toward possible murder?" Joe asked.

Craig shrugged. "It's raised the likelihood."

A figure came their way, and Torie recognized Amelia's son, Noah, dressed in shorts and a tee. She sent an automatic smile his way, and he stopped beside them.

He nodded at the state trooper. "Hey, Craig. If I'd thought I'd run into you today, I would have brought the cap you left at my place last night."

"I'll get it one of these days." Craig gestured toward Torie and Joe. "You guys know Noah? He's Amelia's son and is here for a month or so."

"We met him at Amelia's," Torie said. "Good to see you again, Noah."

Noah glanced toward The Wharf restaurant. "Mom will have my hide if I keep her waiting to eat. Nice running into you."

Once Noah was out of earshot, Craig turned back to Torie. "I do have something else to talk about. Lisbeth had no family, and after consulting her will, I've been authorized to turn over her personal effects to you."

Torie straightened and inhaled. "Personal effects? What do you have that belonged to her?"

She longed to touch anything that belonged to Lisbeth, to remember her friend and all the time they'd shared.

"It's everything the hotel turned over that was in her cottage as well as her car. If you want to follow me to the impound lot, you can take possession of all of it. We've loaded her vehicle with her belongings."

Could there be a lead in the car or in the boxes of her things? Maybe the missing journal pages would turn up. Torie had begun to lose hope of finding Lisbeth's murderer, but the prospect of some new directions invigorated her determination.

Joe took out his truck keys. "We'll follow you there right now."

She saw the light in his eyes. This new information was as exciting to him as it was to her.

==

The red Camaro sat in a forlorn lot beside a patch of weeds poking through the broken concrete. Scraggly pines lined the property and lofted their refreshing scent into the air.

Torie remembered the day her friend had driven the car over to show her. She'd washed it twice a week and kept the interior spotless. If Lisbeth could see the dust on it now, she'd be rushing to get a bucket and rag.

Joe touched her shoulder. "You okay?"

He must have seen her struggling to hold back the tears. "That car was the first new vehicle she'd ever owned. She worked hard for it, and it was her pride and joy. I've seen her so often sitting there behind the wheel, beaming. She didn't have much growing up, and being able to afford something so nice was a sign to herself that her past couldn't keep her down."

"I wish I could have known her better. I only met her a few times." He glanced back to check on Hailey, who was sitting in his truck with his phone with the door locked. The little girl had her head down as she stared at her dad's phone. She'd be oblivious to anything said between the two of them.

Craig exited the building with a set of keys dangling from one hand and a clipboard in the other. "I need you to sign that you've taken possession of all this."

She took the clipboard and signed without reading the paper. "Do I need to go through all the boxes?"

"There's nothing of real value there, so it's up to you if you want to tick everything off the list. It's things like jeans, shirts, personal belongings. I double-checked everything of value like her laptop, iPad, watch, phone, those kinds of things."

She took the duplicate copy he handed her and scanned through the list. The clothing was packed into two suitcases, and the electronics were in a plastic tub. It was a scant list to sum up the total of Lisbeth's life.

She looked at Joe through tears. "Nothing here tells the story of her care for other people. Someone going through these things wouldn't know she loved black-and-white movies or that she was learning to crochet."

He squeezed her shoulder. "But as long as you remember all those things, she'll always be with you. Nothing can take those memories from you and how much you treasured her friendship."

Craig shifted from one foot to the other. "Well, if you don't have any questions or want to go through things with me, I'll leave you to it."

She nodded. "Thanks for your help, Craig. If you get a match for those fingerprints, let me know."

"I'll do that." He walked away at a fast pace as if to outrun the uncomfortable aura of grief around her.

"You want to drive her car or my truck?" Joe asked.

"Her car. Definitely. I'm going to move back into my cottage tonight. I want the time and space to go through her things and see if I can discover what happened to her." She told him about the possible safe in the spare room.

He grimaced. "It's a terrible idea to move back in, Torie. I get it—really. But this guy isn't giving up just so you can take the time to grieve."

"I sent my dad a text and asked him to move in with me for now. Everyone knows our relationship now so it doesn't matter if he stays with me."

"Does he have a gun? Know martial arts?"

"Well, no."

"How do you expect him to protect you both?"

"I think his presence will scare our guy off. He's not going to want to run the risk of being seen."

Joe let loose a sharp bark of laughter. "Torie, this guy took my daughter in a throng of people. He's probably killed two women. I don't think anything but an AK-47 is going to deter him. Do you know how to shoot a gun?"

She wanted to tell him she was a crack shot, but she couldn't lie. "I've shot a pistol a couple of times, but I didn't hit anything with it."

He sighed. "Is there anything I can say to talk you out of this idea?"

"Not really, Joe. I'm sorry. I know you're worried about me, and your concern is touching, but I'm not getting anywhere by hiding away. I'd rather face this guy head on than huddle in my hotel room and be just as clueless about what happened to Lisbeth as I am right now."

"You want company tonight in case the guy skulks around the house?"

Her pulse blipped. "Dad has a meeting and can't come over until nine. We could order pizza for lunch and go through Lisbeth's things. I-I don't really want to do this alone."

"Sounds like a plan. We can walk off the pizza with a stroll to the ice cream shop for dessert after we eat."

She jangled the keys in her hand. "I'll meet you at the cottage, and we can unload Lisbeth's things."

"I want to sweep the car too."

"Sweep? The interior looks spotless."

"I want to check for any bugs. The police would have gone over the interior well, but they weren't looking for murder clues. They still think Lisbeth committed suicide. I want to make sure the guy wasn't tracking her every move."

"I should check her phone too. There are so many electronic ways he might have kept up on what she was doing and where she was going."

Having a goal was a shot in the arm for her. The hours together through the afternoon and early evening might help keep her from dwelling on how she'd been failing in her goal. And this was one job she had to finish.

CHAPTER 28

JOE STARED AT THE BUG HE'D FOUND IN Lisbeth's car. It was more confirmation that she'd been killed. But why?

He put his phone away. "Craig will send someone by to get the bug."

Torie nodded and bit her lip when the last piece of clothing was removed, leaving an empty suitcase. "No clues. I connected her phone to some software, and someone was tracking her through it, too, but they're good, whoever they are. I couldn't trace it. Maybe the police can though."

The living room still held the faint scent of a sweet perfume from Lisbeth's clothing. They'd both had so much hope when they carried the boxes and suitcases into the cottage. Now Torie's dreams were in ruins along with the discarded remains of the pizza they had for lunch, and there wasn't anything he could do about it.

Hailey was watching TV in the spare room, and the faint sound of *Little House on the Prairie* echoed down the hallway.

236

Torie dropped onto the sofa and stared down at her hands. "Nothing. We've spent two hours going through every pocket and poking into every crevice in the suitcases. We're no closer to an answer than we were when I arrived on Jekyll Island. I don't know where to look next."

The quaver in her voice tugged at his heart, and he sat beside her. He moved to put his arm around her before reconsidering the idea. Things were still a little strained between them since he'd learned who she was. Maybe it was him or maybe it was her, but he couldn't deny he felt constrained around her now that he knew she was the heir to a massive hospitality empire.

"We could search for that hidden safe."

She got up, and he followed her to the spare room. The TV was too loud, and Joe told Hailey to lower the volume. At least she wasn't paying any attention to them going to the closet.

He flipped on the closet light, and it shone into the dark crevices. On the back-left wall, he spied the safe. "There it is." He knelt and tried to open it. "It's locked. You find any strange keys around?"

Torie knelt beside him and yanked on the lever that didn't budge. "Just the house key. I'll ask at the hotel if there's a key to this."

They both rose and he trailed her back to the living room. "What was she working on when she was here? Any pet projects she took over at the resort?"

"I asked my aunt for a list of everything Lisbeth had been doing, but she never sent it over."

"Maybe check with HR." He glanced at his phone. "It's only three. You should be able to get someone."

"Good idea." She reached for her laptop and typed up an email. "It's done. I told HR I wanted it within the next fifteen minutes. Sometimes it pays to throw around the Bergstrom name."

He wasn't sure he'd ever get used to the kind of power she was used to wielding. Maybe her best bet of a lasting relationship would be with someone who had the same kind of power and money. He'd always taken pride in taking care of his wife and daughter, of providing for them, even if sometimes that provision wasn't steak and caviar.

He wished he could believe he was reading too much into the inequality of their statuses, but it felt overwhelming right now.

"Tea or coffee?" she asked.

"Coffee sounds good, but I'll make it."

"So you can have it strong enough to dissolve the spoon?" she teased. "I can live with it. I'll have you know I've started adding two more scoops of coffee to the pot every morning. You're corrupting me."

"That's a good thing. There's nothing worse than weak-as-dishwater coffee."

He squeezed her hand, then rose and went to the kitchen where he ground coffee and filled the pot. The aroma of strong coffee began to percolate through the house as he got down mugs and pulled out cream for her.

He smelled the scent of her shampoo before he realized she'd joined him. How odd it was that she didn't wear an expensive perfume like her aunt. She always smelled like soap and fresh air, and he liked it.

She stopped a few feet away. "Are you ever going to

forget I'm a Bergstrom? You haven't been the same with me since."

Maybe she'd been reading his mind. "It takes some getting used to. You know, the fact that you could buy and sell an entire island without a blink of an eye. That kind of money and power is a little off-putting."

"Off-putting? Most men I've met are only too happy to think about spending it for me."

He held her gaze for a long minute and his heart squeezed at the vulnerability in her brown eyes. Being judged by her name and wealth couldn't be easy. And he was just as guilty as the rest of them, only he was assuming she wanted to control him with it all. And maybe she didn't.

"I like to make my own way. Stand on my own two feet and provide for my family."

The shadow in her eyes darkened. "Julie didn't work?"

"Well, yes, she did. She was a paralegal. After Hailey was born, she went to part-time, but she planned to go back to full-time once Hailey was in school." He smiled. "I see where you're going with this. I'm being a little hypocritical, aren't I?"

"Not a little. A lot. In any relationship, there's give and take. It's not all give and not all take. It's not right for you to hold my family name against me. I had no control over which family I came from. It's much better to judge me based on my character and what I do with what I've been given. Do you see me driving a Ferrari or living in a mansion? I'm hardly blowing through money in a reckless way."

He held up his hands in a gesture of surrender. "I

give! You're right, and I'm wrong. I'll try to do better. I liked your take-charge attitude and the way you cared about other people from the beginning. I need to remember you're the same person you were last week before I knew who you were."

The tense line of her shoulders softened, and she smiled. "Think you can do it?"

"I'll try. Just don't show up in a Ferrari, and I think I can manage. A Range Rover might be okay though."

"Picky, are we?"

"Well, I've always wanted a Range Rover. If you let me drive it, I might forget you bought it."

He pulled her closer, and she leaned against his chest. She'd be able to hear how his heart sped up at her closeness, but there wasn't any way he could hide how much she drew him in.

＝＝

There was nothing in Torie's in-box from the HR director, and the lack of response made her want to march to the hotel and demand to see her.

Joe stopped tapping on the wall in the living room and glanced at her. "Still nothing?"

"No. I'll give her half an hour, and if she still hasn't answered, I'll go to the hotel."

"Maybe she's in a meeting."

While Torie knew he was right—meetings were a fact of life for most HR directors—the waiting made her heart race and her palms sweat. Which was silly because there was no guarantee they'd find a clue in what Lisbeth was doing during her final weeks.

Her computer dinged, and she scanned the three new emails. "Finally!" She opened the first email and frowned. "It looks like the main order of business for her for the past month was working on getting ready for the banking convention. She was working on games for it and had a big scavenger hunt planned. She'd been visiting various businesses to see about prizes and clues. It was going to serve as a way to highlight the various businesses as the members stopped by to search for the clues."

"Clever," he said. "But I can't see why anyone would kill her over that."

She sank into the sofa and exhaled. "Maybe I need to retrace her steps, see what she saw and learn what she learned. I know it's a long shot, but I don't have anything better to do."

Doubt lingered in his eyes, but bless him, he only said, "We know it's likely she stumbled on some nefarious plot and had to be silenced."

"Even if that's true, the chances of me discovering what that was are unlikely."

"But not impossible."

It felt impossible, but she had to keep going. Staring out the window at the late-afternoon light, she shivered. Was the killer out there watching her? He'd probably noticed she was back in the cottage, and she was prepared for a new attack tonight. She'd almost welcome it since it would be proof the guy considered her investigation a threat. That had to mean the evidence she needed was out there somewhere. If he felt safe, he wouldn't be trying to scare her away.

"It's nearly dinnertime," Joe said. "Anything special sound good?"

"I'm still full from the pizza, so check with Hailey and see what she wants."

"Fish tacos," they said in unison before breaking into a chorus of laughter.

The laughter dispelled her frustration. "I wouldn't say no to some salsa if you're calling Tortuga Jack's anyway."

"You got it." He pulled out his phone and placed an order. "How about we all ride together to pick it up?"

"I'll be fine for the ten minutes you'll be gone. You can take Hailey with you to ease your worries, but I'll lock up and pay attention to any noises." She swept her hand toward the window. "And it's still light outside. I don't think he'll bother me this afternoon."

Tonight might be a different story, but she wasn't going to bring that up.

"Okay, I'll roust the girl from her *Little House on the Prairie* marathon."

"I think she's up to season three. She's mesmerized. I can't believe I've never watched it before."

He yawned and raked his hand through his thick thatch of brown hair. "We'll remedy that over dinner."

She watched him go down the hall and she smiled at his banter with his daughter. He was a really good dad. She'd always loved and respected her father, but watching the two of them, she realized she'd missed out on a lot. Her dad's constant travel and preoccupation with his work had taken a toll on her childhood. She couldn't recall a day when they'd hung out on the sofa and watched a family show together. He would politely ask about her schoolwork, but she doubted he knew she loved Latin quotes. Did he even know she had a terrible sense of direction or that she loved the Twilight series when she was a teenager?

Not a chance.

She locked the door behind Joe and Hailey as they good-naturedly squabbled about whether she could eat her tacos in the truck on the way back. There was no doubt who would win that battle. Joe would let her eat the whole bag of food if she asked. And so would Torie.

She looked at the stack of Lisbeth's belongings. It had all come down to clothing and books. She picked up the thick book she'd started reading a few days ago. *The Creature from Jekyll Island* sounded like one of Lisbeth's favorite horror novels, but it was about the creation of the Federal Reserve. She rubbed her head. She needed some sleep, but she couldn't stop reading.

The book was eye-opening about how the Federal Reserve was a banking cartel. It should have been illegal, and yet it had steered the money industry for over a hundred years.

She looked up when the doorknob rattled. "What did you forget?" She laughed and rose to let them in.

But no one answered her. With her hand on the door, she paused. "Joe? Hailey? Who's there?"

Still no answer. She backed away toward the kitchen. There were no panes or skylights at the door to see through, but she had a sinking sensation that someone else stood on the other side of the wood. If it was an acquaintance, why didn't he or she answer when she called out?

The danger felt so thick she struggled to breathe. Why hadn't she gone with Joe? Experience had already shown this guy was the boldest person she'd ever encountered. He seemed to walk past cameras and people like a mist that no one noticed.

She stared at the door, and her lips parted but her tongue felt too parched to call out. Her gaze found her phone lying on the sofa, and she moved toward it. Her finger felt numb as she punched out 911 and waited for the dispatcher to answer.

The male disembodied voice spoke in her ear. "911, what is your emergency?"

"There's someone outside my door, and I think it's an intruder who's broken in before." She raised her voice. "I'm calling 911!" She gave the dispatcher the address.

A sudden flurry of noise at the door came, and she grabbed the lamp to use the base as a weapon if he came inside.

"A patrol car is on the way, but it will be a while. Can you get to safety or call a friend?"

"I'll call a friend." Torie couldn't cower in the living room when she should be trying to identify the intruder. Her pulse pounded in her ears as she ended the call and advanced to the door. Holding the lamp high overhead, she unlocked the door and jerked it open.

No one was there. She looked up and down the street again but saw no one. A flash of color at her feet caught her eye, and she saw a board game laid out.

Monopoly.

What on earth did that mean?

CHAPTER 29

THE MONOPOLY GAME SAT ON THE STOOP ALMOST mocking him.

Joe had left the board exactly as the stalker had set it up. The top hat token sat beside a hotel on Park Place, and the wheelbarrow fittingly had found a spot on Water Works. The Scottie dog perched on Reading Railroad, and the sack of money was on Indiana Avenue. Piles of money weighted down with rocks were at each of the four corners as well as deeds to various properties. Off to one side of the game, the intruder had set down the box with its unused tokens.

Torie and Hailey knelt beside the board and studied the layout with him. "I used to hate playing Monopoly when I was a kid," Torie said.

"Your dad always beat you?"

She shook her head. "No, it wasn't that. I hated to bankrupt him. I'd usually cry and tell him not to pay when he'd land on a hotel property, especially Park Place or Boardwalk."

He smiled at her tender admission. "You're a soft touch. This all has to mean something. The stalker took the time to lay this all out in a specific way. Why the top hat piece? Why the wheelbarrow?"

"I had to do a report on a board game when I was a sophomore, and I picked Monopoly because I hated it and everyone I knew loved it. The top hat piece is said to represent J. P. Morgan." She pointed. "His place, Sans Souci, is part of the Club Resort now."

"What about the other pieces?"

"The wheelbarrow represents hard work. The dog was supposedly the top hat's right-hand man. And the sack of money, of course, is all about wealth. It was not a popular piece and was only included as a game piece starting in 1999 and was used less than ten years."

"That means this game was purchased sometime between 1999 and 2009."

"We'd better not disturb it until we are sure we've milked it for all the clues."

He drew out his phone and snapped half a dozen pictures. "I've got all the details, but let's go through the stacks of money and see if anything seems off."

She nodded and picked up the pile of money closest to her. "This one has the deeds to both blue properties as well as all the railroads and the utilities."

"He has a monopoly," Joe said.

"Yes, but I don't know which token it belongs to." Torie began to count the money, sorting it into denomination piles.

Hailey wanted to go through a stack of money so Joe let her while he sorted a pile as well.

"Nothing but money in my two piles," Torie said. "I checked both sides. No notes or markings on any of the bills."

"Same here."

The box might hold more clues, but all he saw was the rest of the tokens. No instructions and nothing marked on the interior of the box.

"Try the top," Torie said.

The intruder had nested the bottom of the box inside the top, so Joe slid it loose and looked it over. "Nothing."

Hailey scooped up the pieces and handed them to him, then scooped up the cards and put them in the designated spot in the box. Torie organized the bills into denominations and stacked them in their place.

Another thought occurred to him, and he took the board and folded it up. "I think you should talk to your dad about this. You've said Anton rarely takes a vacation, yet he's been hanging around here for over a week. What if the stalker is doing this as an elaborate way of getting to him?"

She frowned and rose from the stoop. "But why terrorize me when he's right here to be threatened as well?"

"Have you asked him if anything weird has happened to him?"

"No." She glanced down the street. "But here he comes now. You can ask him yourself."

Joe hadn't intended to leave until Anton arrived, but he'd hoped it would be later. It felt like his time with Torie just got snatched away.

☰

Her dad's smile faded when he saw Torie's face. "What's wrong?" The scent of his cologne wafted toward her on the evening breeze.

Torie picked up the Monopoly box. "This was left on the doorstep."

He examined it. "Why leave it for you to find? You've always hated Monopoly with a passion. The last time we played it, you cried like a baby when I tried to pay you. You'd have thought I'd asked you to beat me with a club."

"It was going to bankrupt you."

His blue eyes crinkled in a smile. "It's a game, honey. You'll never make a mogul, will you? Even now, you're so tenderhearted."

"Which is why I don't manage anything. Let me just fix a few problems any day."

Joe gave a glance up and down the street. "It's getting dark. I suggest we go inside."

Her dad frowned and followed them inside.

Joe shut and locked the door behind them, then drew the curtains. "I have a few questions for you, sir, if you don't mind."

"If it helps my daughter, fire away." He smiled at Joe's daughter. "Hailey, isn't it?"

The little girl sidled up closer to him. "Yes. Do you really own lots of hotels? Daddy says you're as rich as Midas. I know who Midas is because I like all those ancient myths."

Her dad gave a bark of laughter that sounded genuine. "I suppose that's true, but money doesn't buy you a great dad like you have. It only pays for things that don't matter nearly as much."

If it was so unimportant, why had her dad pursued it with such passion all these years? Did he have regrets about time lost together like she did?

Her dad settled on the sofa, and Hailey joined him. He patted her hand and smiled at her again, and Torie was struck at his ease with the child. Did he ever worry he'd never have grandkids? She was twenty-eight without a prospect in sight. Her gaze wandered to Joe.

Well, that wasn't exactly true.

Dad cleared his throat. "Your questions?"

Joe dropped into the armchair, and Torie went to sit on the fireplace hearth. She prayed her dad didn't get riled at the questions. Joe might get a little personal. He wasn't one to pull punches.

"I wondered if you had any enemies. It's possible whoever is stalking Torie is doing it to get back at you."

"Why would you think that?" Dad glanced from Joe to Torie. "There's been no message left for me, has there?" His voice rose.

"No, no," Torie said.

Joe's brows drew together, and his mouth flattened. "So you can't think of any enemies, or you don't want to talk about it? Which is it?"

Whoa. Torie had never heard anyone stand up to her father like that. He was a man who said "Do this" and his subordinates asked what other tasks they could perform. No one ever questioned what he said or how he said it.

Not even her.

Her father's mouth sagged, and his face reddened. She waited for the explosion, but his expression cleared, and he folded his arms across his chest. "A man in my position is bound to have enemies. People I've had to fire. Companies I've been affiliated with that have gone bankrupt. Even in my role with the Fed, decisions I've made have resulted in banks or businesses going under. Such is life."

She winced at the callousness of the words. More and more she was convinced she wasn't cut out to be a cutthroat Bergstrom, but how did she walk away from her heritage? Someday her father would expect her to take over the reins of the company since she was an only child. He'd given her space to find her own way, but she was nearing thirty. He wouldn't be patient forever.

"Anyone in particular stand out?" Joe asked.

"There are too many to remember."

"Anyone ever threaten you?"

Her father let out a mirthless laugh. "Too many times to count. It's always been things like, 'You'll be sorry,' or 'You'll pay.' People feel they have to say something when they're trapped. I give as much leeway as I can, but sometimes you have to take action."

"Could you think about it and give us a list?"

"I could, but I think it's useless." Her dad swept his hand toward Torie. "She's the one threatened, not me."

Joe shot her a helpless glance, and she knew she had to join the fray. Her dad might listen to her more than a stranger. "Dad, what better way to get back at you than to hurt your only family left? Surely you can see that. I think we have to explore every avenue."

He pinned her with a steely stare, then gave a jerky nod. "Fine. I'll work on a list tonight, but I think you're on the wrong railway."

She glanced at Joe. "Send me the pictures you took of the board game and I'll forward them to Dad's email. Something might jog his memory in the placement of the pieces and the tokens used."

But she didn't hold out much hope her dad would help. And maybe he was right. The intruder hadn't said a word about her dad.

The door rattled, and Joe looked out. "It's Craig."

By the time Craig left with the car bug, the phone, and the Monopoly game, it was after nine, and Torie wanted nothing more than to go to bed. Joe left with Hailey in tow, and Torie promised to keep her safe tomorrow while he turned Simon over to the Navy.

Maybe she could call Jason Graham tomorrow while she kept Hailey.

As she locked the door behind Joe and Hailey, her gaze fell to the bookcase again. Could the key to the safe be there somewhere? She stepped to the shelves and ran her hands along the undersides of them.

On the third shelf her fingers hit something metal, and she turned on her phone's flashlight to take a look. A small brass key was taped to the underside. She peeled it off and did a fist pump. This had to unlock the safe.

She went to the spare room and opened the closet door to find the safe again. The key slid in easily and turned, and she threw the lever to open the door. It was dark in the closet, so she turned on her flashlight again. The glow illuminated the interior, but the only item inside was a business-size envelope.

She pulled it out and saw *Anton* scrawled across the front. The flap wasn't sealed so she opened it and withdrew the piece of paper inside. It was a typed letter addressed to her dad.

Anton, I can't take this anymore. This ends tonight. You'll only have yourself to blame at my funeral. Lily

Torie exhaled and sat back on her heels. Had her mom killed herself? The letter implied it could be true, even though she'd never wanted to believe it.

CHAPTER 30

JOE WOULD MISS SIMON. HE'D NEVER BEEN SO fond of one his charges before.

In the prow of one of his boats, he faced the fleet sailing by. The new submarine rode high on the choppy waves, and Joe thrilled to see its majesty. He wished Hailey and Torie could see it, but they were safely at the hotel on this Wednesday morning. The wind blew through his hair, and he inhaled the invigorating scents of sea and salt. His crew exclaimed behind him, but he had to sit and soak in the moment. When had he ever seen a sight like today? Never.

The two aircraft carriers flanked the sub in a simulation of protection, and American flags flapped from the decks. American boats decked out as hostile enemy craft swarmed the starboard side in an attack. Someone onboard shouted, "Battle stations!" An order to fire came seconds later, and a loud *boom* followed the order. The guns held simulated ammunition, but it was awe-inspiring anyway to see the Navy chase off attacking boats.

A sense of pride rose in his chest to realize his small part in protecting American soil. He leaned over and slapped his palm against the hull of his boat. Simon's sleek black head popped up, and Tyrone put the clamp in the sea lion's mouth. Simon dove and they all waited. A swimmer was out there attempting to plant a fake bomb on the submarine, and Joe wanted to monitor Simon's first test as an official Navy sea mammal.

Joe shaded his eyes from the early morning glare with his hand and watched the waves. The swimmer could come from anywhere, and he might be using a diver propulsion device to move faster through the ocean. Joe and his team had no idea how the attack would happen.

"You think Simon's ready?" Danielle asked.

"He's been performing well," Tyrone said. "I think he'll make us proud."

"I think so too," Joe said. "Simon's smart."

He reached for binoculars and searched the water with them. Nothing yet. It could be a few hours still. The wait could be part of the exercise. In fact, it might be. Would Simon perform as well if he was tired?

The morning sun rose higher in the sky as their boat tracked with the grand armada.

Tyrone jumped to his feet. "He's located the swimmer! We've got him hooked." He engaged the winch, and the line began to wind.

A few minutes later Simon's head popped above the water, and Joe tossed him some crab. "Good boy!"

He fed him more crab as the winch continued to yank the swimmer to the boat. The guy would not be able to get away. It took ten minutes before he saw the swimmer's form under the foamy waves.

Simon had done it even when tired. He was ready to leave the nest whether Joe liked it or not.

== ==

Over a dozen black limousines parked in a line in front of the hotel when Torie arrived with Hailey. She entered a beehive of activity in the lobby.

"What's happening?" She stopped her aunt who was rushing past her.

Aunt Genevieve's eyes were wide and agitated. "The bank executives are here already! They weren't supposed to arrive for two days, and we're not ready."

The chaos for such a change in schedule would be massive, and Torie needed to jump in too. "Why would they change the dates without telling us?"

"They wanted to throw off the media. The state police closed the bridge behind them, and every dock and wharf is closed to boats as well after this afternoon when all the fishing and excursion boats get in."

"Are there any guests in the rooms we were planning to use? How can I help?"

"We'd cleared out the guests to give the rooms a thorough cleaning and to put extra touches in them. But the baskets haven't been taken to the rooms. They're all in the Grand Dining Room. Grab a cart and take as many as you can. The room numbers are on the baskets, and you have a master key."

Her aunt rushed off without so much as a thank-you,

but Torie hadn't expected one. This was her business, and she was expected to take responsibility.

"You can help me," she told Hailey.

The little girl brightened at the unexpected excitement of helping out. "I'm good with decorations."

She followed Torie to the dining room, where Torie found two carts along the wall. She had Hailey load one with gaily decorated baskets while she loaded another one. Five minutes later, they were outside the designated guest rooms. Torie unlocked all the rooms and propped them open with the lever.

"You take that side, and I'll take this one," she told Hailey.

In short order they had their baskets delivered. The last room was next to her family's former apartment, which Torie had occupied when she was Hailey's age. Her gaze lingered on the door. The note she'd found in the safe had rocked her world.

Hadn't her mother thought about what her death would do to her daughter? Until reading that note, she would have sworn her mother never harbored any thoughts of suicide. Was she wrong about everything?

"Want to see where I lived when I was your age?" she asked Hailey.

Hailey nodded vigorously. "You lived here in the hotel?"

"Right here." Before she could change her mind, Torie unlocked the door and pushed it open. "This is a two-bedroom apartment."

Light spilled through the floor-to-ceiling windows and sliding door to the balcony. The light scent of Clive

Christian No. 1 lingered in the air just like when she'd been here with her dad. Had someone been in Mom's bedroom?

She moved across the white carpet to the master bedroom. The blue silk bedspread held wrinkles as though someone had been sitting there recently. Her mom's cologne sat on the gleaming marble surface of the dressing table.

Her gaze went to the closet, which stood open. She'd closed it when she was here five days ago, hadn't she? Her throat closed at the thought of stepping into the closet. She shook her head and backed away. Wild horses couldn't drag her into that space.

Hailey's voice broke through her fear. "This was your room?"

"N-No. It was my parents' room. My room is on the other side of the living room." Which she hadn't even gone into when she'd been here with her dad. She exited the room at a near run and walked quickly past the white sofa and gold chairs to her bedroom door. It was closed, and her hand fumbled at the knob. Memories flooded in of playing with Lisbeth here and board games with her parents. Of warm summer days and splashing in the pool and the ocean.

Torie had an idyllic childhood until that awful day her mom plummeted off the roof.

She twisted the doorknob and pushed into the room. It was the same size as the other bedroom, but it held two twin beds covered in pink silk *Little Mermaid* spreads.

Hailey rushed to throw herself on the closest bed. "You liked *The Little Mermaid*!"

Torie touched the fine silk. "My mom had these custom made for me."

She looked around at the original movie posters on the walls. She had a clear memory of herself in this bedroom reading in the fuzzy white lounge in the corner. She moved to the bookcase beside it and saw the complete collection of *Little House on the Prairie* books beside an assortment of picture books and early readers. She nearly gasped when she saw her old notebooks on the bottom shelf.

She pulled one out and opened it to see her childish block letters as she practiced her printing. Her mother's smiling face was more vivid than she could ever remember since she'd left this island. Her mom had spent a lot of time here with her. They'd played games at the table beside the white cabinet. If she opened the doors to the cabinet, she'd find every children's game available on the shelves.

There were some loose pages. She shook them out and gathered them up, then stopped when she recognized Lisbeth's handwriting. The missing journal pages!

Hailey slid off the bed and came to her side to take her hand. "You look like you're going to cry. Are you sad?"

Torie squeezed the little girl's hand. "I haven't been in this room since I was ten, and I was remembering my mom. I miss her." Best not to mention the pages. She couldn't wait to read them.

Hailey's green eyes filled with tears, and she nodded. "I still miss Mommy, and it makes me sad that I can't remember her voice. Do you remember your mom's voice?"

"Yes, but I was ten when she died, and you were only five. Maybe your dad has some videos of her you can watch so you can hear her again."

"He does. I watch them sometimes, and I remember better for a little while, then it goes away." Tears rolled down her cheeks.

Maybe this hadn't been a good idea to bring her in here. Torie hadn't expected to be so emotional. "Let's go see if there's anything else we need to do to prepare the rooms."

When she led Hailey back to the living room, she smelled her mom's perfume again, even stronger this time. She frowned and looked around. A glimmer on the carpet caught her eyes—a glass bottle lay broken. Moving closer, she recognized her mom's perfume bottle. The one that had been on the dressing table just minutes ago.

She pushed Hailey to the door. "Run!"

The hair stood on the back of her neck as she followed Hailey through the door and pulled it shut behind them. She took Hailey's hand and ran for the elevator.

CHAPTER 31

"WE HAVE NO IDEA WHO THAT HOSTILE DIVER Simon caught nearly a week ago was." Commander Chen seemed his normal, unperturbed self behind his large desk except for the way he pursed his lips.

Joe stood in Chen's office and waited for more questions. He'd asked Joe to stop by to discuss the bombing incident last Friday morning that had taken out Joe's boat. It was the second time in a week he'd been in front of Chen, and he could go a long time without being called on the carpet again. None of this had been his fault, but it felt like he'd failed in some way.

Joe stared at Chen. "Was there any clear information about the bomb's origins or the materials the guy had? Or of his identity? Or even what his intent was?"

The commander shrugged. "The materials were common and easily obtained. And while we don't have any clear evidence, I suspect he wanted to incapacitate the sub and breach the defenses to get aboard and steal top-secret details once it sank."

"And the diver? American or foreign?" The question had been burning through Joe ever since he found the swimmer.

"Hard to say. No ID on the guy, no clear ethnic appearance—not that it would have told us much since we're so diverse. We're running his prints, but it will take some time to figure this out."

"You think this attack had anything to do with my boat being blown up? Was I specifically targeted?"

Chen steepled his fingers. "I don't much believe in coincidence, so yeah. While we can't figure out how they're connected yet, it can't be accidental. It would make sense whoever is behind this wanted to take out the mammal guardians. The best way to do that would be to destroy the people who train them."

"Are you ordering extra sea mammal patrols?"

The commander nodded. "And extra patrol boats. Good work out there during the war games, by the way."

"Thank you, sir."

"I'd like you to take charge of all the sea lions for us and get them out in the water, pronto. Your expertise might be crucial in the next few days. I'll arrange for a place for you to stay. And I want to take possession of the three sea lions today. We've already paid for them, and we need them."

"I'll leave the sea lions with you, but I'm sorry, Commander, I can't take over the Navy's work with them right now. I need to get back home. My daughter was kidnapped on Saturday." Joe told Chen about the incident, and the man listened with an impassive expression. "I don't trust anyone else to guard her but me. This is a true hardship. While I'd like to be part of the protection along the coast this week, my daughter is my primary responsibility."

Chen showed no emotion. "Where is she today?"

"With a friend, but I need to pick her up soon."

Chen exhaled, then shook his head. "I sympathize with your situation, but this is a matter of national security. It supersedes all other concerns."

Joe dug his fingers into his palms. "I have other trainers in my employ, Commander. Tyrone could do it, I'm sure."

"But you're our best. I'm sorry. You must do this."

Joe squared his shoulders. "My answer is still no." He whirled and stormed for the door. He barely kept himself from slamming it behind him.

What had he just done? Training the sea lions wasn't exactly something he could take anywhere but the Navy. He had insurance money from Julie's death stashed in the bank, but he hadn't wanted to touch that since it would pay for Hailey's college someday. Much as he loved America, his daughter's safety was more important to him than anything, even his country. His life would be over if something happened to Hailey.

In the bright sunlight he jogged to his boat. Tyrone and Danielle were waiting for him, and he fired up the motor. If he hurried, he could take the girls to lunch.

After several long moments, the guard at the dock approached his boat. "Um, Commander Chen wants you detained. MPs are coming to get you."

"Detained? He can't do that."

But Chen could do whatever he liked on the base. He

could call Joe a terrorist and throw him in the brig until he agreed to his demands. Joe couldn't let that happen. Hailey needed him—now.

He pushed on the throttle and the boat slewed away. Chen had much less power on the open seas than on the base.

He told Danielle and Tyrone what had happened. "Keep an eye out for pursuit."

But there was none. There might be repercussions later, but for now, he was getting Hailey and laying low. Joe didn't see how Chen could force him to work when he'd just quit a contractor job. He wasn't owned by the Navy.

Joe regretted not getting to say good-bye to Simon and his team, but even as he tried to figure out what the future held, he wasn't sorry. And he was a little bit excited to think he might forge his way into something new.

Only God knew what that new adventure might be. Joe had no clue.

==

Someone had been in the apartment with them.

Why hadn't Torie forced herself to check out that closet? She might have been face-to-face with whoever was tormenting her.

She and Hailey sat in her aunt's office waiting for security to arrive. When they exited the elevator, she'd gone directly to security and told them there'd been an intruder in the owner's apartment. They rushed off to check it out, and she sat here castigating herself ever since.

As well as listening to her aunt harangue her.

Her aunt's voice broke into her thoughts again. "You should not have been in that apartment, Torie."

Torie stiffened, tired of hearing the same thing. "I've been trying to hold my tongue, Aunt Genevieve, but you forget who you're talking to. My family owns this hotel, not you. You manage it for Dad, but my name is on the paperwork, not yours. I have the right to go anywhere on this property I desire. I don't want to hear another word about what rights you think I have. I have any rights I want to take."

Red ran up her aunt's face, and her mouth dropped open. She struggled for words, but nothing emerged but a garbled noise. The color vanished as quickly as it came, leaving her angry eyes shooting daggers at Torie.

She pointed her finger at Torie. "Your father will hear about this. Such impudence! Do children have no respect for their elders any longer?"

Torie sighed. "I'm twenty-eight years old, hardly a child. You've never treated me with respect, and I've tried to overlook it, but it needs to end. I'm perfectly competent."

Her aunt rolled her eyes. "Look at you. Your mother would be so disappointed in you. No style. No attempt to even hide those huge, ugly feet of yours." She smiled coldly. "You think those Latin quotes make you appear intelligent, but they only make you seem more pathetic."

"*Non fortuna homines aestimabo, sed moribus,*" Torie said softly. "Seneca said, 'I do not estimate the men for their fortune, but for their habits.' Your behavior speaks volumes, Aunt Genevieve."

"And don't even get me started on your father. He's hardly a role model for anyone."

Torie stared at her. "I know you dislike him. Dad met and dated you first, didn't he? I don't understand how you can carry a grudge all these years over something like that."

Her aunt's eyes hardened. "Ask your father why Lily killed herself. He was having an affair, and it broke her heart."

"That's a lie! Dad loved Mom with all his heart."

"You just don't want to believe it. I saw him with his floozy with my own eyes. He said he was checking on a hotel in Atlanta, and I was there for a conference. I saw him kissing the other woman. It's true, Torie."

"You told Mom, didn't you?" When her aunt looked away, Torie knew she was right.

What about the note she'd found that Lisbeth had hidden in the safe? Was it truly from her mother? It was computer generated, not handwritten.

"You've always said she killed herself. Why are you so sure?" Torie asked.

"She was wild with grief about it. Lily was always volatile. I always thought she'd walk into the ocean one day and not come back."

"I never saw her act in a crazy way."

"You were a child. Of course she wouldn't show that side to you."

Torie was done with this conversation. She rose and took Hailey's hand. "Come with me, honey." Torie managed to keep the tears at bay until they stood outside her aunt's closed door.

She drew in a shaky breath. "Sorry you had to hear that."

"I'm sorry she was mean to you."

Torie squeezed the little girl's hand. "Thank you."

A security guard headed her direction, and she turned to face him. "Anything?" she asked when he drew near. He reeked of her mom's perfume.

The older man shrugged. "We found the broken perfume bottle, so someone must have been in there while you were. The apartment was empty though."

"Any clues to who he was or where he was hiding?"

"I found a couple of caved-in boxes in the closet, so he might have been sitting on them listening to you in the bedroom. No way to know for sure though. You didn't open any closet doors. There's one for coats in the living room too. Could have been in either of those places or even the pantry."

True enough. "Thanks for checking."

"Of course, Ms. Bergstrom. Glad to be of service." He looked past her shoulder. "I'd better tell Ms. Hallston what we discovered."

When he stepped into her aunt's office and closed the door behind him, Torie took Hailey's hand. "It's nearly noon. How about some lunch?"

Hailey nodded and pointed. "And there's Daddy. He can come with us. Maybe he'll buy us ice cream."

Torie turned to see Joe's long-limbed figure loping toward them down the nearly empty hall, past the seating area with its fireplace. Her pulse stuttered at the grim expression on his face. That couldn't be good.

She started to ask him what was wrong, but he gave a

slight shake to his head, and she held back her question. "We're about to go to lunch. You hungry?"

"Famished."

"We've got a Mexican buffet special going on today in the dining room," she said.

"I'm in," he said.

Hailey slipped her hand into his as they started for the Grand Dining Room. "Torie got yelled at."

Torie's face went hot, and she looked away from Joe's probing gaze. "My aunt's always been a little difficult. And she's never liked me."

"She's always been so good to Hailey and me." Joe took her hand and squeezed it. "What's not to like?"

The warmth in his words made her shoot a glance his way, but she found it hard to accept the admiration in his green eyes. Was it only admiration or something a little stronger? She wasn't used to reading emotional undercurrents. All of the subtext went right over her head. Why couldn't people say what they mean and mean what they said?

But maybe Joe was one who did. She'd seen no evidence of him twisting his words. He was only guilty of twisting her insides into a knot. And her heart.

"My dad says she's jealous. That Genevieve has been angry ever since he dated her, then dumped her when he met Mom. I can't remember our relationship ever being anything except how it is right now."

They walked toward the dining room, and Hailey waited until they were seated to announce her second bombshell. "Someone was in Torie's old apartment. He busted up her mom's perfume bottle. And Torie cried

when we were there. You should get her some ice cream
to make her smile again."

Torie went from a flinch to a full-bodied laugh. She
leaned over and tickled Hailey. "Don't pull me into your
little schemes, girlfriend. You're the one who wants the
ice cream."

"I thought you liked ice cream," Joe said.

His deadpan voice didn't fool her. He might not be
interrogating her right this minute, but he'd be firing questions her way the moment they were alone.

But she'd do the same. She hadn't missed the stress
around his mouth and the worry in his eyes. Something
had happened this morning.

CHAPTER 32

A SIREN BLARED, AND JOE JUMPED, SURE THE
MPs were after him.

Once it screamed past his building, he relaxed. Just a
state trooper. Perspiration beaded on his forehead in the
warm humidity near the sea lion enclosure. They'd talked
Hailey out of ice cream with the lure of seeing the newly
arrived group of sea lions.

The sun shone on the water and steel fencing where
his four sea mammals frolicked and barked. One of the
sea lions flopped out of the water onto the decking and
clapped his flippers until Hailey tossed him crab.

"He's glad to see you," Joe said.

A perfect day if it weren't that he'd just quit the best
job he'd ever had.

Hailey was ten feet away talking to a sea lion. Far
enough away he could talk without her overhearing, especially since she was chattering away.

"What about the intruder in your old apartment? You
see or hear anything?"

Torie shook her head. "I had a funny feeling when I saw the closet door was standing open. I was sure we'd shut it."

"You didn't go in, did you?"

If she'd interrupted that guy . . . He suppressed a shudder.

"I should have, but I couldn't make myself take one step that way."

At the shame in her voice, he gripped her by the shoulders. "Never apologize for using the good sense God gave you. Only an idiot would make a move to surprise an intruder. Especially when you were responsible for a child."

The shame fled her brown eyes, and she smiled up at him. "How do you always know the right thing to say?"

"Do I? That's the first time anyone's ever told me that. I'm usually accused of being too blunt."

"I like a man who says what he means and means what he says."

"That's good because I don't think I could change if I wanted to. And I want you to like me. More than like me."

The sparkle in her eyes at his confession made his heart skitter in his chest. Maybe they were starting to get somewhere.

"I found Lisbeth's missing pages—at least some of them." She reached into her bag and pulled out some journal pages. "I haven't had a chance to read them yet." She handed some to him. "You take a look and I will too."

He began to leaf through the pages. "These seem

different from the others you showed me. Choppier. Look."

She leaned over to read where he pointed. "'Tell Torie? Can't decide. Wish I'd never found it. Genevieve saw it on my desk and we argued about it. Why would she do something like that to her sister?'" Torie frowned. "What was Lisbeth struggling with telling me?"

"I don't know."

Torie went back to her pages. "Here's something. This page isn't from her journal. It's a Xerox of my mother's suicide note: 'You'll only have yourself to blame at my funeral. Lily.'" Torie put her finger at the bottom of the page. "This is Lisbeth's handwriting here. 'Found this tucked into a Bible in a nightstand in the master bedroom. Did Anton hide this to protect Torie?'"

He read it and whistled. "We should ask him if Lisbeth called him to ask about it."

"I wondered if Mom even wrote the note since it wasn't handwritten. But I never heard of a suicide note being found at the crime scene, so that must be why Lisbeth wondered if Dad hid it."

Speculation wouldn't get them anywhere. "What happened today with your aunt?"

Torie's smile faded, and she laid down the pages. "She always finds something hurtful to say. Today it was that I was pretentious in using Latin quotes and that I should do something to hide my l-large feet."

Something in Joe's heart broke at the pained expression on her face. "Only a genius knows Latin, so that's a moot point. But a personal attack like the size of your feet? They're proportionate to your height. You're six feet tall. Did she even stop to think how ridiculous you'd look if your feet were a size five? I hope you jumped right back down her throat."

"I'm ashamed to say I did. I tried to keep my temper, but she was just so mean. I dislike meanness."

"I'll keep that in mind." He reached out and stroked a strand of hair that had escaped her crown of braids. "Your mom was beautiful."

She nodded. "She was gorgeous."

"I bet she wore a size twelve shoe."

She arched a brow. "How would you know that?"

"I saw a picture of her at your cottage. You look so much like her, and her feet are in the same proportion. But you're even more gorgeous."

Red swept up her neck. "Now you've gone from truth to fiction."

"Ask any man, and he'd tell you the same thing. You didn't see the admiring glances Craig was sending your way when he met you. You're one of those rare women who have no idea of the feminine power they have. Let's keep it that way, okay?"

An uneasy chuckle escaped her, and she shook her head. "That's an easy request since I don't believe a word of your blather." Her smile vanished. "And what happened to you today? I saw how upset you were when you showed up at the hotel."

"I broke ties with the Navy today."

She held her hand to her mouth. "But you love working with the sea lions!"

"I didn't have any choice."

He told her what had happened, and her eyes grew

bigger and rounder when she heard about the hostile swimmer killing himself with cyanide.

"It had to have been a very serious plot for him to kill himself rather than be taken alive and interrogated. That's the kind of thing a foreign power might have their soldiers do."

"I've been thinking the same thing. I'm sure the Navy will figure out what power is behind this, but it escalated everything along the Eastern Seaboard."

She shivered and hugged herself. "Scary stuff. What are you going to do about a job?"

"I don't know yet. I could work full-time at the hotel instead of part-time. Or maybe I'll find one wherever you're heading when you're through here." The words popped out before he'd even realized that thought had been simmering for the past few hours.

Her eyes widened and her mouth curved into a huge smile. "I'd vote for that idea, but I'll have to give it some thought. Dad's been wanting me to go to Costa Rica and turn around a resort there, but I'm not sure what I want to do. I'm not even sure I want to be in the hospitality business. Ever since that thought bloomed in my head, I haven't been able to get rid of it. What would I want to do if I could do anything at all? I don't even know."

"When you figure it out, let me know and I'll do what I can to help."

He dropped his arm around her, and they strolled along the decking to join Hailey. It was too soon to push Torie, but he hoped he'd planted the thought of what life might be like if they were in close proximity.

≡≡

Her aunt always managed to ruin a pleasant moment. **Pick up the glass globes from Amelia and hide them. There are fifteen globes.**

In the front seat of Joe's truck, Torie stared at the text message on her phone. No *please* or *thank you*. No apology for the morning's insults. But had she really expected anything more from her aunt? It was no wonder she had never married. Who could put up with her sharp tongue for long?

It wasn't the first time Torie wondered why her dad had let Aunt Genevieve manage the Club Resort. The staff lived in fear of her, and there was a constant turnover of positions.

Torie could do so much with the hotel. The idea had been slowly forming over her time here. Every time she thought about leaving, she felt a check in her spirit—a conviction it would be wrong to leave this place where she felt so at home. And where she knew she could make a difference.

She tucked the notion away for further consideration later and turned to Joe, who was turning the truck into the parking lot. "Duty calls. My aunt wants me to collect the glass globes from Amelia and help hide them for the scavenger hunt."

"Ooh, can I help?" Hailey asked.

"I'm terrible at hiding things, so I'd love the help if it's okay with your dad." She glanced at Joe.

"Only if I get to be part of the project."

Was he always this good-natured? Her dad rarely

raised his voice, but it was mostly because he was distracted and focused on his business. He was rarely fully present. It had been her and her mother most of the time with quick trips in and out from her dad.

Joe drove them to the glass shop. "I hope Amelia has tubs or something to keep them from rolling."

Torie shoved open her door and got out. "I'm sure she has it all planned."

"I'll let Amelia know we're here," Joe said.

His tall figure disappeared into the shop, and Torie marveled at the way he took charge, jumping in and helping wherever he could. He didn't stand back and make her do the work, even though it was her job. It made her feel cared for in a deeper way than she could remember experiencing. At least not since her mother died.

Hailey took Torie's hand. "Daddy likes you. Do you like him?"

"I do. He's a very nice man. Do you like living on Jekyll Island?" How would Hailey take it if Joe told her they were moving? She remembered how she felt when her dad had announced they were moving after Mom's death. He hadn't consulted her and just packed her things up. Two days later they were in Arizona, which couldn't be more different from this quaint island.

"I love the beach and all the sea life. I don't remember much now about where we lived with Mommy. This is home."

Did Torie have the right to disrupt the little girl's life when she'd already lost so much? And would it really be a sacrifice to stay here and see what the future held with Joe and Hailey? Maybe it wouldn't work out, but after nearly dying in the ocean, she didn't want to turn her back on such a delicious possibility.

He exited the shop with his arms full of boxes. "I've got six of them. There are nine more."

"I'll get some. They aren't heavy," she added when he frowned.

"I can carry some," Hailey said.

Amelia came out balancing four more boxes. "The others are just inside the door."

Torie opened the door and placed one of the boxes in Hailey's hands. "I can get the other four." She balanced them in her arms and went out with the little girl.

Hailey walked in front of Torie back to the truck. "Where can we hide them?"

"I can answer that," Amelia said. "We want to highlight the island businesses so hide a few at the shops along here and take some to the Jekyll Island Beach Village. Maybe put one at Jekyll Market and The Collection Boutique. The event kicks off tomorrow night."

"What about Driftwood Beach? It's iconic Jekyll Island," Joe said.

Amelia frowned. "It doesn't highlight any businesses."

Why was Amelia taking charge of the locations? This was hotel business, for the club's guests. She'd been paid handsomely for the beautiful globes, but that was as far as her authority went.

"I'll figure it out," Torie said.

"I've planned all this out with Genevieve," Amelia said. "I suggest you follow her plans."

Amelia's high-handed behavior made Torie want to dig in her heels. She had seen all of the plans for the weekend's events. None of the businesses had paid for the privilege of having the visitors search their properties for the globes so this was something she could decide, no matter what her aunt or Amelia had to say about it.

"My aunt said nothing about following any special plan, but thank you for the advice." She climbed into the passenger seat of Joe's truck, and as they drove away, she caught a glimpse of Amelia's tight lips as she pulled out her phone. She was probably calling Aunt Genevieve.

Sure enough, moments later, another message flashed on the screen from her aunt. Torie didn't read it. In that moment she knew what she wanted to do—stay here and bring the hotel back to its full life and beauty. Build up the employees and change the culture here. A year from now she wanted every person working at the resort to talk about how much they loved being a part of it.

In her bones she knew she could make a difference here. All it would take was commitment to this place and these people. Her gaze slid sideways to Joe. It felt like a huge step but the right one.

CHAPTER 33

WHAT WAS DIFFERENT ABOUT TORIE THIS AFTERNOON?

Joe sensed a freer spirit, a lightness in her manner. He wanted to hope it was because he'd told her he wanted to be wherever she was, but he might be reading too much into it. With the blue sky overhead and the tang of the sea in his nose, it would take a grinch not to enjoy the perfect afternoon with Hailey and Torie. Maybe she felt the same way.

Torie sat on a twisted tree on Driftwood Beach and studied the globe in her hands. "This one is beautiful so let's put it on the beach somewhere. There will be a picnic here at dinner tomorrow, followed by fireworks from a boat out on the water," Torie said. "The guests will be milling around for hours. I think we should put two here."

"I saw your back go up at Rogers Glass," he teased.

She flushed. "Was I too unkind?"

"Never. It's not Amelia's business how you use the globes. She was paid for providing them. It's up to the hotel how to use them."

She looked around. "Hailey, you pick out the two you want to hide and figure out where you want to put them. Make the hiding places fairly difficult."

The kindness she showed Hailey touched him. She seemed to always be thinking of ways to please his daughter, something no dad could resist. And he had no intention of trying.

Hailey studied the available globes. "The green one will be harder to see, and I love the orange one. You think it's too bright?"

"I think you can hide it well enough to mask the color," Torie said.

His daughter picked up the orange one first and glanced up and down the beach littered with driftwood and seaweed. "What if I put it in the crook of a tree and drape seaweed on it? I could leave just a glimmer of color peeking through."

"I'll get the seaweed," Joe said. "Since you hate to touch it."

She wrinkled her nose. "It's nasty."

"I'm with you," Torie said. "There's nothing worse than feeling it wrap around your foot when you're in the water."

Hailey shuddered. "I always think it's a sea monster come to drag me down into its depths."

"Like Scylla," Torie said. "Has your dad ever read you Greek and Roman mythology?"

She shook her head. "Who was Scylla?"

"A six-headed sea monster. It lived under a rock in the Strait of Messina."

"Is that why you quote Latin all the time?"

"Our culture was built on the backs of the Greek and Roman civilizations that came before ours. There's a lot of wisdom left behind by those kingdoms. And it's just fun. Even if the stories aren't true, they're heroic and point to how we can have courage in the face of adversity."

"Like when we lost our moms." Hailey stared at the orange globe she held.

Torie draped an arm around her and hugged her. "You're a wise little soul, Hailey. It took a lot of courage for us to go on, didn't it? But we made it. All those hard trials make us better if we let them. And I love seeing how strong you are now. You're a special girl."

Joe's throat thickened at the joy on his daughter's face. Torie affirmed her in so many important ways. He'd thought he was doing a good job of raising her by himself, but there was a softness a woman brought to a relationship. Hailey was soaking it up like a dry sponge—and so was he. How had he forgotten how important that was?

He swallowed past the lump of emotion in his throat. "Where do you want me to hide the green one?"

Hailey pointed back toward the tree line near the parking area along the road. "Into the greenery a little. Not far. Just enough to blend in."

"You've got it." He carried the globe to where the sand ended and the vegetation began and nestled it into weeds and leaves. Stepping back, he could barely tell it was there.

Next up, seaweed. As he turned toward the crashing waves, he caught a glint of something metallic. He squinted in the sun and walked a few feet closer until he saw it wasn't the bike he'd first thought it might be.

A diver propulsion device lay tucked into the vegetation. Someone had pulled boughs of pine atop it. If not for the care someone had taken to hide it, he wouldn't have this tingle of trepidation down his back. It was an expensive piece of equipment too. Military grade. No diver would let this bring him to shore and then abandon it. At least no one he knew.

He looked up and down the beach, populated by a few families strolling the packed, wet sand. No one in a wet suit or carrying dive tanks. This wasn't a great place to shore dive so he hadn't expected to see any scuba divers, but the sea scooter wouldn't likely be used for anything else.

His mind flashed to the hostile swimmers. Could it be related? His commander had said in times like this, there were no coincidences, but Joe stood frowning down at the piece of equipment.

Something didn't sit right, and he couldn't let it go. Chen needed to know about this.

==

"You ignored my text."

Torie turned around at her aunt's irate voice. Genevieve stood at the edge of the sand in her impeccable lavender suit and heels. The wind lifted strands of her blonde hair, and she smoothed it back into place.

"I did. I was given this task, and I'll do it my way, not Amelia's. She's not a hotel employee and has no say in what we do with the globes. They're hotel property now."

Her aunt's lips flattened, and her eyes narrowed.

"Must you always make things so difficult, Torie? Just do what you're told."

Torie could only imagine her aunt's reaction when she learned Torie was going to settle here and take over the hotel. The fireworks between them would continue until her aunt figured out who was in charge.

Torie glanced over to make sure Hailey was still out of earshot and saw the little girl wandering along the tree line with a globe in her hands. "Why have you always believed Mom's death was a suicide?"

Her aunt's gaze narrowed and her lips grew pinched. "I shouldn't have said anything. It was all so long ago."

Should she ask her about Lisbeth's handwritten remarks and the note Torie had found in the safe?

"Lisbeth found a suicide note, but it's not handwritten so I don't know what to think. And Lisbeth mentioned you two had argued about it." She paused and frowned. "Mom prided herself on writing personal notes. What could be more personal than a threat to kill herself? So why would she type it out? It's strange."

Her aunt's face reddened, and she looked down, as if she couldn't meet Torie's gaze. In that moment Torie knew what had happened.

"You wrote my mom's suicide note, didn't you, Aunt Genevieve?" Torie reached into her bag lying next to a big downed tree and pulled out the original note. "Don't lie to me. If I turn this over to the police, they will be able to match it to the paper you have always used. Did you actually *kill* her?"

Her aunt gasped. "I did no such thing!" She glanced from side to side as if searching for a way out, then her shoulders sagged. "It was an accident. Your mom was so angry when I told her about your dad's mistress, and she attacked me. I-I just pushed her off me. She stumbled, and I tried to catch her." Her voice quivered, and she reached a hand out toward Torie.

"But what about the note?"

"I was afraid someone had seen me leave the apartment so I planted the note. The police never mentioned it, and I've always suspected your father took it to protect his reputation. He couldn't let anyone think he'd driven his wife to suicide."

Torie absorbed the news for a long moment. She could imagine the struggle, hear her mom's scream as she catapulted over the railing, and Torie shuddered. "I can see Dad trying to protect me. What about Lisbeth? Why did you argue with her about the note she'd found?"

"The impertinence of that girl. Of course I told her nothing." Her aunt's chin came up.

"Someone broke into the cottage and left Lisbeth a warning note. Was that you?"

Her aunt nodded. "It's such old history. There was no reason to dig into it all again." She sighed. "I suppose you're going to tell your father?"

"He deserves to know."

"He deserves nothing! And if you tell him, my job here is over." She was too proud to beg, and her chin came up.

"You're going to jail for manslaughter! You should have told the truth right from the start."

"It's your word against mine. And your father would be in trouble, too, for tampering with the scene."

"My mother deserves justice."

Her aunt pressed her lips together. "Since you've made it clear you're the boss, I'm submitting my resignation. I'll be gone after this big weekend is over. I hope you're happy that you've destroyed my life."

Such blindness to the pain she'd caused. Torie watched her aunt turn and walk away with her head high. Nothing got through to her.

Joe approached and touched her arm. "You okay? From your body language it looks like you had it out with Genevieve."

Now that it was over, weakness washed down Torie's legs and she exhaled. "She admitted to writing the suicide note Lisbeth found." She told Joe what she'd learned.

Just talking about it made her eyes flood with tears. At least her mother hadn't left her on purpose, but they'd missed out on so much together. Why did life have to be so unfair?

==

Joe walked a few feet away from Torie and called Chen. "Hello, Commander." He turned away from the crashing surf in order to hear better. "You had no right to try to send MPs to apprehend me."

Hailey wandered down the beach toward Torie. He wouldn't want his daughter to hear his worry about the propulsion device. Torie either, though he'd tell her what he found once he had a quiet minute.

Chen still hadn't responded, so Joe pulled the phone

from his ear and looked at it. Still connected. He returned it to his ear. "Sir?"

"I'm here. Just trying to figure out how you had the audacity to blame me after quitting on me today."

"I found something interesting on Driftwood Beach." Joe told him about the diver propulsion device. "It was hidden like someone came ashore here and planned to return to use it. But it's not a shore dive area. Too rough of an entrance. So what's the diver want? I couldn't help but think about our bomber."

This time Chen's silence followed an intrigued, "Hmm," and Joe waited for more. Chen would be running every bit of data he had through his head and correlating it with what he'd just learned.

"So what do you think?"

"I hardly think we can talk about it, Joe. Not when you abandoned me today. Let me just say I don't believe this has anything to do with the Navy. We've defused the danger and apprehended multiple threats."

Shut out. He'd known it was a long shot. Why would Chen tell him anything? "Sorry for bothering you, sir. I'll let you go."

"Wait. What make is the device?"

"It's military grade, but I didn't check the manufacturer. Let me look." Joe went to the propulsion unit and squatted beside it. He raised a brow as he called it out to Chen on the phone. "Pricey. Our SEALs use them."

"Indeed."

This time Joe gave him space to think it through. His pulse increased at the thought of what this could mean.

Whatever plan the morning's diver had put in place might have pulled in this small island. And why come ashore up here? It was too far away from the naval base to be of much use. Unless he had brought something with big firepower that could reach out to sea as the sub came by.

"I'll send some men after it. We'll sweep it for evidence just in case," Chen said. "But I don't believe it has anything to do with our threat."

"Yes, sir."

"Thanks for calling it in. I won't hold your lapse in judgment against you if you decide to come back to work. Go ahead and take the week to see to your daughter. I'll expect you back on Monday."

"Yes, sir." The olive branch was such a surprise that Joe couldn't think of what to say. Chen was usually by the book, so something must have changed his mind, but what? Maybe Simon wasn't cooperating.

"Thank you, sir."

If danger still swirled around Hailey on Monday, he'd worry about it then. Right now, he'd been given an unexpected gift, and he'd pray it all worked out.

He ended the call and settled on a large twisted log near the propulsion device. If the guy came back for it, he'd strike up a conversation to see what he could find out. It might be innocuous, though Joe couldn't imagine how.

Her bare feet kicking up sand, Hailey ran toward him with seashells in her hands. He wanted to fix her image in his head because one day in the not-too-distant future, his little girl would be too grown up for days at the beach with seashells and sea turtles.

"You made a haul." He patted the log beside him, and she plopped down on it.

His gaze went past her to Torie, who strolled along the edge of the water with her high heels in her hands. Her long legs, clad in rolled-up white pants, held a touch of pink from the intense sun, and the wind had teased most of her hair loose from its updo of braids. She looked like Aphrodite rising from the sea with her sun-kissed cheeks and bright eyes.

He was such a goner. The more he was around her, the more compelling she became.

Torie dropped her heels onto the beach. "I'd forgotten how much I loved this beach. It was my favorite place on the island. I have a tree house across the street, and I spent so many hours out here."

"That's *your* tree house?" Hailey asked. "We found it, and Daddy fixed it up. The ladder boards had fallen off, and Daddy put on new ones and made it all safe again."

Torie's brown eyes went soft. "I love that! I noticed someone had repaired it. And it wasn't really mine. I mean, we didn't own the property, but my dad had it built. Let's go over and take a look at it together." She slid her feet back into her heels, then held out her hand to Hailey, who was sitting next to Joe.

Hailey situated her seashells on the sand by Joe's feet, then jumped up and took Torie's hand. "Want to come, Daddy?"

"You two go ahead. I'm meeting, um, a friend here in a little while. I'll be able to see you from here, but holler if you get scared."

At least he still had a job.

CHAPTER 34

THE LEAFY TOPS OF THE TREES SHADED TORIE and Hailey from the intense summer sun as they headed to the tree house. The hum of tourists walking and talking along the road blended with the birdsong in the trees all along the beach. They skirted a few bikers and plunged deeper into the trees.

Torie reached the spot first and looked up into the tree. The thick foliage hid the tree house from view, but she couldn't wait to share a few minutes with Hailey there. She hadn't been here in the daylight since she'd arrived, and it would be a different view from what she'd shared with her dad during the fireworks.

"Can I go up first?" Hailey asked.

Torie stepped away from the tree ladder. "Sure."

Hailey clambered up the rungs nailed into the old tree and disappeared from view amid the rustling of leaves and the indignant squawk of a bird the girl's presence had chased away.

Torie secured her crossbody bag around herself,

then put her foot on the first rung. It gave way a bit. She retracted her foot and jerked on the rungs she could reach. Only the first one felt a little loose, so she scrambled up the tree trunk. Her head poked above the first layer of leaves and she spotted Hailey still a few feet up.

The little girl was sitting where Torie used to perch, staring out over the treetops to the water. She pulled out her phone and snapped a picture of the idyllic scene. If only she had a few pictures of herself at this age in the very same pose. It was the iconic scene of her childhood and would have meant so much to her.

She slipped her phone back into her bag, then climbed up the rest of the way. When she put her foot on the surface of the platform, it felt off somehow—spongy. And that couldn't be with the new boards Joe had installed. She clutched a close branch with her left hand and studied the boards at her feet. There were holes where new nails used to be.

The hair on the back of her neck rose. "Hailey, you need to move slowly toward me. Test the boards before you put your full weight on them. Someone has been up here messing around."

She stretched out her hand as far as she could reach as Hailey, her eyes wide, sidled toward her. "Keep one hand on a branch, honey. Get as close to the tree trunk as you can."

Catching her breath felt like trying to suck air through an empty oxygen tank, and her heart struggled to keep beating. A fall from this height could kill the little girl if she tumbled down the wrong way. Torie couldn't let that happen.

Hailey froze. "I-I'm scared." Her face had lost all color, and her lids fluttered as if she wanted to close them so she didn't have to see what was happening.

Torie inched a few more feet onto the platform. She didn't dare move too fast in case her weight made the whole thing plummet to the ground, but she had to reach Hailey. "I've got you, honey. Reach for my hand. You can do it."

The little girl flung both arms around the tree trunk. "I don't want to fall like Mommy did! I want my daddy!"

Torie could hear the wail building in the little girl's throat. Any minute now and she would be sobbing and hysterical. "Hailey, look at me. We're both going to be okay, but you have to be brave, okay? You've got your daddy's bravery in your genes. He'd expect you to listen and do what I tell you, wouldn't he?"

Hailey's nod was almost imperceptible. She closed her eyes for a brief moment, then opened them and reached one hand toward Torie. "I can't reach you."

Torie glanced at the tree branch she'd been gripping. The rough sensation of the bark against her fingers was her lifeline, but she had to let go of it to grab Hailey's hand. She released her grip on the tree, but it took several long moments to peel each finger away from the safety of the branch.

Without that steadying grip, she inched her way along the floorboards, waiting for one to let go and throw her into the air. It seemed forever before her fingertips grazed Hailey's and she was able to walk the little girl toward her.

"Come on, honey, just a little farther." Inch by inch Hailey moved toward her until she was finally in Torie's arms. "Scoot around me and start climbing down the ladder. I'll hang on to you until you're secure on the ladder."

Tears hung on Hailey's lashes, and she nodded. "Don't let me fall." She swung one leg over the edge of the tree house, then slid down onto the first rung.

Torie held her gaze. "I've got you." She sank to her knees to be able to hang on to Hailey until the little girl pulled her hand away to grip the rung and climb on down.

She closed her eyes briefly. "Thank you, God."

Now to get down herself. Still on her knees, she eased her left leg over the side and felt for the top rung. There it was. As she started to swing her right leg over the edge, she felt the big tree house shift and tilt to her right.

"No!" She flung out her hand to grab for the branch that had been her lifeline moments ago, but her fingers barely grazed the rough bark before it slammed onto a board. The movement tilted the floorboards even more, and she felt a dizzying sensation as the tree house lost its grip on the perch that had sustained it for twenty years.

A scream ripped from her throat, and she plummeted as the ground rose to meet her.

==

Joe turned back to keep his vigil by the propulsion device and heard something on the wind. It reminded him of the shriek of a crow—until it came again. It was a woman's cry. Torie!

He ran for the path from the beach and headed for the tree house. "Torie! Hailey!"

Tourists were already gathering over by the tree house

area, and dread coated his tongue and accelerated his heart rate. He pushed his way through the small group of people and saw the shattered remains of the tree house. Every stick, every board had tumbled to the ground and lay in a twisted mass.

He spotted Torie's purse and picked it up. Her phone was smashed inside, but the other belongings seemed intact.

Where was his daughter and Torie? He called for them again before he turned to the closest spectators. "Did you see a tall woman with dark-brown hair and a little girl with red hair?"

"They went off with that guy." A woman pointed toward the road. "That way. He got them in his four-wheeler to take them to urgent care."

A guy. A helpful tourist or someone more sinister? Hailey knew better than to go off with a stranger, but she might have followed Torie's lead.

"Were they conscious?" The woman hesitated, and he quickly added, "The little girl is my daughter, and the woman is a good friend."

"The woman was unconscious, and the little girl kept saying she had to get her daddy, but the guy told her they had to go or the woman would die. So she went with him."

"You didn't object or try to intervene? Some stranger just took my daughter!"

"The woman's head was bloody. She needed medical attention right away."

Pain pulsed behind his eyes, and he turned to run for his truck.

CHAPTER 35

JOE FOUND IT HARD TO PLAN WITH FEAR PARA-
lyzing his thoughts while Anton organized searchers.

Hailey was out there somewhere with a stranger. And
was Torie even alive? After seeing the wreckage of the tree
house, he couldn't be sure of it. She'd been unconscious
when the guy took her, maybe worse. Anton had called all
the hospitals around, and none of them had Hailey or Torie.

"Joe, over here," Anton barked.

The older man wore a grim expression, and Craig,
standing a few feet away with a grid map, mirrored
Anton. Joe stepped over to join them.

Craig jabbed a finger south of where they stood. "We
have reports of a loud ATV barreling past the shopping
center and turning toward the causeway. It's possible he
took them off island."

Joe didn't want to believe it. Jekyll Island's 5,700 acres
would be much easier to search than to have to expand
out into Georgia and Florida. "Anyone see them go by?
Maybe tourists at Dairy Queen?"

"No other eyewitness that I've heard about, but I have troopers going door to door and asking."

Which might or might not do any good. Tourists would be out and about, not lingering around hotel rooms and condos. And there were day trippers who were often gone by now. He fought against the discouragement threatening to swamp him.

They'd find them both, alive and well. They had to.

"It's already getting dark," Anton said. "We're wasting time here. Let's get out there looking. With all the volunteers we have, we could cover all the roads and search for any ATV we see. We're burning daylight, people!"

Joe nodded. "My truck can handle unpaved roads. I'll start up north and make my way down."

"I'll go with you," Anton said. "I don't have a vehicle, but I've got sharp eyes."

"I'm parked over here." Joe led the way to his pickup.

Anton had little to say as he craned his neck to look out into the twilight. Joe turned onto the first dirt track, and the truck bounced along the rutted pathway. Here in the shelter of the trees, it was even hard to see through the murky gloom. His headlamps only went so far, and they saw no sign of an ATV or the girls.

Over the next three hours Joe turned the truck into any area that looked passable by ATV, but it was a futile search as nightfall obscured anything more than a few feet from the truck. There wasn't even moonlight to reveal a track or any movement. The only light he had during the night was a half hour of fireworks going off by Driftwood Beach after dinner.

At one point Genevieve tracked him down, and he

handed over the rest of the glass globes even though he thought her timing was poor. Her focus was always the hotel.

The clock on the dash read 11:14 p.m. Joe gripped the wheel with both hands and stifled a groan. His daughter was out there in the black night with a murderer, and Torie could be dead. He couldn't wrap his head around something so horrible.

Think, man, think.

He knew this island as well as his own skin. Where could someone take them and feel confident they would stay hidden? There were a few remote places inaccessible to tourists, but others were looking there too.

He braked at the main road and pounded the steering wheel with his fists. "We have to find them! Why is this happening?" The last question was flung at God, not Anton.

Joe'd had to watch his wife die in front of his eyes. He couldn't handle another loss like that.

Anton lowered his window, and the scent of marsh, night air, and mud rushed in. "I thought about what you asked me—about enemies. I wrote down a list of three men who might hate me for their banks failing." He passed a paper to Joe.

Joe flipped on the light and read it under the dim illumination. None of the names meant anything to him. "Have you contacted any of them?"

"Not yet, but I plan to hire a private investigator to see what they're up to."

"You haven't seen any of them on the island, right?"

"No, I haven't, but you asked so I wanted to do what I could to help figure this out."

Joe handed back the useless piece of paper. He

supposed Anton felt the need to do something, even if it didn't illuminate what was going on.

His text notification sounded, and he grabbed his phone while praying it was good news. The message from Craig was short. Nothing here. Any luck on your end?

No, he texted back. What now?

We're wasting our time looking in the dark. I'm calling the search for now. We'll start again at daybreak. In the meantime I have a roadblock on the causeway.

Joe's eyes burned, and a lump formed in his throat. Calling the search? How could they call the search when his daughter and Torie were still missing?

"Was that the state trooper?"

"Yes. They're abandoning the search until daylight. He's monitoring traffic on the exit, but if they're already off island, that won't do any good."

"You think he already got away?"

Did he? Joe examined what he knew, then shook his head. "No. This guy is playing a game of some kind, and none of us know the rules. He's not going to go far enough to miss out on the fun of seeing our reactions."

Anton's face was pale in the sickly overhead light. "You think it's someone we know?"

"I don't see any other explanation. Someone is yanking our chains and laughing behind our backs."

"Maybe that means he hasn't hurt them."

"I hope that's true." Joe bit back the reminder that Torie was already injured. The guy didn't have to hurt her—he only had to withhold medical care.

But that was something no father wanted to hear. And Joe didn't either when he already cared about her so much.

The stench of marsh water came to Torie's senses first, followed by a child's soft sobs.

She opened her eyes and blinked in the darkness. The support beneath her was hard and damp. Her head felt like someone had used it for a soccer ball, and her arms and legs throbbed and burned. She ran her bound fingertips over her thighs and felt something matted on the fabric of her pants. Blood? She was lucky she hadn't broken anything, but her fall had been broken by some branches on the way down.

She struggled to remember what had happened. And who was crying? She blinked and tried to see through the murky depths of the blackness surrounding her.

"W-Who's there?" Her voice was a whispered quaver.

"Torie, you're not dead!"

In moments a small hand touched Torie's cheek. Hailey. It was Hailey. Torie struggled to sit up, and nausea clenched her stomach as the pain in her head became excruciating. She forced bile down. The pain eased back enough for her to try to organize her thoughts and sensations.

"I'm here, honey." She pressed Hailey's hand. "Can you help me try to sit up? My head is pounding."

Hanging on to Hailey's hand, she managed to get to a seated position. "Where are we?"

"Somewhere in the marsh. The man brought us here on a four-wheeler, but you didn't wake up."

Torie's stomach rebelled again, and she took several deep breaths. "What man? Did you recognize him?"

"He had a bandana over his nose and mouth, and he wore sunglasses. He's got brown hair."

Very nonspecific. Torie could think of several men she knew matching that description. She fingered a goose egg on her temple and felt dried blood. All the aches in her arms and legs were likely from tumbling to the ground accompanied by boards and nails.

"Are we in a cabin?" She felt the floor of the space, but it almost seemed to be canvas, which made no sense.

"No, we're in a tent."

"Did you try to get out? And why is it so dark?"

"I couldn't move the zipper on the doorway. It's night-time. You haven't been awake for hours."

Torie's mouth was so dry it was hard to talk. "Is there any water?"

"The man left bottles of water and peanut butter sandwiches. I'll get you some water."

Hailey's hand left Torie's, and a few moments later, she felt the plastic of a warm bottle. "Thank you." She uncapped it and swigged much of it down.

Torie flexed her legs. Maybe she could stand. "Can you help me stand? Maybe I can get us out of here."

With the little girl's assistance, she managed to get to her feet, but she swayed and her knees buckled. She reached out in the dark and grasped Hailey's shoulder to steady herself.

Hailey turned her to the left. "The opening is that way. You can hang on to me."

"Okay. Go slow." Feeling her way with bare feet, she inched across the rough canvas until her outstretched hand touched the side of the tent. Her groping fingers felt the cold metal of the zipper, and she followed it to one end. No tab, so she moved to the other side. Still no tab.

"He's done something to it so the tab is outside and not in here. It can't be unzipped. When it was light, did you see anything I could use to cut the tent?"

"There's only the water and sandwiches. Oh, and the potty pan. I didn't see anything else."

But maybe Hailey was too upset to notice something Torie could use. If only she had a flashlight or lantern. Hands in front of her, she began to map the room with her right hand and feet, but the only thing her stumbling feet found was the pile of water and sandwiches. Nothing else in the space at all.

Hurting all over, she made her way back to the walls of the tent and began to search for another way out. If there was even the slightest rip, she might be able to pull it apart. Her fingers found only smooth canvas that felt stiff and new. That was a clue by itself. Canvas tents cost more but were also more durable, usually lasting many years with good care. The person who'd brought them here had enough money to afford something like this and hadn't opted for a cheap nylon one.

She guessed the size to be around ten by ten or maybe a bit bigger in one direction. It was hard to estimate while wandering in the dark. The man hadn't harmed them. She touched the lump on her head—at least not since bringing them here. So what was the purpose? It had to be the same guy who'd been stalking her. His motive seemed to be to scare her off of investigating Lisbeth's death, and so far, he hadn't shot at her or tried to kill her.

What did that mean?

Her aching legs buckled again, and this time Hailey wasn't nearby. She tumbled down, and her cheek hit the floor of the tent and her left arm screamed in pain. Clutching it to her chest, she lay curled up for a long moment inhaling the smell of the treated canvas before she pushed herself to a seated position.

"Torie, are you all right? Where are you?"

Torie turned toward the little girl's quavering voice. "I'm right here, honey. I fell but I'm okay. Walk toward my voice."

In a few moments Hailey was beside her and had climbed into her lap. Torie smoothed her hair and kissed her forehead. "Are you hungry? We could have a sandwich."

"I want my daddy."

"So do I, but I don't think we can get out until the man comes back. This is a very expensive and sturdy tent."

A roar came from outside the tent, and Hailey grabbed her tightly around the neck. "What was that?"

"An alligator. I don't think he can get in here any easier than we can get out."

And it told her they were probably near Horton Pond for alligators to be so near. Near enough to the nature trails?

"I'm going to call for help. You too. Help!" Torie yelled at the top of her lungs.

Hailey joined her in shouting for help, but no one came. Maybe it was too late for anyone to be out. She'd have to try again at daylight.

CHAPTER 36

EVERY MUSCLE IN HER BODY ACHED.

Torie stifled a moan and rolled over on the hard tent floor. Hailey's even in-and-out breaths beside her revealed deep, peaceful sleep. Good. As long as the little girl slept, she wouldn't be fearful. Once the light of day came, they'd be faced with whatever fate the kidnapper had planned.

Torie couldn't sit back and let anything happen to Hailey. Surely there would be an opportunity to arm herself, even if only with a tree branch or rock. She reached out, and her fingers grazed the case of water, partially gone now. Maybe she could use it as a bludgeon. The full bottles would be weighty.

It was something at least.

She closed her eyes and tried to go back to sleep, but her mind buzzed like a thousand flies. Every plan seemed impossible with them trapped inside this tent. In the blackness of the night, it all seemed hopeless, but she wasn't the kind of person to give up. Not when Hailey's life was on the line. There had to be something she could do.

It seemed an eternity before light began to creep into the tent. It never got as bright as outside, but at least she could see the parameters of the interior. She fumbled to her feet and walked around the space to find any kind of weapon. There was a metal potty chair in the corner, but it would be lightweight, and she doubted she was strong enough to do much damage with it. The case of water still seemed to be her best hope.

Hailey stirred and sat up. "Torie?"

The thread of panic in the little girl's voice sent Torie hurrying to her side. "I'm right here, honey. How about a peanut butter sandwich for breakfast?"

"Okay. I'm thirsty."

Torie fetched them both a sandwich and a bottle of water. "Here you go."

They munched down their food in silence. Torie wanted Hailey settled and strong enough to help when the time came. "Better?"

"I want my daddy." She began to weep, a hopeless sound that pierced Torie's heart.

She pulled Hailey onto her lap. "I know, I know. But I have a plan."

Hailey lifted her head. "A plan?"

"Yes, and I'll need your help. The guy who put us here is bound to come back and make sure we haven't escaped. I need you to distract him when he first comes in. I'm going to stand off to one side with the case of water, and I'll crash it down on his head when he steps inside. If he's focused on you, I'll be able to take him by surprise."

"Okay, I can do that. So I just talk to him or something like that?"

"Maybe yell for your dad. Cry and let him see how upset you are. Most people have at least a little sympathy for a kid."

"I cried all the way here, and he kept telling me to shut up or he'd kill you. So I had to be quiet and sniffle into my arm."

Poor kid. Torie hugged her. "Let me swing this case around in a trial run of our plan."

Hailey scooted off her lap, and Torie rose to grab the plastic end of the case of water where several bottles had been removed. She hefted it up, and though the muscles in her arms protested, she managed to swing it around and pretend to hit someone with the heavy weight of it.

It would have to do.

She set down the water and went to the zipper again to examine it in the light. Her fingers had told the truth last night—there was no tab for the zipper inside. Maybe she could rip it at the seam. She grasped each side of it and tugged as hard as she could, but it didn't give even a little. The tent seemed to be new and very well built.

If only she had a sharp edge of some kind. Her gaze fell on the toilet, but all the metal on it was smooth and round. No help there.

They'd have to wait.

The minutes ticked into hours as they sat in the dimness. The food ran out sometime in the afternoon, but they conserved as much water as possible.

When she thought it would never come, she heard the rumble of an ATV motor. She moved back to the side of the zipper and grabbed the water again. Her arms tired of the weight almost at once, and she prayed the guy would move quickly.

Footsteps came toward the tent, and a guy whistled the tune to the old country song, "Sixteen Tons." It had been playing in her cottage that time he'd broken in.

Her pulse sped to a patter in her chest, and she braced herself for the coming confrontation. She nodded to Hailey, who moved into position and began to cry.

"Daddy! I want my daddy. She's dead, Torie is dead. Let me out of here!"

What a great little actress! Torie wanted to hug her for the inspired improvisation. If the guy thought she was dead, he'd be more likely to run inside to verify it without expecting an attack.

"Quiet down, kid. She wasn't hurt that bad. She's probably just sleeping."

Torie inhaled at the sound of the man's voice. The voice was familiar, but she couldn't place him.

The zippered entrance fell open as the man ran the tab around the teeth. The guy stepped inside, his back to Torie, and she swung the case of water with all her might. Her aim was off from using just one hand, and it struck only a glancing blow that knocked him to his knees and left him stunned facedown on the tent's floor.

Torie reached out with her right hand and grabbed Hailey's hand. "Run!" She lunged through the opening with Hailey close to her side, and they plunged into the underbrush. "We have to hide," she whispered.

With the scent of mud and wildflowers in her nose, she pulled Hailey down behind some dense bushes and underbrush. The foliage was so thick she couldn't see through it to watch for the man emerging from the tent. Surely he'd look for them, but she prayed he would assume they would make for the trail to escape.

Stumbling footsteps snapped twigs as someone moved on the other side of the bushes guarding them.

"I'm in big trouble," he said. "She's going to kill me."

The footsteps faded away, and she held her breath to see if he would return. Once she caught the sound of an ATV engine, she rose and looked over the vegetation. They were alone.

The sound of the ATV's engine sputtered out. "I think he's got machine trouble. Let's wait until he gets farther away."

"What if he comes back?"

"I don't think he wanted us to see his face, so I think he'll walk out. Let's get out of the heat for a few minutes. We can grab some water for our hike out of the woods."

She guided Hailey back inside and listened with a sharp ear to the noises outside the tent. No sounds other than birds chirping and frogs croaking.

== ==

As Joe paced the floor all night waiting for daylight, he'd realized he needed to get into more remote places, areas his truck couldn't go, so at daybreak he borrowed an ATV from Craig and set out. Joe had searched all day, and he was bone weary, but he wasn't about to give up as he maneuvered the ATV into tracks so narrow the bushes scraped his arms.

He'd searched alone since he hoped to be able to have

room to bring back Hailey and Torie. He couldn't let himself think it might be a vain hope. They had to be all right.

At five he drove down a narrow track to Horton Pond, moving in a circular pattern into smaller and smaller trails. He rounded a curve and spotted an ATV in his path. He dismounted.

"Hello, anyone there?"

The marshy ground was soft underfoot, and birds squawked overhead at his intrusion into their space. He saw no one around, but when he touched the hood of the ATV, he found it warm. Someone had driven this thing recently and abandoned it. Had it run out of gas?

He got back on his ATV and veered around the abandoned machine to continue the search. In a couple of minutes he found himself breaking through a hedge into a small clearing. At first he thought it was another dead end until he spotted torn leaves and broken twigs where someone had forced his way through the underbrush to make a narrow path.

He cupped his hands to his mouth and started to yell for his daughter, then shook his head and dropped his arms. If this happened to be the girls' location, he didn't want to tip off their kidnapper. He pulled out his phone to call for backup, but found no bars back here, so he reached into his ATV and retrieved his SIG Sauer. With the gun in hand he walked back to the other ATV and searched for signs of where the kidnapper had gone.

With the ground marshy and soft back here, he quickly found footprints that led away from the ATV and toward the main road. Joe went back to the path he'd found and forced his way into the bushes. He struggled against the thorns that scraped at his jeans and shirt.

His elation deflated on the other side of the barrier at the sight of a canvas tent on the far end of another clearing. Just campers. He started to go back the way he'd come when he hesitated. Why not at least ask if they'd seen Hailey or Torie? It was a long shot, but it was all he had.

The open door revealed the darker interior, and he thought he saw movement, so he moved that direction. "Hello?"

A head popped through the opening, and he blinked. "Hailey?" It *was* her and not a mirage. "Hailey!"

"Daddy!" His daughter tumbled out into the sunlight and ran toward him with her arms out.

He sprang forward and scooped her up. Her heart beat like a frightened bird against his chest, and he inhaled the wonderful *live* scent of her as he buried his face in her matted hair. He didn't care if she reeked of canvas and mud.

He looked past her to the opening and saw Torie step out into the sunshine with two bottles of water. Her hair had fallen out of its braid, and her lovely face showed the trauma of her ordeal. Purple marks marred her high cheekbones, and she sported a black eye. Livid scratches had crusted over on her arms, and she limped as she stepped out of the tent.

"Joe?" Her choked voice trembled. "Oh, Joe."

She moved into a rambling half jog-half stumble, and he moved one arm away from Hailey to catch her as she fell against him. Her trembling transferred to him, and he shook with the intensity of the moment too.

Alive. They were both alive.

He kissed her forehead and embraced both of them with all his strength. "Thank you, God, thank you."

He hadn't even admitted to himself how much he doubted this would end well. His past traumas had shown him that things didn't always turn out okay. Good people died or disappeared. Loved ones left. Jobs disappeared. But as long as Hailey and Torie were alive, he could tackle any other problem.

Torie drew away and gestured to the tent. "We were locked in there all night. The guy came back on an ATV and I clobbered him with the case of water. While he was stunned, we escaped. We never saw him, but he sounded familiar."

"I think he had to ditch his ATV. I found one a little ways down the path."

"I heard the engine cut out, and we decided to wait and let him get away."

"Smart move." He circled one arm around her waist and took Hailey by the hand. "Let's get out of here."

CHAPTER 37

TORIE FOUGHT BACK THE MOISTURE IN HER stinging eyes as she tried to wrap her head around what had just happened. Who had taken them and why?

They needed to find out. Maybe there would be a clue in the kidnapper's vehicle.

Torie turned to the exit. "Let's take a look at the ATV."

His green eyes understanding, Joe gave a nod. "We need to call Craig once we get a cell signal too."

Torie looked around for the ATV but didn't see it. A narrow path forced its way through some bushes, and there were recent shoe impressions in the vegetation.

"It's this way," Joe said.

He held back the bushes for her and Hailey, and they forced their way through the vegetation into a small clearing. She went to the ATV, but as she neared, she saw the police emblem on the side.

"That one's mine," Joe said. "The other one is a little ways along the path."

He helped her along the uneven ground since she was

still so unsteady. He pointed. "There it is. Let me check it out." He climbed into the passenger seat and began to open every compartment and checked under the seats.

"Find anything?"

"Not really." He reached out and grabbed the key ring in the ignition. "Look at this."

He held it up and it took a moment for the metal piece dangling from the ring to register to Torie. "That's the top hat from a Monopoly game!"

He took out his phone and looked at it. "One bar. I'll call Craig. He's going to have a cow that I examined the ATV."

"I don't think we had any choice. We need to find out what's going on. You go ahead and call him."

He exchanged a few short words with Craig. What did all this mean? If she could push back the pain enough, maybe she could see to the heart. The man's voice reverberated in her head. She *knew* that voice—if it would just come to her. Her gaze went back to the keys with the top hat token. The token for wealth.

Joe ended the call. "He'll be here in a few minutes. He's just finishing up with security for the dignitaries arriving."

Torie watched him begin to tinker with the engine. Her memory nagged at her.

Dignitaries. The dinner tonight. Then it came to her. "It's Noah. It was Noah's voice."

He lifted a brow. "Noah kidnapped you?"

She nodded. "And I keep thinking about how picky Amelia was about the globes and where she wanted them. What if they are planning something against the bank and government officials? Noah was reading that book about the Federal Reserve. What if he's part of the protesters against the Federal Reserve? I know he works for the senator, but maybe it's part of his plot. Joe, we need to get to the hotel, to the Sans Souci building. The banking executives are all in danger. I think whoever is in on this with Noah plans to take them all out."

"Why Sans Souci?"

"It's where they're all staying." She was missing something else, but what was it? When the memory hit her, she put her hand to her mouth. "What if Lisbeth found out about his plan somehow? She was poking into things and was part of the hotel's planning for the globes. She might have overheard something, and that's why she was killed."

"Craig's on his way. We need to pass this information along to him."

She shook her head. "There's no time. Guests will be gathering for the opening games very soon. I need to get there. I can take your ATV."

"I just fixed a fouled spark plug on this one." He gestured to Noah's ATV. "See if it starts."

She nodded and the engine fired the first time she tried to start it. "You and Hailey wait here for Craig, and I'll get to the hotel. Meet up with me there."

"Let's try calling your aunt first. Maybe she can get them all to safety."

She put her hand on his arm. "What if she's part of it? She lied about my mom. What else has she lied about? And I heard Noah say, 'She's going to kill me.' We can't trust anyone."

She saw the argument gathering in his eyes, but she

didn't want to argue so she accelerated away. Lives were at stake, and she could only pray she wasn't too late.

≡≡

Torie might be driving straight into danger. Joe paced while waiting for Craig. Her phone was broken, so he couldn't even contact her to see how it was going.

His gaze slid to his daughter. What could he do with Hailey before he went to the hotel? He couldn't take his daughter into danger. He thought through who he could trust. He'd call his parents but he needed someone here on the island right now. Maybe Danielle wouldn't mind keeping her. Hailey would enjoy being with her little twins.

He shot off a quick text to Danielle, and she replied almost immediately, suggesting she send her husband to pick up Hailey.

"You get to go play with Danielle's twins tonight, and it might be a sleepover," he told Hailey. "Mr. Pete will be here in a few minutes."

A frown still creased her forehead. "I don't want to leave you, Daddy. I'm scared."

He pulled her against his chest and kissed the top of her head. "I know, Peanut, but it might be a long, boring wait while I tell Craig everything that happened. You might as well have a fun evening with her littles. They are looking forward to you coming. They're going to get fish tacos from Tortuga Jack's and then have a *Frozen* marathon."

Her eyes lit up. "That sounds fun. You'll come get me first thing in the morning, right?"

"I promise." He turned at the sound of an ATV rolling through the brush.

He waved at Pete and hurried Hailey into the passenger seat before sending them off. They'd barely left when two more machines rolled to a stop. Craig and another state trooper got off their transport, and he stepped to meet them.

"Torie left on an ATV. She recognized the kidnapper's voice. It's Noah Rogers. But there's an even bigger problem. Torie thinks the plot seems to revolve around the Federal Reserve executives. We think it's going down tonight."

He launched into the items left at Torie's house and the connection to the Monopoly game and the Federal Reserve. Craig's mouth twisted, and he took a step back as a frown gathered on his forehead. Joe was losing him.

"Look, I know it sounds like some kind of conspiracy theory, but I believe it's true. You have to check it out."

Craig shook his head and glanced at the other officer. "What proof do you have? Torie finding a top hat token for a Monopoly game on Noah's ATV key ring seems to show he was behind her stalking? What you're proposing is outlandish, Joe. Where's your logic?"

The propulsion device.

But even as he prepared to tell Craig about it, he realized it would sound crazy to the state trooper too. The propulsion device was no real evidence of anything other than someone scuba diving. It didn't have to be something sinister like a terrorist bringing in explosives.

But Joe was convinced it was and that Torie was running headlong into danger. He didn't have time to convince Craig, not when he needed to get to Torie.

"I understand your hesitancy. Will you at least promise me you'll consider what I've told you and do some digging?"

"I can do that," Craig said. "Forensics will be here any minute along with our detective. What can you tell me about what happened here?"

Joe glanced at the time on his watch. After six. The group would be at the cottage by now, and he needed to get there too. "All I really know is that he had Hailey and Torie. He showed up and she managed to escape with Hailey. Look, I have to go."

"We need to talk to Torie. Where is she?"

"It will have to wait until tomorrow." He ignored Craig's command to come back and rushed to his ATV.

Craig ran after him and tried to block him, but he veered to the right to avoid him and zoomed down the narrow track out of there. In minutes he was on the road and rolling toward the historic district. Bicyclers were out in force, and he gritted his teeth at the need to slow down to avoid hitting them. When the coast cleared, he raced around them and finally turned at the mini golf to drive back to the hotel.

He gaped at the big black SUVs parked in the lot. They announced the power and wealth of the dignitaries inside, and he spotted several security men on alert outside. At least he and Torie wouldn't be the only ones dedicated to preserving the lives of the executives and politicians. While the state police hadn't believed him, these men knew him. They would be ready to listen.

He rolled past and drove to the Sans Souci building. It looked deserted. Maybe they'd gone to dinner. He parked and looked for Torie's ATV. When he didn't spot it, his gut clenched. Had someone else intercepted her on the way here? She'd left at least twenty minutes before him so she should be here. Could she have parked somewhere else and walked? Maybe she hadn't wanted to alarm anyone and had slipped in the back way to scope out what was happening.

Wait a minute. Wasn't there an event at the Morgan Ballroom too? Maybe she'd gone there first.

All they had to go on was gut instinct and very few clues to exactly how this was going to go down. He realized that he might need a key. Torie had had a master key, and he prayed it was in her purse. He grabbed it and searched through the wallet inside. There it was. He pocketed the key, then got out and ran around to the front. He'd check here first, then go to the Morgan Center.

CHAPTER 38

TORIE GLANCED AT HER WATCH AS SHE NEARED the Sans Souci building. Nearly six thirty. Maybe stopping to change had been a mistake, but the last thing she wanted to do was cause an uproar or frighten anyone needlessly in case she was wrong. That was one of the first things she'd learned in the hotel business—don't upset the guests. If she burst in looking like a refugee, she'd attract too much attention and there could be a panic that caused injuries.

Her gaze took in the hotel wing. Wait a minute. There was no ballroom here and no real gathering spots. The scavenger hunt couldn't be taking place here. Had she made a mistake? She clutched the top hat token in her palm, and the metal edges reaffirmed her confidence in what was about to happen. While she had no motive for Noah's actions yet, she was positive of her sudden insight.

It had to refer to something about J. P. Morgan. She turned and looked around the historical district. The dining room was in the main hotel, and there was a ballroom as well. She snapped her fingers—the Morgan Center! It was off to her right and close enough to walk instead of drive. She kicked off her heels and sped along the grass past the Island Sweets Shoppe and across the road.

The big building was originally an indoor tennis court for club members back in the day. And she'd been right. Men in tuxedos and women in formal dresses stood outside on the terrace and spread out onto the lush lawn. Cloth-draped refreshment tables lined the area near the trellis, and the tinkle of laughter mingled with the sound of running water from a fountain.

She slipped her heels back on and donned a smile before strolling toward the crowd. Her gaze swept the group of who's who in banking. Some of the faces were familiar, but she couldn't have identified them. Dad could though. She looked around for him. He would help her.

Though she saw no sign of his tall figure, she was sure he'd be here somewhere. This was a huge coup for the hotel and for the Bergstrom Hospitality brand, and he was on the Fed's board. A photographer snapped pictures constantly, and the woman would be able to sell her photos for good sums to the newspapers.

The news had been filled lately with cryptocurrency and how it was going to change the world. She had no doubt the topic would be discussed during the next few days, and the newness of it made for great copy for reporters.

She spied her aunt dressed in a lacy lavender formal, so she changed directions and headed that way.

Her aunt's gaze went wide when she saw her. "Your father is still out searching for you. Does he know you're safe? You've worried us to death. Have you looked at your face? You still have mud and twigs in your hair."

"Noah kidnapped Hailey and me, but we managed to escape. The executives here are in terrible danger. We need to herd them somewhere safe without arousing suspicion that could taint our name."

"Danger?" Her aunt's blonde hair bobbed when she shook her head. "Have you seen all the security? Your head injury must have addled your thoughts."

"I'm serious about the danger. What would be the best way to get all these people back to their rooms? At the very least we have to stop the scavenger hunt."

"Oh no, no. We can't stop that. Everyone is looking forward to it. It's our iconic event tonight. In fact, it's time for it to start." She clapped her hands together and walked a few feet away to an open area. "Ladies and gentlemen, we're so glad you've joined us, and we're honored you have chosen the Jekyll Island Club Resort to host your event. To kick things off in a fun way, we're ready to start the scavenger hunt." She pointed to the table. "Please pick up the details on the table, and remember, if you find a glass globe, you're finished. Bring your globe back to the ballroom and have a seat. Once all the globes are found, we'll hand out prizes. If you don't find a globe, keep looking for the items on the paper, and once you've discovered all of them, return to your table as well."

The excitement hit a new high, and people surged to the table to get their instructions. The laughter increased, and several people teamed up.

Torie clenched her hands together. She couldn't just announce a danger she didn't understand. Once the guests were at their tables, she could make an announcement from the podium and ask everyone to disperse to their rooms.

She needed her dad, but without her phone, she couldn't call him. Her aunt rejoined her with a satisfied expression, and Torie held out her hand. "Could I borrow your phone, please? I need to let Dad know I'm all right. He might still be out there searching."

Her aunt rolled her eyes. "Of course he is. He wouldn't let a little thing like the most important dinner of his career stand in the way of finding his daughter, not even if it destroyed his business. He wouldn't listen when I tried to get him here."

Warmth spread up Torie's chest. Dad would be frantic. She took the phone her aunt proffered and called him. He didn't answer, and she knew he was likely avoiding the call because it was Genevieve's number. She texted him and let him know she was all right. Maybe he'd read that and come.

==

How did Joe get someone to believe the danger?

His shoes echoing on the polished wood floors, Joe walked along the empty hallway on the first floor of the Sans Souci building. The spotless hall was silent and empty and smelled of lemony polish. How many bank executives were at the hotel now? Two from every major Fed bank so that would be twenty-four. Plus several other executives and a couple of US senators. All those security people would be staying, too, so he estimated fifty rooms taken.

They didn't seem to be in this cottage though, but

he wasn't quite ready to give up and leave. There might be something here he hadn't seen. He found stairs and climbed to the next floor. It was just as empty, and so was the third. He retraced his steps and walked toward the front door to exit when he heard a soft sliding sound behind him. He turned and followed the faint noise to a room toward the back.

He pressed his ear to the oak door with its ornate Victorian trim. There was someone inside. Footsteps came toward the door, and he darted down the hall and around a corner, where he pressed against the wall and peeked around to watch.

A man holding a glass globe exited. The guy was in his thirties with light-brown hair. He looked like a typical tourist in his khaki shorts and tee, but Joe's attention fixed on the orange globe. A worker? Or something more sinister?

The guy walked the other direction, and as soon as he was gone, Joe dashed back to the door of the room he'd vacated. Locked, of course. He dug Torie's master key out of his pocket and in seconds he was inside the room.

It was a large suite, but tables had been brought in on the far wall. He nearly stumbled over dive equipment—tanks, BCDs, and two wet suits. The propulsion device! Had the people using this equipment come here via the device?

He didn't touch anything as he walked to the table. There were several broken glass globes on one end. A cardboard box on the other end of the table drew his attention. When he read the lettering on the clear vials, he caught his breath. *Sarin? Like in sarin gas, the potent nerve gas?* His gaze traveled back to the broken globes, and his stomach plunged.

He opened the box gingerly and spotted small glass globules inside. They looked like the smaller glass pieces inside the globes Amelia had made. Did they contain sarin?

Divers could have brought the loaded glass pieces here to be used. He backed away from the ominous box and pulled out his phone to snap a picture, then shot it off to Chen before calling him.

Chen answered on the first ring. "Joe? If you're checking on Simon, we've got him back at King's Bay."

"That's good, but there's something more serious going on." Joe heard the noise on the other end that signaled Chen had gotten the picture. "Check the text I sent you. I just found this box at the Sans Souci cottage in the historic district. There are small glass globes inside the box marked *sarin* in the room as well as discarded diver equipment. I think someone plans to use the gas on the Fed executives."

Chen inhaled sharply. "Hang on." His voice returned after a pause. "That looks real. I'll notify Homeland Security, and we'll start an evacuation. Do what you can there until help arrives. Do you have any idea when this is going down?"

"Any minute, I'm afraid. The scavenger hunt with the glass globes has likely already started."

And Torie was right in the middle of it all.

Chen was silent for a long moment. "I'll call the state police and have them get there right away."

They'd probably listen to Chen. Joe thanked him

and ended the call. He texted Danielle and told her to evacuate. The docks were closed, but she could go to the enclosure and use it to escape by boat. But what about the other Jekyll Island residents? He had no idea how far the gas could travel if one of the globes broke.

Was the sarin in all the globes? Or just the orange one the man had carried out? Would whoever was behind this plot trust it to just one glass globe? He didn't think so.

He ran for the door. If only he had a way of contacting Torie to find out where she was. He stopped and called up Genevieve's name. She'd know where the event was being held.

Genevieve answered on the third ring. "Joe, I hope you're not calling to report a security issue."

"Actually I am, Genevieve. Where is the scavenger hunt being held tonight?"

"We're all here at the Morgan Center. People are out looking for two special globes, and one has been found already. Torie showed up spouting a lamebrain conspiracy theory."

He closed his eyes briefly. "She's still there?"

"She's wandering around wringing her hands and telling me to evacuate. But she has no credible reason to disrupt our guests."

"There's sarin gas on the property, Genevieve. I just found it. Homeland Security is on the way, and so is the state police. You need to get people out of there."

Genevieve gasped. "Sarin gas?" Her voice quavered. "I need help, Joe."

"I'll be there in two minutes." He ended the call and ran for the door.

CHAPTER 39

TORIE'S GAZE SWEPT THE ROOM FOR WHERE danger might be lurking.

Finally, all the executives were back in the Morgan Center, which was decked out in all its glory for their arrival. She recognized the aromas she'd noted on the menu: lobster bisque, filet, sea bass, brussels sprouts with bacon, and three choices for dessert.

Greenery and flowers draped the mezzanine railing, and linen covered the tables to the carpeted floor. Sheer fabric hung in gathers on the walls. Anything might have been placed under the tables or even hidden in the flowers. The globes hidden on the grounds were on two different tables, one near the front of the room and one near the back.

Her nerves felt as taut as a fishing pole reeling in a big fish, and she shifted from place to place. If only her dad and Joe were here. She had no support, no way to prove these people were in danger. Would these modern-day captains of industry and politicians listen to her?

She glanced at her aunt, who was approaching her with wide eyes and pale cheeks. Something was wrong.

Aunt Genevieve clutched Torie's arm. "Joe called. There's sarin gas in the glass globes. The entire island is in danger. I'm sorry I didn't listen to you. Homeland Security is on its way, and Joe should be here any second." She released Torie and wrung her hands. "If only your father were here. He always has such a cool head in chaos."

Sarin gas. The news footage of the horrible effects of the nerve gas flashed through her memory. This was even worse than she thought.

The door opened and Joe stepped through. Torie bit back a cry of relief and lifted her hand so he could see her. He zigzagged between the tables and joined her and her aunt where they stood near the podium.

He touched her arm. "You heard?"

"Sarin gas." She wanted to find out how he knew and what he'd seen, but there was no time.

"I told the security people they brought with them, and they're bringing the limos and vehicles around to the entrance. We need to get everyone out of here now."

She took a step toward the podium and raised the mic higher and leaned forward. "May I have your attention please? We've become aware of a security threat, and we need all of you to prepare to leave in an orderly manner. Your vehicles are being brought around so please—" Torie broke off at the sight of Noah propelling her dad into the room, a pistol jammed in his side.

Her gaze jetted to Joe, who'd seen them too. Noah marched her dad in lockstep to where she stood and jerked his thumb. "So you got away. But you're too late. There's no stopping this now. Get out of my way."

Her dad was pale. Torie stepped away from the podium, and Joe and her aunt crowded beside her.

Joe slipped his arm around her waist, and she leaned into his strength. This was bad, very bad.

The door opened again, and ten security people were ushered in by a group of three men carrying large weapons. The security men were unarmed and their hands were zip-tied behind them. Torie thought the weapons might be AK-47s, though she was no gun expert. They looked big and dangerous.

"Over there." One of the men gestured to a small alcove under the mezzanine. "Sit down and shut up."

The security detail settled onto the floor. They seemed stunned.

Noah shoved her dad closer to the podium, then set the orange globe on top of it before speaking into the mic. "You've all sucked the blood of the common worker for far too long. Conceived right here in 1910, the Federal Reserve is nothing more than a cartel designed to make sure you continued to make money while the rest of us worked and slaved for you. You're nothing more than slave owners keeping us all under your thumb. With your deaths, the world will sit up and take notice of the atrocities you've committed against humanity."

At the word *deaths* the executives and politicians began to stir and talk among themselves.

An older gentleman held up his hand. "Sir, may I speak?"

"Your deeds have spoken for you."

"Who are you?" a woman called.

He squared his shoulders. "I'm Noah Rogers. You bloodsuckers ran my business into the ground. I've tried to change things through the political system, but you've greased too many palms over the years. None of the Washington players are willing to give up the money pouring into their pockets. There's no other way to stop the carnage except to shut you all down."

Noah picked up the orange globe and thrust it into her dad's hands. "All of us are prepared to die with you."

Torie had seen a documentary, and she struggled for the name of the antidote it had mentioned. Could the men have taken it before they came here? What was it?

Atropine.

If Homeland Security knew, hopefully they were arranging for hospitals to be ready to treat everyone. If rescue got to them in time.

Noah's gaze swept her way, then continued on to stare at the executives. "This globe is beautiful, isn't it? Beautiful and deadly."

Amelia came through one of the doors. She wore a flowing gown of dark blue, red, and yellow that made her almost look like Wonder Woman in formal wear with long gloves.

"Mom, I told you not to come in here. Get out!"

Amelia's gaze locked on Torie's dad, and she handed him something silver. "I had to be here to see justice done."

Torie's dad flexed his palm to look, and Torie saw it too—the Monopoly money bag token.

She was clearly part of this with her son.

Torie took another step closer to Amelia. "Can you live with the guilt that you've caused so many deaths in such a horrific way? Your son says everyone is prepared to die here today. Did he tell you that? Are you ready to suffocate when your muscles freeze and you can't breathe?"

Amelia glanced at her son. "We aren't dying. You all are. It's about time the powerful know what it's like to be helpless and at the mercy of other people."

Some of the people sitting at the tables began to shout and stand. Gunfire erupted, and the air stank of gunpowder. A stately man in his sixties fell as the bullets struck his chest. Pandemonium erupted at the attack, and even Noah looked disoriented.

Joe leaped forward, and his arm looped around Amelia's waist. He dragged her back with him as the older woman fought, in spite of being six inches shorter. He managed to get one of Amelia's hands behind her and reached for the other one, but Amelia wrenched out of his grip for a moment until Joe seized her and managed to get his arm locked across her neck. He held her in front of him as a shield.

Noah gestured to one of his men. "Don't just stand there—shoot him before he hurts my mother."

Joe turned toward the gunmen with Amelia in front of him. He stared at each of the three men, then at Noah. "Throw down your guns or I'll kill her. I can break her neck with one move. This is already over."

Torie stepped to his side. "Homeland Security is

already on their way. Your plan is over. You'll never get out of here alive."

Joe tightened his grip on Amelia's neck, and the older woman began to sag as her air was more restricted. "Throw down your weapons!"

"Do it," Noah said. "I don't want my mother hurt."

The big guns clanged to the floor, and one of the guests rushed over to pick up the guns. He found a pocketknife to cut the zip ties and freed the security guys, then handed them the guns. They cuffed the three terrorists.

"Let go of my mother," Noah said.

Joe nodded and released Amelia. The older woman stumbled and nearly fell, but Noah grabbed her and guided her to a seat. He shot a poisonous glare Joe's direction.

Even a man like Noah loved his mother. Torie should have felt sorry for him and Amelia, but she couldn't find any sympathy. What he'd been prepared to do was horrible.

Joe grabbed a spare set of cuffs and seized Noah's hands, forcing them behind his back. He snapped on the handcuffs but left Amelia's hands free. She was still panting and didn't seem to have the strength to fight anymore.

The fight drained out of Torie, and her knees felt weak. She sank to a chair at a nearby table and exhaled. Her hands shook as she reached for a glass of water.

Joe's hands came down on her shoulders. "You okay?"

"All the adrenaline left me." She tipped her head back and looked up into his face. "You were amazing."

"I wanted to hurt her. I never would have guessed I could grab someone like that." He leaned down and kissed her gently. "You figured it out, Torie. You saved all these people."

"And you. If you hadn't found the sarin gas, no one would have believed us."

"We make a pretty good team."

She leaned her cheek against his arm. "I guess we do."

A shriek pierced the air, and she jerked around to see Amelia holding the orange globe above her head as she advanced on Torie's dad. Tears mingled with mascara tracked down her face. "You've ruined my son! I hate you!"

Her dad held out his hands. "Give me the globe, Amelia. You don't want to do this. If you break the globe, I'll be dead, but so will Noah. And so will you. I'm sorry. I never meant to hurt him or you."

Step by step he advanced until he was right in front of her. "Hand it to me carefully. You don't want to be the one to kill your own boy. Easy."

She lowered her hands a few inches, then dropped the globe. His hands shot out and he barely caught it in his left hand. The room gave a collective gasp as he clutched it to his chest and staggered away from her.

The doors burst open, and men poured into the room. Torie spotted Craig and some other state police officers. It was finally over.

CHAPTER 40

THE CRASHING WAVES AT DRIFTWOOD BEACH swirled foam around Torie's feet and she relished the calming scent of salt and sea after last week's horrific events.

She retreated to sit on the sand with her back against a tree the ocean had tossed there especially for her. She lifted her face to the sunshine and let it bake into her skin. Somehow, against all odds, they'd survived.

"I thought I'd find you here." Her dad spoke from her right.

She opened her eyes and found him dressed in shorts and a tee, standing barefoot. His tentative smile told her he wasn't sure of his welcome. Behind him, looking just as uncertain as her dad, stood Joe, incredibly handsome in swim trunks and a muscle shirt.

She patted the soft sand beside her on either side. "Have a seat."

Her dad's clouded gaze cleared, and he dropped down beside her, but Joe tossed his towel down. "I'll let you have some time with your dad while I take a swim."

The strong muscles in his tanned legs flexed as he

ran across the beach to plunge headlong into the crashing waves.

"You like him a lot, don't you?" her dad said.

She smiled and scooped up a handful of sand. "He's a stand-up guy. We might all be dead except for him."

"I think that's likely. And except for your quick thinking when you saw that Monopoly piece." He shifted and leaned his head back against the driftwood.

If they were ever going to talk about her mom's death, now was the time. "Dad, Lisbeth found Mom's suicide note. Aunt Genevieve wrote it, but you took it, didn't you?"

He gaped and his cheeks paled. "Your mother didn't write it?"

"You thought she did?"

He nodded. "We'd had a big fight. I didn't want you to have to deal with your mom's suicide at such a vulnerable age so I took the note."

"Aunt Genevieve told Mom you'd been seeing another woman, and they fought. Mom fell accidentally. I saw Aunt Genevieve rush out of the apartment that day, but I never thought anything about it. I thought she was upset because she saw Mom's body." Sand sifted through her fingers, and she shook her head. "This wasn't your fault, Dad. I wanted to tell the police about Genevieve's confession, but it's her word against mine."

"Perhaps it's best not to. She's an old woman, and it's been eighteen years." He drew in a deep breath. "It's poisoned my life for a long time. At least we know the truth now. You never know what lurks behind people's masks. I never would have dreamed Noah and Amelia could do something like this."

"After reading more last night in that book *The Creature from Jekyll Island*, I understand the Fed and the harm it's done. But what Noah did wasn't any way to eliminate it. It has to be done through the law, not with violence."

"The Fed has done a lot of good keeping the economy stable," he said.

She arched a brow. "I don't think so, Dad, but I'm not going to argue with you about it."

She watched Joe, his tanned muscles glistening with seawater, pop up out of the ocean. He took the towel she offered and dried his dripping hair before he spread it out and dropped down beside her.

"You talk to Hailey this morning?"

He nodded. "My parents picked her up, and they'll keep her all weekend."

She turned back to her dad. "Lisbeth's last job was helping coordinate the creation of the glass globes and how that scavenger hunt was going to go down. I would guess she somehow heard what was about to happen and had to be eliminated."

"Craig said during interrogation Noah said he recognized you right away. He'd seen a picture of you with your dad in a business magazine."

"Why did he kill Lisbeth?"

"She was helping with the globe arrangements and went to Rogers Glass. She went in the back door like we did and overheard them talking about the plot."

"Who was the diver bringing in the sarin?" she asked. "You found two dive suits, right?"

Joe took her hand in his, chilled from the water. "Two of the guys with AK-47s. They had their weapons here and transported the nerve gas underwater. They knew security would be tight and figured they could bring stuff in by sea without being seen."

She clung to his hand. "What about the incidents with your boat being bombed and that other diver poisoning himself?"

"I talked to Chen. We found out that diver we captured was part of a plot to get nuclear sub technology. It had nothing to do with Noah."

Her dad sighed and rose. "I'm going to head back to the hotel. I've got a flight out tonight after dinner. Want to eat together before I go?"

"Of course." She stood and embraced him, relishing the comfort of his arms.

When it came right down to it, he would always be her dad, no matter what he'd done. Her parents' marriage was none of her business. It wasn't her job to pass judgment on how he'd failed or how her mother had failed. Torie would let the Holy Spirit take care of things in his heart.

She stepped back and watched him walk gingerly across the hot sand. He was getting older, and it made her a little sad to realize things were changing. At dinner she planned to tell him she was staying on Jekyll Island, that she didn't want to take the reins of Bergstrom Hospitality. He had many excellent VPs who could step into that role, and she could attend the occasional board meeting to make sure they stayed in line. She'd take this one hotel and turn it into something world-class.

Her gaze strayed to Joe's broad shoulders, and she prayed her news would make him happy.

There was something different about Torie today. Joe couldn't put his finger on it.

Relief? Happiness? Contentment? They all played a part in the curve to her lips and the sparkle in her eyes. As for him, he felt the weight of the world off his shoulders. She was safe, his daughter was tucked away in Brunswick with his parents for now, and he could think through all that had happened.

He pulled her down onto his lap. "I'm going to get you all wet, but it's hot anyway. I'll cool you off."

Her sandy fingers laced against the back of his neck, and she leaned against his chest. His skin was sticky with salt, but he didn't mind them being stuck together. Her soft hair brushed his chin as she nestled into his shoulder.

"So it's all over here. You did it," he said. "It doesn't bring back Lisbeth, but I hope the justice feels sweet."

"Not as sweet as I'd hoped. We walked through the fire together and came out the other end though. I wish she were here to know that I'm free from the past."

"So when is your flight out of here? You going back to Scottsdale?"

"Probably sometime next week. I haven't bought a ticket yet. You're urging me on, are you?"

He caught a note of caution in her voice and pressed a kiss on top of her hair. "You know better than that. I'm trying to prepare to let you go for now. And I needed to know where to look for a job. I thought Scottsdale might be a possibility, and I sent a résumé to the aquarium there. I already got a response back asking for an interview."

He felt her chest heave as she gasped and sat up and stared into his face. Her dark-brown eyes filled with moisture. "You'd do that for me?"

His hands trailed up her arms to cup her face. "I already told you I wasn't ready to let what we have slip away."

"I won't be gone long, Joe. I'm going to fly to my house, pack up my stuff, stage it, list it, and drive back across the country to stay here."

Joy threatened to launch his heart right through his chest. "You're sure?"

She nodded. "Completely sure. When I was in that tent with Hailey, I knew I couldn't leave her or you. I've never had such a sense of belonging, of family. No pressure on either of us, but I want to see where our relationship might go. I already love Hailey."

"I can promise you my feelings are real. Real enough that I'd already told Hailey we were going wherever you were. She was ready even though she loves it here."

"And you can continue to work for the Navy, doing what you love and what you're good at."

"Maybe. Who knows. I might do something totally different. As long as you and Hailey are here, I don't care what I do."

"That's all I wanted to hear."

She lifted her face to his, and he lowered his lips to hers. Her kiss held tenderness, passion, joy, and promise. They had a road to travel yet and so much to learn about each other, but he could see the ending from here. And it was so beautiful.

A NOTE FROM
THE AUTHOR

Dear Reader,

If you've ever been to Jekyll Island, you know all about the rich history there. I was enthralled the first time I visited and knew I had to pull in some of the fabulous buildings and setting. But that meant instead of having the liberties I'm used to with imaginary settings, I had to tweak some things with the island.

Right now Jekyll Island is owned by Northview Hotel Group and not by Bergstrom Hospitality. I started to plop an anonymous hotel onto the island, but I loved the fabulous Club Resort so much, and its history was so compelling, I took the literary license of changing it up while acknowledging it here.

I was very interested in the makeup of the Federal Reserve and stumbled across the controversy in its creation while researching. *The Creature from Jekyll Island* by G. Edward Griffin was eye-opening, and you might find it interesting as well.

As always, I love hearing from you and can't wait to hear what you think of the story.

Lots of love,
Colleen

colleen@colleencoble.com

ACKNOWLEDGMENTS

NINETEEN YEARS AND COUNTING THAT I'VE BEEN part of the amazing HarperCollins Christian Publishing team as of the spring of 2021! I have the best team in publishing (and I'm not a bit prejudiced), and I'm so grateful for all you've taught me and all you've done for me. My dear editor and publisher, Amanda Bostic, makes sure I'm taken care of in every way. My marketing and publicity team is fabulous (thank you Nekasha Pratt, Kerri Potts, and Margaret Kercher!). I'm truly blessed by all your hard work. My entire team works so hard, and I wish there was a way to reward you all for what you do for me.

Julee Schwarzburg is my freelance editor, and she has such fabulous expertise with suspense and story. She smooths out all my rough spots and makes me look better than I am. I learn something from you and Amanda with every book, so thank you!

My agent, Karen Solem, and I have been together for twenty-two years now. She has helped shape my career in many ways, and that includes kicking an idea to the curb when necessary.

My critique partner and dear friend of over twenty-two years, Denise Hunter, is the best sounding board ever. Together we've created so many works of fiction. She reads every line of my work, and I read every one of hers. It's truly been a blessed partnership.

I'm so grateful for my husband, Dave, who carts me around from city to city, washes towels, and chases down dinner without complaint. Right now he's been getting radiation treatments for recurrent prostate cancer, and we're praying for good results. But my Dave's even temper and good nature hasn't budged in spite of the trials of the past year.

My family is everything to me, and my three grandchildren make life wonderful. We try to split our time between Indiana and Arizona to be with them, but I'm constantly missing someone. ☺

Over the past year, I've had Covid, a broken ankle, and knee replacement surgery as well as cared for our daughter who nearly died of sepsis. So life has thrown some rocks in our path, but God is good all the time! He's been carrying us through these challenges, and I'm grateful for his loving care each and every day.

And I'm grateful for you, dear readers!

DISCUSSION QUESTIONS

1. People can tend to make snap judgments when they meet others. Have you ever been pegged as someone you're not?
2. Torie didn't want anything to get in the way of her search for the truth, and she lied about her identity. Is a lie ever justified?
3. Torie's lack of truthfulness had repercussions. How do you feel when you find out someone lied to you?
4. Joe struggled after learning about Torie's true identity. Would you have found it hard to forgive Torie?
5. Torie noticed how fire shaped glass and correlated it to her own life. Have you been shaped by some kind of tragedy?
6. Lisbeth loved Torie enough to do something to help her move forward. Have you ever been a friend like that?

7. Torie had an epiphany that she had to follow her own path, not necessarily what her father wanted. How hard was it for you to follow your own path?

8. One of the perpetual questions we can have even as Christians is why God lets bad things happen. What conclusion have you come to about that?

ABOUT THE AUTHOR

Photo by Amber Zimmerman

COLLEEN COBLE IS A *USA TODAY* BESTSELLING author best known for her coastal romantic suspense novels, including *The Inn at Ocean's Edge*, *Twilight at Blueberry Barrens*, and the Lavender Tides, Sunset Cove, Hope Beach, and Rock Harbor series.

== ==

Connect with Colleen online at colleencoble.com
Facebook: @colleencoblebooks
Twitter: @colleencoble
Pinterest: @ColleenCoble